FEARFULLY
UNMADE

This is a work of fiction. Any references to places, people or historical events are used fictitiously. Any resemblance to real people, living or dead, is coincidental.

Pill Bug Publishing

ISBN: 978-1-7349472-0-5 (paperback)

ISBN: 978-1-7349472-1-2 (ebook)

www.jmrutherford.com

To Sidney,
Our struggles can break us or they can build us.
Let them build.

J.M. RUTHERFORD

FEARFULLY
UNMADE

ONE

Taite couldn't have explained why, but she often considered herself a regular misfit. No one knew this, since she had told no one. Not her father or her friends. No one. Still, she played the part of the good student, the good daughter, and whatever else they wanted her to be. But it was getting old.

It seemed she was living someone else's life.

This was the last thought that ran through her mind before her world changed. The last thing Taite heard was a low deafening rumble. The last thing she saw and what she would remember most was blinding white light before everything faded to black.

But the day had started so deceptively normal.

Taite sighed and cupped her face in one hand as she leaned toward the window to peer out at the scene rushing past. The pink haze of sunrise lingered, and gray snow clouds sprawled low over the horizon. Few other cars shared the road as the tranquil quiet of falling snow replaced the usual traffic noise of the city. She spotted only one pedestrian bundled up as she jogged beside a frisky malamute. In the driver's seat, Taite's father droned on about something as he lifted a long-fingered hand off the wheel in a dramatic gesture. She wasn't listening, as she had tuned him out several minutes ago, her mind meandering down other roads.

"Aisea, are you listening to me?" he asked, using her first name as always. She hated that name and had disowned it by the time she turned ten, preferring her last name instead.

"Huh?" she snapped out of her daze with a jerk of her head.

"You know I hate it when you do that." Her father's eyes still focused on the road.

"Do what?" Taite asked with an eye roll.

"Zone out like that. I'm talking to you." He paused and cough into his hand. "As I was saying, I won't be home until tomorrow. I have a conference, so when you get back from the exam I won't be there."

"When are you ever there?" Taite asked under her breath, as her father pulled the car up to the station.

"My work is important, Aisea," he said, looking at her with a strange expression. As usual, he sounded serious, but something in his eyes made Taite rather morose.

"Of course."

As she got out of her father's sleek black Mercedes, her feet plunged ankle-deep into a mound of fresh snow. "Guess I better go," she said. For once, she wished she would come above his job.

Much to her surprise, her father stepped out of the car after her, and a glimmer of hope surged within her. It dissolved as he walked around and said, "Eat something healthy for lunch, not any of that fast-food junk. It's dreadful for the heart."

"Fine," Taite said as her healthy heart sank. Why her father bothered to stand in the snow in his best shoes only to tell her what to eat, she didn't know. She scanned over the slush-splattered bus. A few people had already started climbing aboard. Her father glanced over at her. She couldn't help thinking even as he looked at her, he didn't see her at all.

"Well, see ya later," she said, not knowing she wouldn't. Any other father might give her a hug, but Taite's father wasn't any other. He only patted her shoulder and leaned against the car. While he had never been the most affectionate person, today he seemed even more distant.

Taite stopped for a moment with one booted foot on the step of the idling Bethesda city bus. She turned back and waved, her warm breath clouding in the crisp winter air.

Wrapped in a black trench coat, her father's isolated figure stood in the distance. He held up one hand, but he didn't smile as he turned and stepped into the car. With a shrug of her bony shoulders, Taite adjusted the bag slung over her back, and climbed onto the bus. It was going to be a long day.

She found an empty seat toward the back and tossed her green backpack before sliding down with a grunt. All morning, butterflies fluttered in her stomach. In two hours, she would sit down to take an exam that could very well decide her entire future. No pressure.

Crammed into the corner, the cold of the icy window pane exhaled against her cheek. Snow already accumulated on the steamed-over windows in gentle arches. On a normal day, Taite liked snow, but now she wished it would stop until she made it back home to the comfort of her cozy room. She didn't want to get stranded in Baltimore alone, and according to the weather report, it might snow all day.

Settling in for the ride, she pulled a notebook out of her pack to go through the paperwork for the test. The exam would help award scholarships for university freshmen in the fall. Taite wanted to be just that.

She had asked her father to come along. Missing the point, he had told her she was almost an adult and needed to do this alone. It was rare that they spent much time together. Work always took priority. Her father, the walking contradiction; always telling her what to eat, how to act. In that way, he seemed to care, but spend his precious time with her? Not a chance.

The seat squeaked as someone crowded down next to Taite. She didn't bother to look up but continued watching the wet snowflakes flutter to the ground and disappear into the drifts. No two snowflakes are alike, but it was impossible to tell from her vantage point. Their individuality disappeared into the crowd. Sometimes, she felt like that, like she dissolved into the background.

The person next to Taite turned out to be a woman wearing a black pantsuit. She pivoted to her young neighbor and asked where Taite was heading. And this was exactly why she hated riding the city bus. It was so obvious she was busy, but did this woman care?

"To take a test in the city. I'm studying," she said and held up her notebook. Taite looked away to focus on her notes.

"I didn't mean to bother you," the woman said with a stiff smile on painted lips.

Taite sighed and gazed at her, realizing the woman might be about the same age as her father. It would have been nice if her mother was seated next to her instead of a stranger. Well, how could she be sure? Maybe she was. Taite had never known her mother, and her dad's entire face tightened up if she dared to mention her. He refused to talk about it, other than to say that her mother had abandoned Taite at birth.

Taite often wondered if she looked like her mother. Because she didn't resemble her Dad with his long face and large features. Taite's nose was narrow and straight, with a slight bump on the bridge, not her dad's prominent arched nose.

It was always an odd feeling to find herself staring at a random woman, searching her face and wondering if this might be her mother. Even as a child, she had attempted to give up the habit. It never worked.

Taite tried not to stare at the stranger, dark hair pinned up at the base of her neck. She broke her gaze away and tried to think of other things. When she was younger, she would often stay with the neighbor, Mrs. Dalton. About sixty now, her own children grown. While she was always nice to Taite in her way, helping her with homework, playing the occasional board game, it wasn't the same.

Taite went back to studying, but it was hopeless. Why did this woman sit there, sending her mind reeling? She picked at a tear in the seat in front, poking a bit of fluff back into the gray crevice. As she adjusted her slight frame, she tried to ignore the woman sitting next to her.

Taite grew restless, and she fiddled with the zipper pull on her backpack. It was bursting at the seams from the spare change of clothes her father insisted she bring. Because of the snow. Wrapping her heavy pea-coat tighter, Taite tried to lose herself in a sci-fi thriller she bought earlier. But her thoughts turned gloomy until she drifted off.

+++

Without warning, the bus gave a hard jolt, waking Taite and knocking the novel from her limp hands. The woman beside her let out a startled squeak as her shoulder slammed into Taite's. A sharp pain shot down her arm.

"Sorry," the woman said as she hurried to right herself.

Taite scowled and rubbed her bicep before reaching to retrieve her book from where it fell. They lurched again, and she tumbled headfirst toward the floor.

"What the heck?" Taite said aloud, as she recovered and crammed the novel into her backpack. Her stomach rolled from the commotion, but she looked out the window anyway. What was happening out there? She saw nothing but the soft white of the still-falling snow.

As she sank back in her seat, hoping for a smoother ride, the bus swerved hard and came to a sudden screeching halt. Taite looked to her dark-haired neighbor who appeared undaunted. The other passengers must have already reached their stops while she slept. There was no one else left.

"Everything will be fine," the woman said.

Such an odd thing to say. Nothing seemed fine. Taite crinkled her brow and started to ask what she meant, but she didn't get the chance.

The woman reached into her pocket, pulled out a hypodermic needle, and stabbed it into Taite's thigh. With a scream, Taite shoved the woman away, but it was too late.

"Just relax, Aisea," the woman said. "It's pointless to struggle."

How did she know her name? What was going on? Taite gaped at her, dumbfounded as her head began to spin and her vision blurred. A man appeared, dressed like a faceless shadow. The image rippled and twisted. Her memory cut out to a fierce light and a thunderous, resounding boom.

TWO

It was pitch-black when Taite woke with her face pressed against a seat and her legs folded at awkward angles beneath her. While she glanced around, her eyes adjusted and her head throbbed. Taite pushed herself up with muscles that proved stiff and sore. A pulsing pain filled her skull, and nausea rushed up her throat. Coughing and spitting, she wiped her mouth clean on a sleeve and leaned her head against the back of the seat as she cursed her weak stomach.

As her head began to clear and the throbbing in her temples began to wane, Taite peered over the seats. The woman had vanished. She was alone, and the bus seemed smaller than she remembered. Disoriented, she couldn't quite grasp at a clear thought. Something was wrong though. Then it hit her, it wasn't the same bus.

Had someone kidnapped her? If so, where had they gone? A chill crept into her bones and fear prickled at her skin. Strange memories skirted the edge of her mind, but she didn't trust them. Nothing made any sense.

An unsettling, piercing silence met her ears, as she listened in the blackness. Inhaling, and slinging the green pack over one shoulder, a weakness clung to her limbs as she crept toward the front of the empty bus. As soon as she pulled the bi-fold doors open, a cold breeze thick with scents of soil and cold metal forced its way toward her.

Fingers of a thick haze crept near the ground as she stepped down from the bus. A night sky heavy with clouds stretched overhead, but not a trace of snow remained. Wherever she was, she couldn't tell, but one thing was clear — she was far from where she should be. The driver seemed to have stopped in the middle of nowhere, but even that was somewhere. She saw no trees or buildings, just a complete absence of civilization. That wasn't the only thing bothering her. It was also the geography. An empty plain sprawled in all directions. This was not the Northeast.

A thousand thoughts flooded her mind like a breaking dam. Everyone had vanished, and nothing looked familiar. The chilling hand of complete panic crept up her spine, but her Dad's calm scientific voice echoed in her mind — *There is always a rational explanation for everything under the sun.* They were the words he lived by. Not helpful at the moment, Dad.

"Well, shit," Taite said, her voice cracking with disuse and fear. This was impossible. As she began to crumble, she chewed her lip. No, she would not let herself fall apart. Her dad had always told her that in a crisis, panic only inhibits one's ability to comprehend and make rational decisions. A few more inhales, and she stood up straight and focused on getting home.

Once she shook her head to clear away the mental cobwebs, she began searching for her cell phone. Digging through spare clothes in her backpack, she pushed aside a pair of clean socks rolled into a ball and shoved her journal out of the way. Her fingertips brushed the smooth surface of her phone, and she tugged it loose from the tangle of clothes. Taite powered it on and prayed for a signal. The screen lit up. The blue glow illuminated her hands and face, but died away with a musical chirp. No signal, and no battery.

"Wonderful," she said, her breath a small cloud. She always kept it charged. What good is a phone for emergencies if it won't turn on? Taite swore and threw it back among her belongings. She let the bag lie and walked a few steps to get a better view.

Before her, the horizon was a wide-open expanse. An icy gust hurtled itself across the plain to brush against her cheek and send her brown hair flying. Far ahead, a few small lights twinkled. If she had to guess, it must have been at least five miles.

No car engines rumbled along, no crickets chirped, only the eerie wind whispered in her ears. She walked the short length of the bus. There were no city markings, not even a license plate. Her skin crawled, and her heart began to race as her instincts demanded she get as far away as possible.

A flat lot of nothing went on for miles behind the bus. In the other direction, the shadowed forms of hills rose from the horizon. The choice wasn't difficult. She would walk to the lights. It looked like a perfect habitat for coyotes or wolves, but she wasn't staying there one second longer. She pulled her coat tighter as she shivered. Dawn might be hours away.

From the first steps along the slate-smooth surface of the road, it seemed as if any minute she might drop off a cliff. The night was black and empty. It would have been comforting to hear the crunching of her boots against gravel, but the surface absorbed all but the faint padding of her rubber soles.

A mile past beneath her feet, and then another. The air grew colder by the minute, her teeth chattered and her fingers went numb. She began to worry all over again when light edged in from behind. Taite froze as the soft glow engulfed her.

When she whipped around, a car was closing in on her. Her brain said she should run, but her feet failed to react and stayed glued to the road. Finally, Taite willed a foot to lift but found her stiff knees only buckled. She fell to her hands, staring at the blinding lights of the approaching vehicle.

While a second was all that passed, it seemed time moved at a crawl. Her quickening pulse pounded in her ears. It was the only sound besides a low growl from the engine as it came to an abrupt stop only inches from her stone-still face. Taite stared underneath it as she struggled to catch her breath.

Taite only just regained her senses when a latch clicked — footfalls on the pavement, a new lump of fear in her throat. She lifted her eyes to the shoes that stopped before her. Brown leather hiking boots; thick-soled and caked in pale mud. The boots were not too far from her own size, smaller even. A woman. Taite looked up to confirm her guess. Close enough. But she would have called her more of a girl. She appeared no older than Taite herself with light curls crowning her head and framing her round face. The girl looked as concerned as Taite — shocked to almost run over someone. While Taite was just glad she wasn't a freakish psychopath.

They stared at each other until the blond spoke, her voice rougher than Taite expected. "Are you all right? What are you doing out here?"

"I think so," Taite said, getting to her feet with quivering arms. She brushed herself off, more from habit than need and asked, "Where is here anyway?"

"You don't know where you are?" the girl asked, cocking her head and arching an eyebrow as she watched Taite stoop to grab her backpack.

"No. I was going to Baltimore with a bus full of people, but something happened. Everyone's gone. Something weird is going on, and I need to reach my dad. I was walking to those lights up ahead," Taite said, knowing it sounded rather ridiculous. "Is that a town up there?"

The girl sighed and raked a hand through her curls as she shifted her weight on her feet. After a brief pause, she said, "I wondered why anyone would be out here. I passed the bus a little while ago. That isn't a town, but it's better than nothing. I'm headed there myself. Not much else out here. You better ride along."

Before it occurred to her this might be a bad idea, Taite nodded her agreement. None of Taite's friends would pick up a complete stranger like this. They wouldn't take a ride from one either. Then again, they hadn't been inexplicably lost. Anyway, she wasn't going to argue. It relieved her to see another person at all. Taite took a couple steps over, her feet now solid under her body. She shoved her hand out toward the girl and said, "Thank you. I'm Taite."

The girl raised her eyebrows and one side of her upper lip and stared at the outstretched hand. Her only comment was a dry, "Lanie."

Lanie jerked her arm away after a brief handshake and nodded toward the passenger side of the car. Spinning on her heel without a word, Taite walked to the side of the beige-colored car with tires like an army truck.

"A little help?" she asked when she didn't find the door handle. Lanie was already sitting in the driver's seat and slammed the door while muttering under her breath. At the click of a button, the passenger door cracked open. Taite flopped down hard in the too-low seat. Again, she wondered if this was the best decision as she looked over at Lanie. Well, she was in it now.

Relaxing against the soft gray seat, she would have killed to take her boots off. Her feet were sore and cramped, but she didn't think Lanie would appreciate that.

Lanie didn't even look at Taite, only strapped a safety harness around herself. It was not a typical seat belt but pulled down over her head like a race car. Taite watched, copying her movements to secure her own. To start the car, Lanie pressed her palm to the dash, and the car's gentle roar vibrated in their ears.

At the risk of adding to the obvious annoyance her companion felt at Taite's existence, she asked, "So, um... starts with your hand? Classy."

Despite her obvious irritation, the girl looked over, amusement playing in her light green eyes. "Observant, aren't we?" she asked with a smirk.

Whoever Lanie was, she came off a little demeaning. Brushing it off, Taite asked, "When can I head home? Where are we exactly?"

Lanie shook her head and said, "One question at a time."

Taite shrugged her shoulders as Lanie said, "I'm not sure about getting you home right now. I guess we'll need to talk about where home is first. There's a checkpoint and rail station ahead and not much else. It's the only one this far north. The road ends there... well, the finished road."

Maybe this was a dream. None of it made any sense.

"Listen," Taite said, "I don't have the first clue what you're talking about. This far north? North of what? What state is this? All I know is I'm far from where I should be, and I need to get home. I don't want to go anywhere if there are no finished roads. Is there a phone at this checkpoint? Can I call my dad?" Taite's head whirled, and this girl worried more about pointing out her ignorance than giving her any real answers.

"Slow down. No reason to get angry. I'm trying to help you, but this is the only way I can. There are no phones this far out, and you'll have a difficult time finding one anywhere. Phone service is limited. You might not be able to reach your father anyway." She paused and tucked a curl behind her ear.

"You may not want to go with me, but you're better off with me than walking back. Anyway, it's too cold."

"Why should I trust you? I have no idea who you are. I thought you could take me closer to home, closer to civilization, but you're taking me further away."

Lanie sighed and said, "It's the only place I can take you. I have somewhere to be. I'm not a chauffeur. We'll get through the checkpoint, then I'm on way to meet my brother. You can either come with me or stay at the checkpoint. Trust me, you won't want to do that. It isn't the safest place to linger, ya know?" She drummed her fingers on the wheel as she continued, "And speaking of trusting me, what else can you do? I could have left you back there to freeze. Calm down already."

"Fine," Taite said. "I guess you're right. We'll see about this checkpoint place. Maybe I'll stay. Maybe I won't."

"Suit yourself, but I wouldn't stay if I were you."

The lights remained in the distance, further than Taite estimated from the bus. Lanie said there were no phones, but there had to be a way to reach her dad. Taite was half-convinced this wasn't happening — it was one of those hyper-realistic dreams she had sometimes. Thoughts whirled as she watched the featureless night streak by the window.

The checkpoint lights grew larger, and a small nest of buildings began to take shape beneath them. In the center stood a long, low structure. This must be the checkpoint itself. On either side, there was

19

a short line of buildings; barracks or something. They weren't close enough to make out details, and it was the dead of night. The cluster of civilization didn't amount to much, but it was a welcome sight.

Lanie continued driving in silence though she didn't appear to do much behind the wheel. The road was so straight she only perched there looking important.

When they came closer to the buildings, details came into focus under the lights. The structures were all very simple with little architectural detail — modernist concrete boxes. Few windows interrupted the dull facades, and some buildings had none at all. Where there were openings, they came equipped with large roll-away shutters. Taite had only seen something similar when she had taken a rare vacation with her father to Florida. There, they called them hurricane shutters. Why they used them here with no evidence of a coastline, she couldn't guess. Security perhaps. It seemed to be an issue, as a tall fence ran as far as she could see in either direction.

Nothing decorative existed anywhere, not even landscaping. It was depressing and dirty. Judging by the fragmented bits of clean, the buildings had once been white. Now they looked like they were painted in grime or had been hit by one heck of a shit-storm. There wasn't much else. Only the road that washed out to a pale gray under the lights and the faceless dirty cubes.

The checkpoint sat at the far end of the formation of buildings. As they drove up among the glowing lamps, the train signal lights became visible to the left. It would have all reminded Taite of a ghost town in an old western movie if the buildings weren't so blocky and bare.

Lanie broke the silence. "Let me do the talking. Don't open your mouth and don't ask questions."

"Fine," Taite said with a grunt before realizing she might need to ask questions to figure out if these people would help her get home. "Wait a minute," she said. "You can't order me around. Besides, I might not go any further with you."

"Whatever. Just be quiet and try not to bring attention to us. This place isn't safe."

Lanie slid the car to a stop in front of one of the smaller boxes where the road extended into a large parking slab. There was only one way in and one way out. Like Lanie said, the road ended. Taite started for her backpack, as Lanie walked around and opened the hatch. After pulling on a heavy coat, she slung a tan pack to her side.

"It's Taite, right?"

Before Taite answered, Lanie said, "Hold this," and flung a canvas tote. It was heavier than it looked and sloshed as Taite pulled it over her free shoulder.

"We'll need that later," Lanie said. She adjusted her gear, slammed the hatch, and marched off toward the low building without waiting for a word from Taite. "Follow me and be quiet."

"Yes, sir," Taite said under her breath. Taite trailed after Lanie, observing the sign stamped in the concrete. It read 'Checkpoint'. Whoever designed this building, definitely put function over form. Lanie slung open the bare metal door and slipped through the threshold. Taite hurried in after her, catching the door as it rushed toward her face.

+++

Armed guards stood on either side of the entry. Further in, two more manned a metal detector or some kind of scanner. The guards by the door didn't turn their heads, but Taite could feel their piercing eyes at her back. Lanie never wavered as she marched across the gleaming gray floor toward the scanner in the center of the room. One soldier held an electronic tablet and slid a finger across the screen as he studied the girls. His pale eyes seemed cold, making Taite feel self-conscious.

Lanie stepped forward and said, "We need to board a train as soon as possible, sir."

"No one boards without a pass, miss."

"I'm aware of the rules, but there's been an emergency. We didn't have time for all the red tape."

"Not that it matters, but what type of emergency?"

While Taite listened, Lanie said, "My uncle works at the Eastern camp, and I need to get a message to him. There was a terrorist raid and his son is missing. Most likely dead."

"Yes, I heard about the raid," said the mouth under the cold eyes. "You realize we can notify your uncle ourselves, right?"

"Of course, but under the circumstances, it's better to come from family. You understand," Lanie said while widening her eyes like a dog begging for scraps. As she chewed her lower lip, she added, "Besides, you realize how long all that can take."

Breaths were held.

The young man shifted his weight from one foot to the other and looked the girls up and down, scanning for a sign of the lie they were desperate to hide.

"There were reports of possible fatalities. I don't know what harm it would do to let you go. I'll need to sign you in and do the usual checks of course. The train arrives in a few minutes, but you'll be able to make it." He again activated his tablet and maneuvered around the software.

"Names?" he asked.

"Caitlyn Green. This is Gabby Thorne. She's traveling with me for, well... safety in numbers, right?"

The guard's fingers raced over the screen as he nodded. "The system has been having problems today. Some minor damage occurred during the raid. I've entered the names. I'll manually clear you when the system is back up."

Lanie watched with an innocent expression. She glanced at Taite, who was nauseous all over again. After setting down his tablet, the guard continued by having the girls walk to the scanning area to confirm they carried no weapons or illegal items. Taite shot Lanie a questioning look. What would he find in those bags? But Lanie didn't return the glance. She was watching the guard who had picked up his tablet again.

"Finally. The screen is up," he said.

Lanie leaned over to Taite and mouthed, "Be ready to run."

"What?" Taite asked with a raised eyebrow and a quickening pulse.

"Miss Green, you're cleared. Step through the scanner while I search your friend's name. Is there an 'e' on the end of that?"

"Yes, sir," Lanie said, stepping through the portal-like scanner. Taite became over-conscious of her heart pounding against her ribs. While the guard focused on his screen, Lanie stood on the other side of the scanner, peering at the tablet from behind.

Her eyes flashed up at Taite as the guard said, "There seems to be a problem. I can't find the name in the system."

"Now," Lanie said as she bolted. Adrenaline shoved Taite forward. She sprinted through the portal before the guard even looked up from his screen. The tablet tumble to the floor, but they kept running toward the track exit beyond. He shouted, but Taite didn't hear what he said through the blood rushing in her ears. Seconds later, the cold

23

night air flooded in as they burst through the door. Behind, voices echoed off bare walls.

Lanie said, "We'll go on foot — past the tracks. They won't follow." As the door slammed shut behind, Lanie exploded toward the platform without a glance. Taite sprinted after, her pack bouncing and weighing her down. A door slammed, and she risked a glance to see two officers running from the building.

Taite gasped through sputtering breaths and asked, "What's going on?"

"Run!" Lanie said, as they neared the tracks and veered off to the left. A bright light rushed toward them with a deep rumbling that Taite could feel in her bones.

"Hurry!" Lanie said as she led the way around and behind the building. "We have to beat the train."

"Are you crazy?" Taite asked, panting for air. "You're gonna get us killed!"

"What do you think'll happen if they catch us?" Lanie asked over her shoulder as she ran.

We're going to die. The thought jumped in her mind. Taite sprinted, aware of only her feet pounding against the ground. The girls ran hard through the dry brush that dotted the area as they approached the monorail. The hum of the train engine grew louder.

Taite gasped, her heart raced, and pained stabbed her side. But she pushed on, fear coursing through her veins. Shouts came from behind, but Taite didn't dare look back again. The train hurtled toward them, only feet away, and she knew it would be close.

Lanie reached back and jerked Taite's arm as they jumped across the single track, throwing themselves to the ground beyond. The sleek silver train thundered by short seconds later, horn blaring as it glided along the rail. It isn't easy to take a flying leap with a fifteen pound bag strapped to one's back. As Taite fell to her knees in the gravel along the track, she noticed Lanie caught herself before she toppled.

While the train still rumbled along, the two righted themselves. They looked back at the line of speeding silver and continued running. Taite had no clue where they were going. She only reasoned that when a pack of strange men pursue you, it's best to get away. There was no time to think of anything else.

They kept a pace too brisk for much conversation, but she had a hundred questions for Lanie once they were safe. She asked between sputtering breaths, "Aren't they going to catch up with us once the train is through?"

"No, I told you, they can't leave their posts. They'll send for back-up, but that will give us time," Lanie said as their feet trod the uneven ground.

She seemed pretty certain of herself, almost like she had done this once or twice. By the time the air was silent again, they had covered a few hundred yards. To Taite's relief, Lanie slowed the pace to an easy walk.

After her pulse slowed and her lungs stopped burning, Taite turned to Lanie. "What just happened back there?"

Lanie sounded annoyed as usual, as she adjusted her pack and said, "I made up a name for you. I didn't exactly have time or resources to find a real one. I had mine ready, so he cleared me."

"You had a fake name ready?" Taite asked, as her legs came to a dead stop. She was traveling with a criminal or a delinquent at least. Did that make them fugitives? Her dad was gonna kill her when she got home, assuming she got home. She asked, "Did you even plan on boarding the train?"

"No," Lanie said with a shrug. She tossed her pack down and grabbed the black bag that had been slamming against Taite's hip as she ran. Taite was glad to relinquish it, and Lanie handed her a bottle of water that she cracked open and tipped back.

"I'm not a career thief or something, if that's what you're thinking. It's hard to explain. Like I told you, I have to find my brother. They don't just let anyone walk past the platform."

Taite sighed as she sipped the water, her thoughts racing. "You knew that would happen."

"You saw what kind of place it is. Not exactly somewhere you want to hang around for too long, regardless."

"And Gabby Thorne was the best you could come up with?"

"Well, you hardly stop talking, and you're becoming a real thorn in my side. Seemed fitting."

"Beautiful," Taite said as she rolled her eyes. "So, where are you meeting your brother anyway? Why are we out here?"

"There's a military outpost and maintenance stations for the rail. We'll be going to one of those. That's where my brother is expecting us... me. He won't be too happy to see you," Lanie said, scowling.

"But we're gonna freeze."

"It's a long walk there, but it's only an hour until dawn. That's good and bad. Good, since it'll warm up. Bad because it'll warm up a lot. I only brought water for one, but we'll manage. I would suggest you go through your stuff. You probably have a lot of useless crap in there. Might as well lighten your load."

Taite huffed as she stopped to dump what possessions she could, wondering how things could get any worse. But she was glad of the lighter weight on her back... until Lanie gave her another bag to carry. Of course. She scowled as she swung the bag up and scanned the landscape. But the only thing of note was a few scattered trees standing sentry in the night. Their skeletal frames were black on black in the night.

For what seemed like hours, they trudged along the rocky, dry terrain. Taite's arches were aching and her head was drooping when a faint blue glow crept along the horizon, revealing a large stand of bare trees in the distance and patches of long-dead grasses rattling in the wind.

Lanie pointed to a small gray spec near the trees. "There," she said, "It isn't as far as it looks."

Taite hoped she was right. Right now all Taite wanted was to lie down and sleep. She sighed and willed her feet to keep up the monotonous march as she worked to match Lanie's pace. She wished she'd slow down. While Taite knew she was no track star, she had thought she was in decent shape. This journey was proving her wrong. But Lanie seemed to have a spring in her step as she trotted along. How someone that small could walk so far with twenty extra pounds on her back, Taite couldn't fathom. She interrupted her own rambling thoughts to ask, "Hey, Lanie, after we meet your brother, then what? I mean that works for you, but how do I get home?"

As she stopped in her tracks, Lanie said, "One thing at a time. Besides, if my assumption is correct, getting you home could be more difficult than you think. My brother may know more." She dropped back into silence as if she had given a complete and thorough answer.

"That's it?" Taite asked. "That's all you can tell me?"

"You know," she said, "you aren't my problem. I have my own. I'm helping you how I can. You can come with me. We will try to figure it out, or you can turn back and trek all day and hope those creeps at the checkpoint are feeling more generous. That's your only other choice."

Taite didn't bother to reply. They both knew she was right. How did she get into this mess? And how could she get out of it? Until now, life had been dull and uneventful. Nothing weird ever happened to her. Now, she may as well have walked into a nightmare.

THREE

The sun began to rise behind them with a pale glow. Taite must have been getting tired, because she found her eyes were playing tricks on her. The sky lightened, but dimmed again before transforming into a massive expanse of thick golden clouds. The ground turned a warm ocher beneath their feet with dark shrubs dotting the desolate surface.

Once, the distant blaring of a train whistle met their ears, and Lanie described how the track curved back in their direction as it headed further north through the hills.

They continued walking until Taite thought she couldn't take another step. Her legs ached from her hips to her feet, which were blistering. Finally, Lanie stopped without a word and dropped to the ground.

Since clouds covered the sky, Taite had no guess of the time, but it seemed a few hours later when two large buildings came into view. Like the others near the checkpoint, they were concrete and simple. The flat roofs angled back. Although it didn't look like this place had need of drainage. A few windows and a set of wide double doors marked the front facade and entrance. The only attempt at landscaping came in the form of aesthetic boulders and two rugged, gnarled trees with small,

29

sickly black leaves. The trunks were spindly, and it looked as if the trees were being forced to survive, kept alive by the will of their caretaker. Lanie slowed her pace, while for once, Taite had to resist quickening her own. There would be water, a place to sit, shade, and perhaps food. Please God, let there be real food.

Meanwhile, Lanie considered the scene, taking more interest in the second building. As large as the first, it had no windows, only a wide doorway that stood agape. It resembled a large barn or an airport hanger, and Taite thought it might actually be one. But Lanie described this place as a maintenance station. This must be a workshop or storage building.

Lanie pointed, reaching her arm across Taite's view. "That's where we're headed," she said, pointing out the obvious as she stopped to sip from her water bottle. "We need to be cautious. The man who runs this place doesn't much like us."

"Great," Taite said, smothering the word in sarcasm. "Seems like you're real popular around here."

"Funny," Lanie said with a smile that appeared less than genuine. "You don't understand much, and there is no way you could, so I will ignore that. If you will allow me to continue... his wife is fond of us. 'Us' being my brother and me, not you.

"They're an older couple with none of their own kids, so she sorta adopted us. That's why we meet here sometimes. As long as the old man is out working, we can get a meal or two, a chance to rest and clean up. It works out. If he's home, we'll see, and we'll wait. She usually leaves the shed door open when he's gone."

"Is he here?" Taite asked. The idea of sprinting again made her more aware of the exhaustion tugging at her limbs.

Lanie provided an answer before the sound of her words died in the air. "Door's open. Like I said, he's gone. We go to the house."

Taite became anxious but swallowed her hesitation. "I guess you know best."

Lanie grinned, not the sarcastic smirk Taite already came to expect. They adjusted belongings on their backs and walked in unison to the cubic house. Taite imagined it must have been much larger than two people needed. It looked like an awful waste of space. Lanie's stride remained confident and steady, so Taite ignored the anxiety creeping through her limbs.

The door reverberated with a deep rumble as Lanie pounded her small fist against it twice. They waited. Then they waited some more. Taite's traveling companion stayed silent and unfazed by the lack of response. Taite grew impatient and tapped her foot against the dry soil. She ran her hand along the gnarled bark of the closest tree. It was light gray and felt softer than it looked. Twisted and misshapen, but worn on the surface like a carving polished smooth. Lanie stood firm in front of the door as if to will it open with her presence.

After a moment, the door pulled inward with a slow creak. Taite entertained the thought Lanie opened it somehow. She didn't see a soul inside, only the darkness of the interior. She glanced over Lanie's head as she followed her over the threshold and into the shadows.

As it turned out, the house was occupied, and inside it was not so dark. A cheerful woman stood to the side with her hand on the door. Taller than either of the pair, she seemed eroded like the tree outside. Despite her creased face, something told Taite she had even more years than her squinted eyes implied. Her hair cut short and left to gray. She had a kind look about her, and Taite's apprehension eased. Lanie's adopted mother beamed with a wide smile, almost too wide for her face.

31

+++

Taite fluffed her pillow and stretched out full length on the cushions that Karina provided. That was their hostess's name, although it didn't quite suit her. Lanie slept on a small couch, her dusty boots kicked off onto the floor by her pack. The two already feasted on a generous meal of thick, meaty stew with the perfect amount of salt. Afterwards, they indulged in all the water they could drink.

As luck would have it, Karina's husband was on an overnight job at the far end of his jurisdiction. According to Lanie, this was perfect, since her brother hadn't arrived yet. Taite tried to charge her cell phone, but Karina's solar-powered service wasn't effective. The phone sizzled dead in her hand. Probably no towers nearby anyway.

At least, Karina's home was comfortable and cool, despite having no obvious ventilation system. The floor plan was open-concept, that's what the shows she watched with Mrs. Dalton would have called it. Ceilings rose high with a loft along the back wall over the kitchen. A few pieces minimalist pieces of furniture hinted the interior designer and architect were one and the same.

An arrangement of dried grasses sat on a rough-hewn end table. Above the couch, hung a painting of the northern lights. The colors looked all wrong though. Maybe Karina had an imaginative streak.

After eating, the travelers followed Karina to the loft above the kitchen, forcing their weary legs to move. Later, Taite would have few memories of the conversation between Lanie and Karina. She barely recalled climbing the loft stairs and dropping to the bed made up on the floor. Karina had prepared it as Taite and Lanie took turns in the small bathroom.

To wash away the dirt from her dry skin, to be clean was a luxury.

She was drained, her eyes lids heavy with sleep. Yet she could not seem to relax. Though it was not yet dark, Lanie must have fallen asleep as soon as she hit the pillow. But Taite's mind raced on, trying to make sense out of what she had experienced. The task was going nowhere fast, and she drifted off to bizarre dreams.

+++

Taite woke in confusion and panic. Sometimes, before the rational side wakes up and remembers the day before, there's a moment of terror. As a child, Taite would wake up disoriented only to realize her father had moved her from the couch to her bed as she slept. This was different. Recent memories were not reassuring. Surrounded by strangers, she woke in a place she couldn't name.

Soft breathing came from Lanie's couch behind. She wished Lanie was awake, so she could ask her if this was real. Taite rolled onto her side to face the pale sun beaming in the window as it peeked through the cloud cover. A lump of pillows, padding, and a person had appeared on the floor near the end of the couch. It startled her before she concluded that the tardy brother must have arrived.

Under normal circumstances, Taite was a light sleeper. The thought of a man creeping in while she slept distressed her. No matter whose brother he was. This whole thing was weird. Who the hell were these people? Taite rolled away. She hugged an unnecessary blanket to her chest and ignored the stinging in her eyes.

When she woke again, she was alone in the room. All signs of Lanie and her brother had disappeared. Her heart jumped into her throat as it occurred to her they may have left her. This was a bad situation, but at least she hadn't been alone. Taite scrambled to her feet and ran to peer over the side of the open loft. Over the railing, at least fifteen feet below was a table set with breakfast. The familiar smell of coffee wafted up in a welcome greeting.

Their weathered hostess glanced up and said, "Oh good. Come down before the food gets cold."

With a sigh of relief, she noted three figures around the table. Her heart slowed to its normal rhythm as she returned to dismantle the makeshift bed and slide on her waiting boots.

She crept down the stairs to meet another person who preferred she wasn't there. The siblings continued muttering to each other. Taite was glad no one bothered to look up as she walked into the room. Being ignored had never felt so good.

At first glance, she guessed the brother to be in his early twenties, taller than average. He shared his sister's sharp chin, but otherwise, they didn't look much alike. Dirty blond in all ways, his hair unkempt like he didn't own a comb. Seemed he didn't own a razor either. Taite sat a few chairs away from him, where Karina set down a plate. It didn't concern her if he owned a comb or a razor, but if he was traveling with them she prayed he owned deodorant.

Lanie neglected introductions, which suited Taite fine. She was almost sure she shouldn't exist as far as the brother was concerned. She would pretend he didn't exist either, and they would get along fine. Exactly like most of the a-holes back at school.

"Coffee, Taite?" Karina asked as Taite filled her plate.

"No, but thank you. I've just never cared for the taste."

Breakfast was quiet but out of politeness, Karina scattered a few questions. How did they sleep? Did she like the food? Lanie stayed too preoccupied with her brother to take much notice of Taite. Neither of them looked very chipper.

"Why can't I stay here and try to get in touch with my dad?" Taite asked of no one in particular.

"You can't," Lanie said as she took a drink from her steaming mug. "You'll need to leave with us."

No surprise there. Taite was getting used to that answer. She sighed and turned her attention back to buttering her toast. "Where will we be going, and how long is it going to take?"

Lanie opened her mouth to respond. Before a sound escaped her throat, the brother interrupted.

"About a week," he said in a raspy voice. He cleared his throat and continued. "We all know you shouldn't be here, but here you are. I need to sort this all out, so just hold off on questions for now."

He looked tired and irritated, and his words made Taite furious. She wasn't a piece of luggage to be hauled around. She didn't like this any more than they did, but she needed answers. It was crazy for them to think she would follow them like a lost puppy.

Taite slammed the butter knife to the tabletop. "Hold off? You must be joking. I have gone along with everything so far, knowing nothing. Now you expect me to go traipsing after you both to yet another place in the middle of nowhere. You won't even tell me what the hell is happening. You know where we are. I'm not walking another step unless somebody tells me something."

Burning with anger, the words came out louder than she intended. The raised eyebrows on the faces around told her the sudden burst of temper surprised them too. She felt like an idiot. Not for raising her voice, but for getting into that girl's stupid car in the first place. Lanie broke the brief silence.

Her voice was kinder than Taite expected. "Taite, there's a lot you don't understand."

Her brother looked over with a cautious expression. "Lanie's right, and there's no time to explain it now. We have need to keep moving."

Taite slumped back into her chair, defeated. Always the same answer; there was a lot she didn't understand. Of course. No one wanted to tell her anything. She hated to admit it, but even if she made a big scene, she would have to go with them. Her lower lip quivered, and she bit it. While she wanted to cry, there was no way she would now. Taite didn't know if her expression betrayed her emotions, but as Lanie's brother continued, his voice was slower, almost like he would have talked to a child. It made her even angrier.

"Anyway," he said, pausing to swallow a mouthful, "I will tell you everything when I can. For now, all I can say is that you'll be safer with us and unfortunately, you'll have to trust us. This isn't ideal for anyone."

She opened her eyes, clenched her jaw and stared right at him. His eyes were gloomy and serious, but there was no lie behind them.

"Fine," she said and returned her attention to breakfast.

A clock chimed on the wall, and Lanie jumped in her chair. "Baylin," she said, "we need to go soon."

"I'm aware. Get the rest of the supplies ready, would ya? I gotta take ten minutes to clean up."

He left the table, opening a side door for Karina as she entered with an armload of small, wrapped packages and bags. Taite hadn't even noticed her leave the table.

Karina smiled and said, "This should help you out. There's bread and dried fruit, jerky, and I even tossed in a few of those emergency ration packs they give us. It isn't much, but it might get you through. You've got your water ready, Lanie?"

Lanie nodded, walking over to help fit the packages into every free nook and cranny in their bags. They both seemed to be a bit glum. As if Karina didn't want to see them go, and Lanie would have rather stayed. No one spoke, but the sounds of rustling paper and plastic filled the otherwise quiet room.

Shortly after Lanie forced the last of the food into Taite's backpack, Lanie's brother, Baylin, returned. He had cleaned off the dust and shaved the stubble off his chin and hollowed cheeks. A small scar sat pale against his cheekbone. Back home she would have been staring at his biceps as they contracted beneath his clean gray t-shirt. Now, she watched with suspicion and curiosity.

Baylin glanced at his sister and exhaled with relief. "Better. Let's get going."

For what might have been the thousandth time, Taite heaved her backpack onto her shoulder. It was much heavier than she recalled and contained almost nothing of her own belongings. Lanie now seemed eager to leave. She kept looking from the door to her brother, who was hanging back to exchange a few words with Karina.

"Bay," Lanie said, "we have to leave. We have a long way to go before dark."

"Be right there," he said with a quick glance across the room.

Karina wrinkled her face into a smile as she patted his cheek before he turned to go. "Be careful and come back safe."

As Karina stood in the doorway looking after them, the trio marched into the sun and an uncertain future.

FOUR

Waves of heat radiated from the ground like slithering snakes as they walked miles. Occasionally, a break in the clouds allowed a hint of sky to poke through. Taite didn't remember if she had ever seen it such a shade of blue. She'd been in the sun too long.

The water supply already ran low, and they all grew a little irritable. Sweat trickled down backs, stung their eyes, and made hair shades darker as the trio climbed a steep hill. What few words were spoken often stayed between Baylin and Lanie. Behind them, Taite trudged on, too miserable to care what the siblings talked about. But as she caught up with them at the top of the hill, she froze.

Taite couldn't count how many miles they traveled, but the barren hill turned into another landscape altogether. They now stood gazing down at a forested abyss. Level with their feet, a vast expanse of forest canopy sprouted from a canyon and stretched to either side as far as they could see. The foliage was deep green, nearly black against the ocher soil dusting their boots. To Taite, it looked scorched.

The drop off was immense, and the trees were as high as the ledge — growing ever-taller to escape the shadowed walls of the gulch.

Creeping toward them from below, the blackness of the forest floor blended into the leaves. It was impossible to tell how far down it went. A tangle of twisting branches and blackened leaves rocked in the wind before them. Taite had never heard of anywhere that looked like this. Astonished, she turned to Lanie, who threw off her pack and was pulling out ropes and clasps. Her brother stared out at the trees, looking for what, Taite didn't know.

"What is this place?" she asked, her voice sounding small. Baylin's face snapped around.

"I'm not surprised you had to ask. Don't worry. It isn't as sinister as it looks."

Taite shook her head. Neither of her companions looked surprised by the view. Chilled air rushed up from below, giving the impression the forest exhaled. Her sweaty shirt clung to her back and bloody blisters adorned her feet. In that moment, she was only aware of the chilled breath of the enormous forest. Taite closed her eyes to focus on the cool relief. The updraft dried the sweat in her hair within minutes.

Baylin stayed silent, enjoying the view or doing his best to ignore her. Turning, he stooped to help his sister with the pack.

"Are we going down there?" Taite asked as she observed the careful uncoiling of nylon ropes. "It's so dark. How far is it?"

"It's over a thousand feet and yes, we're going down," Lanie said as she unwound a thin rope. "This is the best part," she added, a spreading grin crinkling her eyes. "We've only got two harnesses, but the rope is strong enough to double up. It would be best to improvise a knotted harness for you, but I don't imagine you know how to rappel. You'll go with Baylin."

Preoccupied collecting the harnesses from his pack, Baylin remained silent.

"Wouldn't it be better if you and I stayed together? We'd be lighter, right?" Taite asked with concern, as she crouched to run a length of rope through her fingers.

"Lighter, yes, but if something happened, neither of us could stop the other from falling. I've rappelled down many times, but you haven't. You'll go with Baylin. It's safer."

Taite turned away and rolled her eyes in exasperation. This is crap. She did not want her life or her anything else in the hands of some guy she just met. This kept getting crappier and crappier. She forced her stiff joints to the ground and sat cross-legged, resting her head on her hands. Lanie was tying a series of knots in one rope. Taite watched and agonized over their thinness.

Lanie stepped closer, testing the strength of her knots with a hard tug. Then she instructed Taite to step into the homemade harness. With a shudder, Taite watched as Lanie formed the rest of the harness around her waist. The loops went tight around her legs, and a twisted rope ran flat across her stomach. It was not comfortable, and Taite was not convinced it would prevent her from plummeting to her death.

"You've never climbed at all?" Baylin asked, his question sounding more like a statement. He walked toward them with more rope and metal clips.

"No," she said, shaking her head as she continued examining the ropes that hugged her hips.

"Well, this is a carabiner," he said in his low voice, clamping a metal clip over the rope across her waist. "This isn't the best way to do this, but I didn't plan for a third person when I packed the equipment. The carabiner on your harness is attached to this length of rope. The other end will anchor you to my harness."

"Lanie," he said over his shoulder to where his sister tested her rope, "wait, so I can test the anchors. We haven't used them for a while. Let's make sure we all get out of here alive."

Baylin turned back to Taite and looked her over. "You can't be that heavy. The gear is already take care of, so we should be good. The worst part for you will be getting over the edge of the cliff."

Behind him, the rocky, curving surface worn smooth by erosion disappeared into the trees. He pointed to a loop of metal wedged into a crack in the rock. "I'll clip onto the anchors there, and we'll back off the edge, rappelling over and down." He continued, holding up a little metal contraption. "This releases the rope to slide down. I'll control that. Don't worry about it. Stay out of the way and do what I say. Simple, right?"

"Guess so," Taite said. She understood little of it, but if she was just along for the ride, it didn't matter. Baylin must have believed her or he didn't care, whatever the case he walked off to check the anchors.

As she sat beside her, Lanie handed Taite a bottle of water and reassured her that her brother knew what he was doing. Taite sipped on water that tasted a little like rust and tried to calm the sick sensation in the pit of her stomach. Heights weren't her thing in the first place, and dangling like a spider was not appealing.

Only minutes later, Taite swayed mid-air against Baylin's back. One hand gripped a safety rope attached to the main, the other clung white-knuckled to his shirt. Below, the cliff face faded to total darkness.

To their right, Lanie rappelled away from the wall as she zipped downward. With a grin and far too much enthusiasm, she yelled, "Woo! I've missed this!"

Taite's tension grew as Baylin's hand worked the metal release. With every drop, her breath stopped, and she squeezed her eyes shut. Once, a small squeal escaped her lips as they plummeted downward. As she tried not to imagine falling, she knew she would never enjoy this like Lanie.

During the descent into the dense canopy, the ambient light disappeared. Lanie switched on a lamp attached to her belt, and a pale glow illuminated the wall before them. Baylin stopped the rope and braced his legs against the dry cliff wall. He was breathing hard, and Taite worried she was heavier than he planned. As he fumbled with his own light, Taite craned her neck back. Forget driving a car through one of the trees, these things would each take up almost the whole block. For their size, they grew close together and had ribbed bark with strange fan-like growths, covered in scales.

Several times Taite's diameter, limbs jutted out in every direction. Sharp leaves scratched against her shoulder, as Baylin shifted his weight and adjusted his hands on the line. Beside them, Lanie's lamp was sliding slowing downward toward the blackness.

Baylin turned his head back. "You good back there?"

"I'm OK," Taite said. "but I'll be glad when my feet are on solid ground."

"You and me both," he said under his breath. A familiar click, and they crept down the wall again. The pale light created an eerie atmosphere, turning Baylin's light hair to blue. Distorted shadows crept in from every angle, and a breeze sent leaves into a rustling frenzy.

With each cool updraft, came the sweet smells of damp soil and rotting vegetation. It was a calming smell that made the descent a little less terrifying.

Brushing near another branch, Baylin shoved off the wall and swung them over to it, switching the rope to a different anchor. Above, another limb widened toward the trunk of the massive tree.

With a fistful of Baylin's damp shirt, she twisted around for a better look. The muscle of his shoulder tensed under her fingers as he tightened his grip.

"Hey, what are you doing?" he asked. "It's dangerous enough without you squirming."

"Sorry. These trees are unbelievable." As predicted, she wasn't enjoying being tied to a sour-tempered guy she didn't know. On the upside, at least he didn't stink.

Out of breath, Baylin said, "You'll have plenty of time to admire the view later. For now, hold still before you send us off the side of the branch and into the wall."

From then on, her sightseeing was limited to the cliff wall and Baylin's wavy hair. It had started to curl with the increasing humidity. The ground remained far below from what Taite saw, which wasn't much. Along with the sunlight, went most of the sun's heat as they sank toward the distant ground. As she shivered, she held on a little tighter.

Hours later, Lanie's lamp was motionless as she sat about thirty feet to the side, legs stretched out on a large limb. Taite stood, enjoying a bit of personal space, though she stayed tethered to Baylin by five feet of rope. He crouched to catch his breath and wipe drips from his brow.

Minutes passed, and he signaled Lanie with his lantern. Odd. She would have heard him if he called out. Lanie rose to her feet in the small halo of light surrounding her. An apparition in the false night around them.

Back on his feet, Baylin said, "We've gotta keep going."

"What's the rush?" Taite asked, swinging her arms. "Can't we rest longer?" She was in no hurry to relinquish her freedom, and Baylin still appeared to be recovering.

"We don't have the time. Besides, I told Lanie yesterday, I suspect the two of you were followed to Karina's. There's no point spending more time out here than needed."

"Followed?" Taite asked, finding herself instinctively dropping her voice. "By those guards? Lanie said they never come past the rail."

"It isn't that. I spotted a scout earlier. I'm not sure why, but I've got a feeling it might have something to do with you. You shouldn't be here," he said, as he tested the line again and pushed a strand of hair from his forehead.

"You think I want to be here?" she asked. She wanted to go home. Her father must be frantic. If this was even real... she still hoped she was hallucinating.

"No need to get upset, Taite," he said, calling her by name for the first time that she recalled. She assumed he didn't bother to remember it.

"Something just feels off about all this."

"You're telling me," she said with a groan.

He snorted as he pointed past her and said, "Down we go. Lanie is already moving. Not too much longer before we can take a real break."

+++

At the bottom, it was darker than a moonless night, and Taite had no idea how much daylight remained in the world above. Her winter boots hit the ground with a muted thud as she and Baylin ended their rappel at last. The forest floor crunched and gave underfoot, littered with layer upon layer of dried leaves, twigs, and other detritus. Stretching out her muscles, she was grateful to be away from heights, ledges, and limbs.

Already there, Lanie waited in her dim light. They caught only shadowed glimpses of each other as she suggested they tear into some

44

jerky for dinner or lunch, whichever it was. Afterwards they had to keep moving, but Taite didn't complain — the lanterns wouldn't last forever. Besides, she wanted out of the woods, rising overhead like a crowd of angry giants.

The branches overhead creaked with the breeze and leaves rustled. If any wildlife lived in this forest, she saw no signs. Taite saw no wildlife — no birds, not even bugs scurrying along the branches. On a different day, she would ask about that. No one was in the mood for conversation now. Her head drooped, as she hugged her knees to her chest. Sleep tugged seductively at her eyes and pulled her below.

The next thing she knew, Lanie was shaking her awake. "We have to go, Taite," she said in a hoarse whisper. "Quietly."

"What... what's going on?" Taite asked. Blackness engulfed them — the lantern extinguished.

"There are lights in the distance. We need to get back up in the trees."

Eyes adjusting to the ebony black, Taite focused on five distant lights twinkling before her.

"I see them," she said as her pulse quickened in her neck.

Baylin and Lanie were shuffling nearby as they attached carabiners to harnesses and tied packs to be pulled up after them. And no light to help them this time. The lanterns below were growing closer as they bobbed and rocked silently among the trunks. Then they vanished, reappearing several minutes later on the other side of a tree.

They only needed to reach the first branch Baylin said. But from Taite's estimation, the way up looked much more difficult. Though the three were tethered together in case someone lost their footing, she had to make it on her own this time.

The wide irregular ridges of the bark made for great finger-holds, and the climb was easier than Taite had feared. Lanie was a good climber, and she scrambled up the enormous trunk as easily as if she was walking. Baylin moved slower. Taite liked to think he wasn't as inhuman as he acted and was getting tired. In reality, she was slowing him down.

It was a battle with the bark for Taite, and she wished she had been more athletic in school. Hand over hand, her fingers were becoming sore from the knotty surface. By the tickle down her arm, she was pretty sure her elbow was bleeding. And then she slipped.

Clumsy winter boots were not made for climbing anything except snowy stairs. In an instant, Taite's dangled free in the air. Her fingernails dug into the course bark, but with the full weight of her body on her fingertips, it was too much. She let out a gasp as she fell. Her heart raced into her throat. With a sharp yank, the rope tightened, and she slammed against the trunk of the tree with a grunt and a scrape. Several feet above, Baylin braced and strained to keep his footing.

"You all right?" Baylin asked.

She groaned and muttered an affirmative. Her feet crammed in crevices, trying to take a little weight off Baylin's rope. The line slackened, and she ran her quivering fingers over the tree as she searched for a hold.

Safe on a branch at last, they sat in silence, watching the continuous march of the approaching lights. Taite was too afraid to speak and was over-conscious of her breath as it forced its way out with a low shaking hiss.

The lights were closer, revealing subtle hints of their carriers. Enigmatic figures emerged, striding alongside the lanterns. Sometimes a stray voice drifted up on the air. Against the blowing breeze and whispering leaves, the words were indistinguishable. They passed by in a dismal, lumbering procession. A shiver ran up Taite's spine.

Breaking the tense silence, Baylin said, "We'll stay in the trees for now. We can continue branch to branch once we can light the lamp."

Lanie protested. "That's too dangerous. We can't risk falling."

"The real danger is down there, Lanie. We'll go slow, and we're tied together."

"All right," Lanie said with hesitation. "I trust you."

Taite fumed, not bothering to speak. She didn't have a say anyway.

Long minutes later, their lights glowing, the group made their precarious way through the towering trees. The branches were wider than a sidewalk in places. Still, she was not at ease strolling along the elevated walkways. On the narrow branches, they moved one foot in front of the other with hands on each other's shoulders. Sometimes a limb creaked or gave under their feet. It was far worse than either the rappel or the climb back up had been.

Forward progress was excruciatingly slow, and Baylin was behind her muttering about the delays. He added to them by stopping every few minutes to listen to an imaginary crackle of twigs or to watch for lights in the woods. The limbs were numerous, and often they could step or climb from one tree to the other at their intersections.

Once in a while, to reach another tree it was necessary to jump to one below or grapple to one above them. It was exhausting and only sheer willpower kept Taite going. Arms shaking, she struggled up to the next branch. Her legs felt like lead as she threw herself up and tested her footing. Above, Lanie had already collapsed on the branch. Taite couldn't make out her form in the dim lamplight, but the sound of her breath was heavy in the air. So, even Lanie was spent. Baylin followed, moving slower than usual. After pulling up the packs behind him for the hundredth time, he crouched down and gave Taite a slap on her back as she lay with her face against the bark.

"We'll stop here to sleep."

The light on his harness faded as he sat between the girls. The forest was quiet, and Taite's stomach growled. She ignored it and closed her eyes as Lanie told Baylin to save his light.

"Taite, are you awake?" Lanie asked minutes later. But Taite was too tired to answer — too worn out to be drawn into a pointless conversation. She ignored her. Lanie continued talking. But not to her.

"What are you going to tell her?" she asked in the darkness.

"So you're leaving that to me?"

"You told her back at Karina's you would tell her. Anyway, I thought you might have a better idea what to say. You've known a few of them. She is one of them, right? That's what I guessed."

Sleep was out. Taite didn't intend to eavesdrop, but she couldn't do anything about that now. Whenever an opportunity to learn something materialized, she had to take it.

"Probably," he said, "but something else is going on. She doesn't belong here, and I'm almost sure we're being tracked. Those lights weren't random. But maybe it's nothing."

"When I picked her up on the road, I worried she would be trouble, but I couldn't leave her. She looked completely lost. I hoped you would know what to do about her."

"Sorry to disappoint you, sis. I don't have all the answers. But we'll have to tell her something. No telling how she will take it or if she'll believe it."

Lanie said, "There's one way to find out. We should get it over with as soon as we can. Besides, she needs to hear it in case they find us."

"As usual, you're right. I'll take care of it, but you gotta back me up," he said through a yawn.

Lanie laughed and asked, "Don't I always back you up? I'm all the way out here, aren't I?"

"Yeah, I know," Baylin said, a smile in his voice. "You're the one person I can count on Lanie. Now, shut your trap and get to sleep."

FIVE

With straining muscles and creaking bones, Taite forced herself upright as the others stirred hours later. To sleep on the ground is one thing, but knowing one wrong move might send you diving to your death is another. While Lanie had made sure they were anchored to the tree, she did not slept well. Dreams of strange, faceless figures filled what little sleep she had. Though sore muscles were grateful for the break, Taite felt she had not slept a wink.

She tried not to speculate about what she overheard, but questions plagued her. Who did they think she was? Who were they?

Lanie's lamp glowed, as she and Baylin sat sipping water and nibbling dried fruit. Taite asked Baylin for his light and unclasped the carabiner that tethered her harness to him. Standard procedure among the trees when one needed to take a pee. She lowered herself to another branch for a little privacy from the others — the only time the dense canopy proved useful.

She was getting the hang of the whole rappelling thing and made it down the trunk with ease. Getting back up was another story. Taite lit the lamp and grabbed the rope with both hands, looping the end into a makeshift step as Lanie had demonstrated earlier. She tried to pull herself up like she had done hundreds of times by now. Her thin biceps burned, her elbows shook, and she went nowhere.

"Dang it," she said aloud, giving up and kicking the tree with her boot. Of course, she couldn't climb back up, she could barely lift the lantern. "Can I get some help?" she asked to the branch above her head.

"I don't want to get involved in your pee break," Baylin said.

"Hilarious. My arms are too tired."

With a light laugh, he said, "Be there in a minute. Keep your light on... and your pants."

The sounds of boots on bark overhead told her Baylin was heading down. She strained her eyes to see his shadow in the dark. Only the rhythm of boots, the faint whirring of the rope, and small sounds of the metal release broke the silence. As the sounds stopped, she waited. He paused on the tree, and she asked, "You are coming down, right?"

"Yeah. I'll be right there," he said, only a few feet above her head. A few more seconds, and he was fumbling the carabiner on the harness around her waist.

"Let me do it," Taite said. "I know how."

"Oh, OK," he said, as he dropped his hands to his sides.

"What were you doing up there anyway?"

"What? Just thinking. We need to talk before we go any further today, but let's get back up to Lanie. You must be hungry."

"I'm starving. Hey, why didn't you pull me up like you did the packs?"

"Are you kidding me? There's not much room to work with up there, and no offense, but you're heavier than a bag of gear. Hold on to my shoulders, and we'll see if I can manage this."

With the loop step Taite had fixed in the rope, he lifted them both back to the elevated camp. Earlier, she learned talking to Baylin, even to ask a question, was pointless during an ascent. Taite supposed that was expected, but questions were ready to burst out of her. The moment they landed safe on the limb, she wasted no time.

"What's up? What did you want to talk about?"

Baylin and Lanie exchanged a glance. Lanie handed a piece of fruit to Taite as she said, "It's about you, Taite and everythi—"

Baylin interrupted. "Thanks, Lanie, but I got it this time." Taite tilted her head and waited for him to continue.

After a pause and a deep breath, he said, "Taite, it won't be easy to hear this, but I need to be honest. Well, you've never seen a place like this, right?"

"No, I haven't. Never heard of one either. What can you tell me about it?"

"Lanie says you woke up on a bus alone. Everyone had vanished. I think they brought you here on purpose."

Bewilderment must have shown on Taite's face, as Lanie shook her head and said, "What Baylin is trying to say is... well, you're from Earth."

Taite's jaw dropped, then she cracked a smile. They were making fun of her. "From Earth? Oh, heck no, I'm from Saturn. Didn't you realize?" she asked and rolled her eyes.

"This isn't funny, Taite," Lanie said. "You are from Earth, right?"

"Of course. You two are messing with me. Talk about not funny." Lanie gave Baylin a look Taite didn't see. He shrugged his shoulders and waved her on.

She said in a halting voice, "This... is going to sound weird. We aren't on Earth."

Baylin snapped his head around. "You can't just blurt it out like that, Lanie."

"Your way would take too long."

Taite scrunched up her face, expressing an indiscernible emotion. Then it hit her. They were nuts. "I see," she said with a sarcastic smile. She laughed awkwardly. "You've escaped from a mental hospital."

Then she was angry in spite of herself. "Is this a joke to you? Let's have some fun with the lost clueless nobody we've been dragging around. Real nice," she said through a clenched jaw.

Baylin rolled his head toward his sister. "Thanks sis, that was helpful."

"Well, it's true. No one is playing games with you, Taite. We aren't crazy either. Baylin is right. Someone brought you here, and you aren't the first. Hundreds have been brought here."

"Enough, Lanie." Baylin's voice was sober and carried a subtle warning with it. Lanie shrugged and said nothing more.

"You're either joking or insane. Either way, what you're doing is just sick."

"Taite, listen. Think about what you've seen. When we reached the gulch, you looked a little shocked. It doesn't match up to what you know, does it?"

"Well, no, but I'm sure there's an explanation. There are plenty of places I've never seen. What you're saying is impossible."

"Many things in history first seemed impossible. Didn't flying used to seem impossible, traveling to the moon, visiting Mars? It all used to be impossible. Can't you imagine that they don't want everyone to realize what's possible anymore?"

Taite remembered newspaper headlines about government conspiracies and secret weapons. And she thought of her father — the work he never discussed. She knew nothing about it, but this was too much to accept.

"Let's say you're right for the sake of argument. If not Earth, where are we and what am I doing here? What are you doing here? Are you going to tell me you're an alien or something?"

Lanie let out a sharp laugh, and Baylin fought a smile. "No, listen, and I'll do my best to explain. Give me a chance. About a hundred years ago, the nations on Earth were freaking out. They were terrified of the end of the human race... global warming, meteors, whatever. Together, they formed a program, a coalition to search out inhabitable planets. Well, they found one and started colonizing it in secret. It was a win-win scenario, preserve humanity, new land, rid the Earth of the people no one would miss and— "

"Hey!" Taite said, "What are you saying? Plenty of people miss me."

"Not you, Taite," he said in frustration. "Let me finish. They started with criminals and those on the outskirts of society. They became the labor force. Then they got selective — picking and choosing, faking deaths, unexplained disappearances. That sort of thing. You may have heard of some of them. Scientists, physicians, anyone they needed, anyone they might use and control.

"Everything's about control here. They decide everything... who's born and who dies. Lanie and I... well, our father was one of them. He came here as a boy. He was raised thinking this was an ideal society. Anyway, they brought you here. I'm not sure why yet. New transplants from Earth are rare anymore, and they aren't abandoned in the desert. It doesn't make sense."

"Stop, stop!" Taite said, waving her hands. "You can't expect me to believe all this? What proof is there? What does this have to do with the people following us?"

"I'm not certain," Baylin said, "but what I've told you is the truth. Crazy as it may sound. As for proof, you'll have to wait till we get out of the forest."

Taite looked to Lanie for help.

The girl's green eyes returned the gaze, but she shrugged her shoulders and said, "For four years, we've been fighting them. That's where we're going. Past the outposts and stations, there's— "

Baylin cut her off and said, "Not now, Lanie. One thing at a time."

Taite raised her eyebrows, suspicious that more details were being kept from her. Truth or fiction, she still couldn't tell. "If what you say is true, how did I get here? Where's my family? What am I supposed to do here? How can I get back home?"

"I can only assume you arrived like everyone else — on a transportation ship in stasis. The trip takes about seventy-five Earth years. So, whatever family you had is probably gone. So, I suggest you forget going home and come with us." He shrugged.

"We may not be the best company, but... what else you can do? There's no way back. Even if there was, that's another seventy-five years. What's the point?" he asked.

"No, you're both psychotic," Taite said and hugged her arms around herself, scared to admit that there might be a grain of truth to their ludicrous story. Her stomach did a flip-flop. Determined not to vomit in front of them, she clung to her anger. "This is stupid. Can we get out of these freaking trees? I'm sick of this."

"We'll talk more later. I'm gonna go scout ahead. Lanie, you two sit tight. Keep your eyes and ears open though."

With a mock salute, Lanie said "Yes, sir!" Baylin, looking frustrated, shot Taite a glance and prepared to climb higher. Lanie and Taite sat alone on the branch, one faint lantern emitting a warm halo. In the dark, it was easy for Taite to imagine how terrifying this would be if she was alone. It was strange. Demented as they were, she still felt safer with them.

Minutes passed, five, ten, fifteen. She had not been thrilled to meet Baylin, but Lanie often looked to him for answers, so Taite found herself doing the same. Now that he was far above and out of sight, she fidgeted with the empty carabiner at her waist in impatience.

Lanie seemed to realize what her companion was thinking and broke the silence. "We'll be fine. He won't take so long now that he's on his own. Then we can get out of here."

"How many days have we been in the woods? It's hard to keep track of time."

"Yes, it is," Lanie said. "I'm not sure exactly, besides our diurnal cycle differs from Earth. The sun rises and sets about every eight Earth days here. It's a little confusing, since we still keep a twenty-four-hour clock for the sake of our biorhythms. Terms like 'day' and 'night' aren't always about light and dark here. By the remaining rations, I would guess we're halfway there.

With no acknowledgment of Lanie's explanation, Taite asked, "Why can't we all climb up and through the canopy? Wouldn't that be faster? I want out of here."

"We used to have zip lines up in the canopy where we had cleared a path. It was like flying through the treetops. It was great, not to mention fast. I loved it," she sighed. "The O.R.D.E.R. found them. That's the Organization of Reconditioning, Disbandment and Eradication of Rebellion. It wasn't safe anymore. They knew exactly where to look. A couple of our guys died that time. So, we can't use the lines anymore. When they find the anchors in the cliff, we'll need to change those."

Taite changed the subject as her mind wandered. "All that stuff — you expect me to believe it?"

Before answering, Lanie folded her legs under her and adjusted her nylon harness. "It's true, Taite. I understand it's difficult to accept, but this place is what's real to Baylin and me. We were born here. Earth, the whole idea of Earth, seems like a fairy tale.

"They told us it's like Earth in ways, the atmosphere. Sometime if we can see the stars, Baylin can show you the Earth's sun. I never cared to remember it. He was always more interested."

"He's a little different, isn't he?" Taite asked.

"What do you mean? Different from what?"

"Different than I expected him to be... even after I met him."

He and I aren't much alike if that's what you mean, but he has a lot more responsibilities than I do," Lanie said. "People depend on him, expect things from him. It's always been that way. First, it was our father, expecting Baylin to be his mirror image. That didn't turn out so well. Now, it's everyone, the whole resistance."

"What resistance?"

"He wouldn't want me to get into it," she said, pausing before launching into an explanation anyway. "Baylin and I are part of a group called Duratio. It's an opposition of sorts. In the past few years, we've manage to sabotage several government operations. About a week ago, Baylin led a small group and broke into a warehouse and collected supplies and information there. That's the raid I mentioned at the station.

"We have to stop them. If no one stands up to them, this will be a planet full of mindless slaves. How is that right? They even control who has children and who can't," she said, lifting her shirt to reveal a small scar on her lower abdomen.

"What?" Taite asked with widening eyes before she considered the possibility that Lanie only had her appendix removed or something. A little scar didn't make this true.

"When I was younger, I began acting up, as my father called it. Or showing signs of too much independent thought. The Order recommended me for the Population Restraint Protocol, the PRP — sterilization. Any female colonist of child-bearing age that has a mind of her own..."

"Wow. That's scary." She didn't understand why Lanie was telling her this or what she expected her to say. Given the fact she still suspected Lanie might be a wacko, it was even more challenging.

"I don't know why I'm telling you all this. It's something you might need to know."

"Sorry to backtrack. But what does 'duratio' mean?" Taite asked to change the subject.

"The word?"

"Yes."

"It's from 'derecho'. It's like a storm — a wall cloud that wipes the surface clean. We want a fresh start here," she said. "With the weather, it's fitting."

Panic began to creep in at Taite. It was getting to be too much, and she needed space. She made an excuse that she needed to pee again, her arms less gelatinous after eating. Since they only had one light, it was more complicated, but the next limb down ran across directly below. She would manage. Taite unclasped herself from the shared rope and was down in no time.

Lanie's sat the lantern where Taite could see it from below, and Baylin could see it from above. As Taite stood on the limb below and inhaled to clear her head, a chill ran up her spine with the cool breeze, her shoulders trembling. She was beyond skeptical of their whole story, but it still freaked her out. After they got out of here, she would find out what was going on. It would be fine. Things had a way of working out.

Taite stood rubbing the cold from her shoulders when she caught a twinkle in the corner of her eye. As she turned, five lights appeared on the ground. Though she didn't know who to trust, her whole body told her this was bad news. Taite fumbled for the rope. Not that long before, she had been too weak to pull herself up, but as her heart pounded, that didn't cross her mind. She forced herself up, over and over.

Dim figures gathered below, and their murmured voices drifted on the air. Taite braced herself with one foot on the trunk of the titan tree. To the right, she saw Lanie standing in the pale light. She was looking up, unaware, searching for Baylin in the treetops. Taite wanted to warn her, but there wasn't time.

Someone shouted as Taite stepped back onto their branch. Lanie whirled around. A sharp flash of light from the floor, a deafening crack, and Lanie crumpled to her knees. In the chaos, Taite couldn't move. Everything happened at once.

Lanie's gray shirt was running red. Her face twisted as she looked straight at Taite. Voices shouted below, but Taite didn't hear what they said. Her head spun.

Lanie tried to get back on her feet, swaying and fumbling as the lamplight spilled over her. She groaned as if she wanted to speak, but blood trickled out instead of words. Taite lunged forward as a reflex — if she could only reach her.

"Stay there," a voice said from above. Taite looked up to where she knew Baylin must be, where he must have seen everything. Taite couldn't fathom why he would say this. A second more, and it was too late. Because Lanie was falling, lost to the obsidian of the forest floor.

A statue in the dark, Taite stared at the shadows below. The lights formed a circle now. Lanie must be there. Maybe the ropes stopped her from hitting the ground.

Why would anyone hurt Lanie of all people? She was harmless and helpless. Taite may not have known her well, but she didn't deserve that. It could not be real. This couldn't be happening.

While her own breath was shaking and shallow, there was no sign or sound from Baylin. Out of pure fear, she couldn't move — fear of falling, fear of those below, fear of Baylin to a degree. The voices drifted away to nothing, the lights flickered and faded into the distance, and even the steady breeze seemed to die. After, her knees shook and went limp below her. Sliding down the rough bark, it tugged at her shirt and scraped her back until she was sitting on the branch choking back sobs that refused to be silent.

SIX

"We'll go higher until we're out of range. We're only a couple days away," Baylin said, standing a few feet to the side.

What was wrong with him? Didn't he care about his own sister? By the light of the remaining lantern, Taite watched him stoop over Lanie's pack and rifle through, removing what might be useful. It was sickening. Disbelief turned to fury.

"How can you do that?" The words escaped in a harsh whisper before she could stop them.

Baylin spun around, his jaw set, a vein on his forehead looked close to bursting. "Not. Now," he said. He stared until she exhaled and lowered her eyes to her feet.

With no further words, ropes were attached, the metal clasps clattering. For a nanosecond, Taite considered refusing to go with him. What if she wasn't on the right side? But they shot Lanie, most likely killed her.

The climb was quiet, a draining journey with many breaks. Hours crawled by before the pair recovered in silence on a knotted, twisting limb. Baylin tossed a piece of fruit in her direction. Sweet and chewy, she choked it down, resisting the urge to gag. Then they were moving again. Branch to branch, they continued their path across the forested canyon. All day, they traveled, and neither offered many words. There was nothing to say. Baylin spoke only to give directions when gestures didn't suffice.

Another hour and they had climbed high enough to have the faintest of ambient light. The surrounding tree limbs streaked upwards as if begging for mercy.

Finally, Baylin broke the silence. "We'll stop here. If we push, tomorrow we should be out."

As usual of late, Taite didn't bother to reply. Instead, she positioned herself as far away as possible, curled up against her pack and attempted to sleep.

When she woke later and her eyes adjusted, Baylin was seated at the edge of the lamplight. Wide awake already or he hadn't slept, he leaned his back against the tree, staring off into space. If Taite were not so angry with him, she would pity him. Hair fell in his eyes, dirt smeared his face. Scratched, torn, he looked miserable. She must be in a similar state. His eyes darted over, feeling the pressure of her stare.

"You know, we couldn't have done anything," he said without hesitation or emotion. Maybe he said it to assure himself it was true.

With the conversation open, Taite buried her sympathy. "You're her brother. You didn't even try to help."

"Don't be naïve. They shot her in the chest. You think we could have helped her? Out here? If you had gone to her, they would have shot you too. You would have accomplished nothing, and you'd be dead. It was too late. That's the way things work sometimes. If it had been me in that situation, Lanie would have done the same. I expect you to do it too."

The response was so cold and matter-of-fact, but it was also true. There was no way to help Lanie. Perhaps they could below. "Do you think there's a chance she survived?" she asked.

Baylin closed his eyes. "I've been asking myself that, and I don't know."

"I'm sorry," Taite said after a long pause. She forgot that some people refuse to feel their emotions. Her father was like that. Not once had she seen him cry, not even when his mother died. Taite had never even met her. The concepts of life and death seem so basic, but few things can muddle the mind as can the fundamental facts of existence.

"For what exactly?" Baylin asked with a disdainful snort.

"That it happened. I'm sorry for everything. For being here. I threw everything off."

Baylin sighed. "It isn't your fault. It might have happened anyway."

"Probably not." Taite dropped her voice to a whisper, her words lost in the faint breeze.

+++

"God, Taite, will you keep up? There's enough on my mind without looking after you," Baylin said as Taite lagged behind after an hour of climbing the next day.

"I know you're upset, but I've got problems too. Stop taking it out on me," she said, the stress of the last week bubbling up.

"Don't even start it. Shut your mouth and move your ass."

Blood rose to Taite's face as anger jumped up her throat. And then she shouted, "You have no right to talk to me like that. I don't want to be here anymore than you want me here. You're upset about Lanie, I get it. But I've lost my whole family. Everyone is gone. So cut me some freaking slack."

After glaring for a moment, he lowered his eyebrows and relaxed, his expression softening. "All right, Taite. I didn't mean to be— we need to keep moving. I don't want anyone else to get hurt. It's my responsibility."

"Fine," Taite said with diminished anger. "I'm..." She was many things: scared, confused, and struggling every minute to breathe and not burst into tears. She said none of this though. Instead, she continued, "I'm not used to this — climbing for hours. And I'm not as strong as you. Can you keep that in mind?"

"I'll try."

+++

Taite's eyes adjusted every so often during the slow ascent, taking in the dappled light streaming from above with tragic beauty. When they pulled themselves up past the dense canopy, leaves brushing the wall, the sunlight blinded by comparison. Twilight neared, and the sun poured orange-gold light down on them. Brilliant purples streaked through the sky. Hints of magenta and teal speckled the mottled clouds. It was breath-taking, but her eyes burned, and she shielded her face with a free hand, and wedged a foot against the rocks.

As with the light, the air temperature increased during the climb. While the heat of the scorching evening pressed down like a physical weight, Taite scrambled onto the edge of the canyon wall. She didn't care, it was better to be away from the endless night that swallowed Lanie whole.

Baylin stayed uncommunicative as usual. When Taite asked him where they were going, he pointed to the horizon. Like storm clouds full of hail, his irises were a dark pewter. But it wasn't clearly sorrow Taite saw there, more like grim determination.

"Baylin, are you OK? You know with..." her voice trailed off.

Without turning, without stopping, Baylin replied, "I don't want to talk about it. Not with you and not with anyone else."

As she lowered her chin and her eyes, she dropped the conversation.

The two traveled for hours at a steady pace across the alien landscape, and the silence between them was deafening. Sometimes familiarity erases the awkwardness between two quiet companions. Both relax and no longer struggle for words, and small talk is pointless. This was not like that. But it was clear Baylin preferred not to talk and little by little the mute tension began to ebb.

Lost in a memory or a daydream, Taite was always aware of his presence as she walked — not that it made much difference. She turned her focus to the shrubs and plants spotting the ground. Plants she couldn't name. Many were navy blue succulents with cylindrical fat leaves. She wished they were edible.

As they trudged mechanically through the plain, hills emerged on the horizon. The light was just beginning to fade as Baylin stopped for water. Pointing toward the hillside and announcing between swallows, he said, "In the hills, there's a recluse, you might call him. He has water, supplies. We can rest for a day."

Taite usually would have kept quiet, but she had enough of her own thoughts and tried to keep him talking. "What's this guy doing out here?"

"Running like the rest of us. And avoiding the authorities," he said with sarcastic emphasis on the last word. Untying his bootlaces as he spoke, he poured out fistfuls of sand, though the boots came halfway to his knees.

His mood was better today, and Taite risked more words. "Whoever he is, I hope he has a shower. I'm disgusting."

His eyebrows lifted with one corner of his mouth. The first hint of anything other than a scowl. "Another perk of the job. Filth, isolation, sudden death, you name it."

Anger edged into his voice, and Taite had no reply for it. It was still difficult to think of Lanie. As the uncomfortable pause stretched out, she needlessly tightened her own boots. She kept her eyes well away from Baylin's without knowing what she feared to see there.

"Anyway," he said, "it's a long way before we reach the hills. We won't get there before dark."

As the sun made its slow way toward the horizon, the pair continued toward the hills as a sympathetic wind rushed across the sweltering sand. By the time the last glimmer of sun dipped behind the hills with an explosion of color, the clouds had broken overhead. The first few pale stars appearing in the sky, Baylin stalked off to look around and get his bearings. Taite plopped on the ground and pulled out her journal to vent.

SEVEN

As he walked away from Taite, Baylin surveyed the landscape to adjust his sense of direction. The sun would set soon, and they couldn't afford to lose their way out here. They — not the same they he had expected.

He had been tough on Taite, but this wasn't her fault. This all came new to her. At first, Lanie needed extra help too. But now he had failed Lanie.

She had been hit by the time he saw the danger. He never looked forward to climbing through the gulch, but this time a feeling of dread haunted him from the minute they came to the canopy. He should have trusted his instincts and kept her close.

Lanie had always met the climb with thrill-seeking enthusiasm. To her, it was a big adventure. He couldn't stand to think of her for long, so he returned his focus to a blister rising from the callused skin of his palm, stinging with every move. But pain always helped keep his mind on the present.

As he bit the inside of his cheek, he pushed the past away. Grief helped no one here. He considered it a pointless emotion, but its dull ache still burned within his chest.

A half an hour passed, and color streaked across the darkened sky in undulating curtains as Baylin stared out at the distant hills. Glad to be away from the trees, he felt he had finally put some space between himself and a nightmare.

His mind turned to his new travel companion. Taite was a mystery, and he wasn't sure what to make of her. She was definitely an inconvenience, weak and ignorant of everything about life here. The only life he had ever known. Most of the transplants from Earth were the same; spoiled and unaccustomed to the physical work of survival.

But they always piqued his curiosity. He had never known a life that wasn't strenuous, exhausting. Even in the colony, there was little time to relax. Structures needed built, water systems maintained, and everything done in suffocating heat or bone-chilling cold and darkness.

With a sigh, he pulled himself back to the reality before him. Baylin shoved his hands into his pockets as he watched the sky fill with stars. It would only last minutes before the clouds rolled back in to blot them out.

EIGHT

Locked in her mind, had been a hint of a memory she couldn't explain. She had convinced herself it had been a dream — a needle stabbing her leg and bright white lights around a shadowed form. But it wasn't a dream, and the truth was hitting hard.

As the night deepened, stars glittered above, terrifying in their strangeness. The sky danced with the faint colors of an undulating aurora. Ursa Major was absent, and Sirius the dog-star was missing. The unfamiliar filled the sky, including the brightest stars she'd ever seen. Patches of clouds did not conceal the rising alien moon, or the second that appeared only minutes later. Not until she saw the third, larger than the others, did the pressure in her chest turn to tears streaming down her face.

At home, she used to stare at the night sky for hours on warm summer nights. Here, it served as a dizzying reminder of how far away she was from everything she remembered. The cool night was quiet with only gentle sounds of the wind as it caressed her cheek. Taite buried her face in her hands.

Moments later, she heard Baylin's returning steps and forced her tears away. He said nothing, only coughed as he stretched out on the sand. As the minutes ticked by, he remained silent.

"Baylin, are you awake?"

"I guess so."

"Can I ask you something?"

"You can ask. Doesn't mean I can answer."

"Which one is Earth?"

"Oh, what? I'm not crazy anymore?" he asked, a note of surprise in his tone. His silhouette sat up, hands draped from his bent knees. He sighed. "I can show you. Trouble sleeping?"

"I guess so," she said, mimicking his words. "Seems to be going around."

"You see that bright star right above the hill?" he asked, ignoring Taite's comment.

"Yes."

"Above that, there are two stars sort of close together. See 'em?"

Taite searched the sky with eager eyes. A satellite blinked as it made its lazy way around the planet. "Um... no, not really. Oh wait. One of them is a little flickery? Is that right?"

"Yeah. The flickery one is Earth. Well, it's the star the Earth orbits. That's what I was taught. It flickers because of the gravitational pull of the planets on the star, the sun."

"That's it? Are you sure?"

"Yes."

"It looks so small. You're sure that's it?"

"What did you expect, Taite?"

"Something more."

Baylin only made a scoffing sound in his throat.

"Lanie told me..." Taite said before stopping herself to wait for a

70

reaction. None came, and she continued, "she said you were always interested in Earth. Why?"

Baylin paused in thought and replied, "It's part of our history, something that I... that we were meant to have. They took it from us. And you. I'm sure it's worse for you. The Earth was dying, they said. That's why they started searching for another planet, but so much of what they taught us was a lie. Was that true?"

"I wouldn't have said dying. There were problems: pollution, overpopulation, mass extinctions, melting ice caps. Lots of problems, but I imagine the planet itself was all right," Taite said.

"Things I heard used to worry me, but whenever we flew somewhere, I would look out the window after take-off. The cars, roads, and everything faded into little specs and ribbons.

"I'm not sure we could do so much damage to something so massive. But my dad always said that the ecosystem is all connected, like building blocks on top of one another. If too many are removed, it collapses."

"Nothing surprises me anymore. One way or another," Baylin said.

Taite shrugged, barely visible in the night. Then in spite of the dark, the weight of Baylin's gaze grew heavy.

"Taite," he asked, "You think I'm a bastard, don't you? For leaving her?"

The question hit like a brick to her gut.

"Uh..." she stammered, searching for words and stalling for time as she rifled through her thoughts. "Why do you care what I think?"

"I don't want anyone to assume I'm the type of person to throw my sister to the wolves, ya know?"

"I'm sure you wouldn't have if there was a choice," Taite said, muttering the words, only half-believing them.

"You don't believe me. I get it. That's OK. I may be a lot of things, but I'm not a liar," he said, his voice raspy in the dry air.

"There's just too much for me to handle now. And I don't understand what's really happening."

"Then you aren't so different from anyone else," he said in a low voice. "I had talked to her about what would happen if... we agreed it was the best thing to do. Besides, she had a better chance of surviving with them than with us. That wound was beyond us out here."

Taite couldn't help but notice he avoided saying Lanie's name.

"Listen," she said. "it wasn't your fault, and there probably wasn't anything you could do. It was terrible. I can't believe any of this is real."

+++

The next day's journey was through darkness. Taite kept expecting the sun to rise, but several hours later the night lingered. Hills surrounded them, and according to Baylin, he knew exactly where to find the entrance to the dwelling of the infamous introvert. This proved to be not quite true, but Taite chalked this up to him being male. As she stood shivering in the increasing cold with arms crossed over her chest, Baylin surveyed the area for landmarks he recognized.

"It's right around here," he said to himself.

"We've been going in circles. Are you sure it isn't over there?" Taite asked and pointed behind Baylin's shoulder. "There's an overhang that might be concealing a cave."

"Taite, I have been here at least five times. I know where I'm going. The entrance is difficult to find. That's the point."

"Uh-huh," she said, rolling her eyes. Typical.

A large rock made a comfortable seat, as she gave up and waited for

Baylin to realize he was wrong. They had been searching for over a half an hour.

About ten minutes later, as Taite sat bouncing her legs, it became obvious they were both wrong. They turned as a large, burly man came strolling up from the opposite direction, chuckling to himself and shaking his head. Dressed in dirty desert camouflage, a scruffy beard obscured much of his face.

"Baylin, Baylin, Baylin," he said through his breath as he walked toward the lost pair. "I will never understand how you can find your way across miles of open desert and shrub land, and yet you can never find my cozy abode." He smiled and ruffled Baylin's tangled hair the way an uncle might.

Baylin ducked away from the man's broad, rough hand like a squirmy little boy and said, "All right, all right, Gage." Baylin tried not to smile as the man, several inches taller, grabbed him in a bear hug.

"Where's that cute little sister of yours, Baylin?" Gage asked, but before he had finished his sentence his face fell, and he lost the gleeful chuckle in his voice. As Taite looked up, it was obvious why. Baylin had gone white in an instant, his blank eyes lowered to the ground.

For a split-second, Baylin's eyes darted up to Taite's. Gage followed his glance, noticing Taite for the first time.

Baylin shook his head. "She didn't make it through the canyon. We were followed, and they— there was nothing we could do." His expression strained when he looked back in Taite's direction. No one said a word. They both stared at Taite as one might stare at a problem.

"This is Taite," Baylin said at last, pausing again as Gage at looked her. "She... uh... Lanie picked her up wandering along the road."

Taite lifted her hand in a slight but solemn wave of acknowledgment.

"Oh, God, Baylin," Gage whispered as the truth settled. "I'm so sorry.

Lanie was a great girl, she was."

Baylin nodded, his shadowed eyes back on the ground. "There's something else I want to run by you." His eyes darted over to Taite again, and he leaned over and murmured something to Gage.

"Hmm..." Gage mused, pulling his short beard as he studied her from the corner of his eye. "That is strange, Bay."

Baylin waved Taite over. Gage towered over her by almost a foot and was a broad-shouldered, mountainous man. He looked to be in his fifties. He seemed to be a friendly sort who didn't need to intimidate anyone with his behavior. His appearance was enough. If he wanted to, he could snap her in half. Good thing he was on their side. Or at least she hoped he was.

"Taite, is it?" Gage asked.

"It's my last name. My family name, but most everyone calls me that." She looked away, realizing she hadn't mentioned this to Baylin, not that it mattered.

"Ahh. Might I have the privilege of your first name then, Miss Taite?"

She smiled a crooked smile, surprised to find she liked this gruff, yet formal man. "It's Aisea, but no one ever calls me that except my father."

He plucked a twig from a dying shrub and said, "Aisea — pretty name. Better than Taite if you ask me, but whatever you prefer, lass." After chewing on the twig for a moment, he slapped a heavy hand against his thigh, jolting himself out of thought. "We'll have time to chitchat later. How 'bout something to eat? Skinny thing like you is gonna waste away out in this wilderness. Baylin, where's your manners, making her carry all that? That pack's near as big as she is."

"I don't mind," Taite said in protest, but Baylin came around and swung her pack over his shoulder. She couldn't shake the impression something had changed in how he looked at her. Like he was studying a mystery through narrowed eyes.

"Come on," he said and followed Gage who was disappearing down a rocky slope.

Gage led them through an obscure, narrow path. It wasn't long before he ducked into a black slash scarring the face of the darkened hill.

"Home sweet home," he called from within.

Taite followed, eager for shelter and rest. Inside, dim phosphorescent lights cast an eerie glow along the cave walls. Slanted shadows shifted and bent as they crossed the entryway. Gage lived a simple life, but it was not entirely primitive.

There was no furniture in the traditional sense of the word. Well-worn cushions were scattered here and there along with a large flat rock that must have functioned as a table. But it wasn't without its own rustic charm. What surprised Taite was a panel of electronics, lights gleaming green, on the far side of the room.

Gage had already vanished somewhere further into the cave. As Taite and Baylin lowered the gear to the uneven floor, sudden illumination sprang up from all around. Formations of rock jutted out from the shadows, glistening with moisture. In other places they were soft with a velvety blue moss. Metal columns stood for support, and a rack of several guns hung from one of the smoother walls.

"Look up. That's the best view." Baylin's voice broke the silence.

He was right. The ceiling was alive with color. The cool lights of the cave bounced and reflected off a shimmering, mufti-faceted ceiling. Crystals encrusted the uneven plains, colors bouncing from the reflected flickering lights. It must have been twenty feet over their heads, twinkling like stars and throwing color in every direction.

"That's amazing," she said, her voice straining in her upturned throat.

Turning around to take it all in, Taite wobbled on the heel of her boot. Baylin's hand gripped her elbow while she steadied herself, her eyes still on the dazzling natural dome.

"Nice, huh?" Baylin asked with a sad smile. His voice sounded far away as he added, "Lanie always looked forward to visiting Gage. She called him Uncle Gage. No real relation."

As if on cue, Gage reappeared from a side tunnel, carrying an armload of food. Baylin's hand dropped from Taite's elbow, and he rushed forward to relieve Gage of his burden.

"Don't be shy, Miss Taite," Gage called from the rocky table. Taite had torn her eyes from the ceiling to glance after the retreating Baylin.

"Between the three of us, I'm sure we have plenty to go 'round. I don't do too bad out here, not what you might expect."

The impromptu meal composed of canned beans, dried fruit and hard bread, but at that point, it was a feast. Baylin and Taite had been running low on supplies and had little to offer except information. Baylin took care of that, describing the events that led up to Lanie's death.

Before Lanie and Taite met him at Karina's, a small team, Baylin included, had been gathering intelligence of some sort. This was part of the raid that also disrupted communications at the checkpoint. Taite zoned out since it had little to do with her.

With her hunger satiated, her eyelids grew heavy. She fought to keep them open as deep, slow voices muttered around her in a gentle hum.

"Taite," a voice said through the fog of sleep. "Go lie down. You're tired."

It was Baylin. With a jerk, Taite opened her eyes.

"Go on. It's fine." He gestured to a heap of cushions in a far corner. He looked tired himself.

His mouth curved in a sympathetic smile as he repeated, "You can't keep your head up. I'll wake you later. Go on."

Taite was too tired to tell him to stop bossing her around, so she nodded, rolling sideways to her knees and fumbled across the floor. The idea of what might be crawling over the cushions crossed her mind, but only for a second before her head sank into the thick pillow. The hushed voices continued, fading into the sweet silence of sleep.

When she woke later, the rough fabric of the cushion against her cheek served as the first reminder of where she was. In the soft glow of the cavern lights, Taite rushed to her feet, still in the sandy boots she had not bothered to remove. A quick glance around revealed she was alone, and the panic of abandonment rose again.

"Baylin," she said. No answer, nothing.

"Baylin, where are you?" Taite called, surprising herself with the sudden fear in her voice. Seconds later, Baylin emerged from the depths of the cave.

"What? Something wrong?"

Taite wasn't sure. She stood staring, trying to come up with an excuse for screeching like a child waking from a bad dream. "Um, I guess not," she finally said, stammering in embarrassment. "I didn't know where you were."

Baylin smirked. "Didn't realize you were so attached, Taite."

"Oh, please," she said, trying her best to sound disgusted. "That isn't what I meant."

"Relax, Taite. Just kidding."

As she rolled her eyes to the ceiling. "Of course."

Baylin smiled and gave her arm a pinch. She shook it out of her head, astonished by the alteration of his mood. "Where were you, anyway? What are you doing back there?"

"Well, boss, I was helping Gage repair a piece of equipment. I should get back to it, if it's all the same to you."

"Is there anything I can do?"

"Nah, we got it. But you mentioned cleaning up and believe me you need it."

His mouth opened in a boyish grin that creased the corners of his eyes. As he did, Taite noticed he had scrubbed away the grime from the journey.

"Ha. Ha," she said, "That sounds good though. After sleeping on those cushions, I think I might have something crawling in my hair."

"You may by the looks of it," he said with mock revulsion. "I'll show you the way. Gage has an underground spring at his disposal, which of course, has a lot to do with why he chose this cave."

The pair walked along a downward sloping passageway where sections had been carved into rough-hewn steps. Down and back, it curved around; the humidity increasing as they descended. The air smelled slightly of eggs, and moisture was already clinging to her skin. It collected above her lip, just as it gathered on the walls and ceiling. The ceiling sloped lower and lower as they strolled further down until it suddenly opened to a vault above their heads.

Beneath the vaulted ceiling was a small pool, fed by a trickling stream flowing from a ragged crack in the wall. Gage, or someone, had installed the same flickering green lights here too. They reflected off the undulating water surface, and patterns of twisting lines bounced onto the wet embankments.

"Here we are," Baylin said, "I'll be above with Gage, if you... get all frantic without me again."

"I can handle it. Thanks," she said, dropping her pack to the damp floor.

"Come back up when you're done and don't take too long. Don't make me walk back to make sure you haven't drown." With a quiet, sly smile, he stomped back up the path.

Stripped to her underwear, Taite shook out the cleanest of her cloths, and rinsed the rest for later. She stepped into the thigh-high warm water and scrubbed.

After, she was chilled, soaking wet, but glad to be clean. She gave her hair a good wringing and combed it back with her fingers. It fell loose and dripping around her shoulders as she dressed.

"How did you enjoy the spa, Miss Taite?" Gage asked, as Taite entered the main room. Gage and Baylin were sitting on the floor, tinkering with a broken light.

"It was great. I feel much better," she said with a satisfied sigh. Legs folding beneath her, she plopped down a few feet from the boys.

Still focused on his work, Baylin asked, "Got all the creepy crawlies out of your hair?"

"Yes, thanks for your concern."

Gage chuckled as Baylin's eyes darted up at her.

She asked, "When do we need to start moving again? Didn't you say we had time to rest?"

"We have time. A day or even two. We can catch our breath."

"Good. And where are we going?" she asked as Baylin and Gage exchanged a glance.

Baylin met her eyes and shrugged. "Home."

As she held his gaze, her mind went blank at the sad expression in his eyes. He looked away, asking, "So, Taite... or should I call you Aisea? Where d'ya get that name?"

"I dunno. My dad I guess. He's the only person who ever called me that. What kind of name is Baylin?"

With a shrug, he said, "Just a name. Look, I asked for a reason. I wonder if it can be a coincidence. This planet is Aises. Similar root. No idea what it would be, but I keep thinking there's a connection. What can you tell us about your father?"

"What are you saying? I don't like where this is going."

"I'm not saying anything. I'm only asking."

"This is stupid, but whatever. To clarify, the name is Polynesian or something. Dad traveled a lot when he was young. I suppose he heard it somewhere. It's supposed to mean 'God Saves' — not that he's real religious. He's a science geek. We didn't talk much about his work. Guess, he assumed it would bore me to tears. I can't tell you much more. To be honest, we didn't spend much time together.

"That's all?" Baylin asked, sounding surprised. "Hmm... kinda odd."

"Well, that's all I know. All I will ever know."

NINE

Taite woke in the middle of the night, half-aware of an unremembered sound. Afraid to move, she listened, her heartbeat thumping hard in her chest. There was only the humming of the electric panel and the far off dripping of water. While she forced out the breath she'd been holding, Taite convinced herself the sound had been a dream.

But there it was again, a muffled voice she didn't understand. She recognized it though.

Baylin, but who was he talking to? She strained to listen. His low voice a murmur across the room. The words of the muttered monologue were lost, but after a moment it was clear Baylin was dreaming. Upon this realization, she tried to ignore the whispers in the dark, but his raspy voice was the only sound. As his mutterings became more urgent, she pulled a few syllables from the jumble. He dreamed of Lanie's death.

The soliloquy grew louder, laced with panic. Taite couldn't sit through it. It became almost painful to hear, unrelenting — like digging a splinter from beneath the skin.

Her own harsh whisper tried to break the spell. "Baylin."

A muted groan, and his voice continued. A frustrated sigh escaped Taite's lips. She didn't want him to know she had heard. How awkward would that be? But she couldn't lie there and listen either, so she shuffled over to where his outstretched form tossed in his sleep. Kneeling beside him, she hesitated. Sweat beaded on his neck, his breathing quick and shallow. If he freaked out, he might fling her across the room.

"Baylin," she said again, shaking his shoulder. She called his name louder. Nothing. He stayed lost in his mind. Taite leaned in closer with her face inches from his ear. "Wake Up," she said as loud as she dared. She gasped as a hand clasped her wrist like a vise, and Baylin bolted upright.

He took a deep breath, and in the dim light, she saw the gleam of his open eyes. Guess it worked. But her wrist ached, as he still had a tight grasp while he struggled to wake.

"Hey, you're hurting me." She squirmed to free her hand.

His face snapped around to Taite, and his grip slackened. In a dry murmur, he said, "Sorry."

"I didn't want to wake you, but you were having a nightmare." The heat of his hand still radiated through her arm.

"Yeah," he said, shivering.

Taite felt a surge of empathy. She already knew more than she wanted to know, but she asked, "You wanna talk about it?"

"What'd I say?"

"Nothing I could really understand."

"I scared you?" he asked.

"A little," she said, meeting his eyes in the faint light. "It's ok. Not a big deal."

"Sorry about that. Guess you want to get back to sleep?" he asked.

"Well, yeah, but you need to let go first."

His fingers dropped to his knee. "Would you mind doing a favor for me, Taite?"

"That would depend on the favor."

"Just stay here for a little while? I don't mean anything by it. Just thought we might talk. To get my mind off everything."

"Um... OK. I guess," she said with reluctance. Sleep had been her real preference.

"Thanks."

"What do you want to talk about?" Taite asked as she folded her legs beneath her.

"Anything. I don't care. Earth. Tell me about it."

"Fine, Earth then. I haven't seen much of it really — cities, a few other places. They say it's perfect for human life. Strange that anyone would want to leave it then. I guess, nowhere's perfect, but we had it pretty good. There was always so much to do... concerts, plays, museums. No reason to be bored in the city. I loved the museums. Whenever they had a free day, I tried to go. I miss it. What do people do for fun here?"

"Fun?" he asked with a laugh. "In the colony, most of time is for work. Once in a while they have entertainment. Everything has to be approved, so it amounts to brainwashing. Nothing I would call fun. Except music, sometimes we had music. I liked that. When I as a boy, some of it put me to sleep. My father punished me for it later." Baylin's voice grew lower, and he yawned.

She echoed it and smiled. "My dad would play soft jazz when I was little to help me fall asleep."

"That must have been nice."

"I guess. With him, it was probably to avoid reading to me."

"You say he was a scientist, huh? That's interesting. Anyway, you're tired. I should let you get back to sleep," he said and yawned again.

"Yeah. We should both sleep. Goodnight, Baylin."

"Goodnight."

With no more words, Taite adjusted her head on a flattened pillow nearby. The glow on the ceiling faded as her eyelids grew heavy and her breathing slowed. It was still hard to relax when Baylin was an arm's length away watching her through tired eyes.

+++

"Taite, get up."

Her eyelids fluttered open at the sound of the voice. The lights were still low, and she rolled to her side and mumbled, "Five more minutes."

"No, Taite. Now!" Baylin said again louder. Gage was talking too — something about needing water.

In Taite's drowsiness, she rubbed her eyes and asked, "What's going on? Is it morning already?"

"No, but we have to go," Baylin said as he filled canteens from a large barrel of water.

Taite sat up, confused. The phosphorescent lights cast a sickly green hue over everything.

"They've caught up with us. We gotta get out of here. Grab your pack. We need food and water. And we have to move fast." He sure was talking fast, but she got to her feet and tried to collect herself.

"Lucky you couldn't sleep Baylin," Gage said, "Otherwise, we all woulda woke with rifles in our faces."

Taite looked at Baylin who appeared to be searching for something.

A satchel was thrust into her hands as she stood watching the boys scramble around. Rifles and pistols came off the wall.

In a matter of minutes, they were sneaking through back passages and emerged into a calm, moonlit night. Still not wide awake, Taite scrambled to keep up as the three of them trekked down the hillside in the moonlight. Loose stones bounced and spilled downward with each step.

Halfway down Taite stumbled, Gage's over-sized hand seized her arm to prevent a fall. He swung her heavy pack from her shoulder. The crunch of boots on rock and the clatter of their gear filled the air. Taite's heart raced. Her breath burned out of her as her feet fought for traction along the pebble-strewn path.

Faint voices came from behind and grew louder as the trio ran further into the hills. A thunderous crack echoed off the rock. A spray of dust flew into Taite's peripheral vision. A second crack, and something whizzed by her head. Taite gasped and forced her tired legs faster.

A few feet ahead, Baylin turned and grabbed her arm, yanking Taite behind a boulder. But they couldn't stop. A fleeting second, and they were running again. Gage was surprisingly fit and not even breathing hard. He led the way and beckoned Baylin forward.

Another shot and a dark spray exploded on the side of Baylin's calf.

"Dammit," he said with a grunt when he stumbled to one knee, but he pulled himself up and forced his feet forward. Dark droplets stained the ground, as Taite traced his staggering steps.

Gage reeled around, jerking Baylin up and tugging him forward. Taite watched, time stretching as another gunshot sang off the hills. She ran to keep pace, but her legs were heavy with sleep, and she fell behind.

"Taite! Come on!" Baylin shouted.

Lanie's red-splattered face presented itself in her mind as she met Baylin's eyes. Gage still pulled him along as blood trailed on the ground after him.

In the next instant, pain ripped through Taite's body. A roar filled her ears, a warm mist hit her face. She fumbled on her feet, lurched forward, and fell to her knees. Baylin's face whitewashed as he pulled against Gage's grip. His mouth moved — he was trying to tell her something, but Taite's ears were ringing. Gage tugged Baylin further along the hill. He was wrenched away, and the world softened at the edges.

Blood trailed from her like a garnet red ribbon among the rocks. Her shoulder, her chest... everywhere, was on fire. Sounds grew soft, distant and then went white like someone pressed the mute button. The world spun above and below and faded to black.

TEN

The contents of Taite's backpack lay strewn on the sand at his feet. A few scraps of paper fluttered away in the night wind. While he didn't want to invade her privacy, he hoped to find a clue why they had been after her. In hindsight, that was obviously the case. They didn't continue the pursuit once they captured her.

He adjusted the bandage on his leg. He was lucky. The bullet only grazed his calf. Taite had not fared so well. A spray of dark crimson had exploded from Taite's right shoulder. Blood spattering and pouring down in a continuous scarlet stream. For the second time in a matter of days, he had been helpless on the sideline. For the second time, he failed.

His numb fingers tossed aside the dust-covered clothes and fumbled through the remains of her pack. An assortment of items littered the ground: a clip for her hair, a brown strand drifted from it in the breeze, a small electronic device, and a small leather-bound book, its cover embossed with an intricate pattern. He reached out and ran his palm over the worn leather.

Gage was calling him, telling him they needed to pack up and start moving. Baylin returned everything to the bag. Everything except the book which he tucked into a pocket of his cargo pants. After slinging the pack over his shoulder, he limped over to where a glum Gage stood waiting.

In a few more days, they would arrive to a greeting of mixed emotions. There would be questions that needed answering. Inevitable emergencies always sprung to life once they arrived. That's how it always went. But this time, it would be worse. He would have to explain about Lanie.

Things would be different for Gage, too. He couldn't return to his underground retreat any time soon. Add that to his list of things to feel guilty about these days. At first, Baylin was angry at Gage, but it only took seconds to realize that he had done the right thing by forcing him forward. The same as Baylin had made the only decision open to him with Lanie. If he had gone back for Taite, he would be dead. Even if by some miracle, they got her out, she would have bled to death or died of an infection in the desert.

The whole business with Lanie, losing her how they did still weighed on his mind, and now Taite too. She was a kid with no experience. At least Lanie had known what she was getting into.

Gage led the way, walking at a slower pace than either of them would have liked. Baylin's wound may have been superficial, but the pain still forced him to hobble along as they made their way. A few hours later, he looked down at his leg; it was bleeding through the gauze again.

"Gage," he called ahead, waiting for him to turn before continuing. "I need to take a break. My leg's bleeding again."

"OK," Gage said, as he doubled back and dropped the pack he carried.

Baylin sat on the ground, rebinding his leg in silence. Gage had said little about the incident, and Baylin hadn't wanted to bring it up either.

So it caught him off guard when Gage said, "I woulda helped her if there was a way."

"I know. You were right. It's... first Lanie, then Taite. Makes me wonder if I'm fit for all this.

"You know as well as anyone, Baylin, sometimes things are beyond your control. All that's left is to accept it and move on," Gage said, his eyes glistening and his voice low.

"Sure. But it doesn't make it easier."

Gage clapped a hand on Baylin's back. "We should rest here for a spell. We aren't in too big a hurry anymore. Looks like they got what they wanted for now."

Baylin nodded as he pulled his pant leg over the bandage. In his pocket, the book's square edge reminded him it was there. Gage sprawled on the ground, a thick hood over his head to keep out the growing cold. Baylin figured he was too proud to say he needed to rest.

Baylin folded his legs beneath him and pulled the leather book from his pocket. Across the cover spread a branching tree — leaves curling and floating as if being blown in the wind. The brown leather was soft and pliable under his fingertips. He cracked it open with growing curiosity.

The first page stared blank and white, except for the printed words 'This book belongs to'. Underneath a slanting, looping signature read 'Aisea M. Taite'. Baylin flipped the page to see more of the sloped writing. Thumbing through the pages, several were filled, and a random sketch popped up here and there. It was a journal, and he was struck with guilt. He shoved it back in his pocket, still wondering what it might tell him.

ELEVEN

Taite was dizzy, floating in the dark with pain radiating throughout. Her shoulder was on fire. Then white lights glared all around, pouring through her eyelids as she fought to open them and failed. Against the black nothingness of unconsciousness, the light blinded. Was this what dying felt like? She struggled to stay awake but darkness pulled her back.

Hours or even days later, she regained consciousness again. With a better grip on it now, she peeked out through narrowed eyes. As she willed her lids to remain open, she thought again she must be dying or already dead. Though the intense pain had faded away, she didn't feel much of anything. And she couldn't tell if she was lying down or floating in space. Her eyes watered and squinted at the light, but as they grew accustomed to it, shapes came forth from the glaring brightness. Grates along square tiles, a silver dome of a lamp. A room, and she was alive.

Her memory was murky as swamp water, but she had one clear image of Baylin's back as he and Gage disappeared from view. So she must be with them — the shadowed hunters who had pursued them through the hills. Baylin had all but turned her over. No, that can't be. But if he left his sister, why wouldn't he leave a near stranger?

Shaking these thoughts away — they would do no good now — she wiggled her fingers and balled her fists. They had tied her down, her ankles too. The straps were tight and pulled at the skin on her wrists. She tugged at the bands, but they were fast and thick.

Her body began to burn again, and a slow seeping red spread across the crisp white gown. A vague memory presented itself. Someone had shot her. Tears welled up, but she bit her lip and clenched her jaw shut like a vault. She would not cry.

Despite the dull ache in her shoulder and the widening streaks of red, she continued the struggle. Then a click, the swishing of clothes. A tall man in a white coat appeared over her, his blond hair short and neat with a few strands of white at the temples.

"Now, Aisea," he said. "You mustn't struggle. You will aggravate your injuries." He spoke in a voice so calm it became patronizing and annoying. How did he know her name? No one called her that.

A sharp pinch on her shoulder as a needle pierced her skin. Then a slow warmth spread over her. Muscles relaxed and her eyelids grew heavy.

+++

When she woke again, she wasn't aware how much time had passed. The room had no windows — no distinguishing features at all. There was only the simple hospital bed, a tall metal lamp, and a painted cabinet. The air was crisp and smelled of antiseptic and bleach. While her feet moved unrestrained, but her hands were bound in front.

She sat up, swinging her legs over the side of the bed. Restrained arms and a wounded shoulder made everything difficult. Sliding her feet to the cold floor took a fair amount of painful wriggling, but the front of her gown remained white. First, she pointed herself to the small cabinet, hoping to find a way to cut herself free.

The flimsy sterile gown did nothing to keep out the chill of the room, and she shivered. The cabinet was locked. She started to the door on the other side of the small room. But again, it was locked. With a grunt, she threw herself at the door. A lonely rumble echoed through the room.

She raised her bound fists and pounded on the metal door until her shoulder and triceps burned and her hands ached. Minutes passed and no one came. Out of breath and sore, she leaned against the wall and allowed herself to slide down to the floor. Curled into a seated fetal position, frustrated tears ran down her face.

Moments later, a short middle-aged woman walked in and turned on the lights. She carried a tray in one hand and set it down on the empty bed while Taite watched in silence. The woman didn't seem surprised to pivot and find the girl sitting on the floor. Ice-blue eyes glared down with disapproval, as if Taite had done something wrong by existing.

"Doctor told me you were awake and out of bed," she said in a bland voice. "Time to change the dressing on your wound."

"Whatever," Taite said as she shuffled to the bed. "Am I a prisoner here?"

"This is a hospital. There are all kinds of people here." Focused on her work, the nurse pried at the bandages, as Taite gritted her teeth.

The gauze peeled off, and red, swollen stitches crisscrossed along the bony ridge of her shoulder. It seemed to belong to someone else, like a mannequin in a store window... or a corpse. In a few moments, it was hidden from sight again, and the nurse exited the room.

Taite started to drift off from boredom when the door opened again. A tall blond man strolled in. She had a fuzzy recollection of seeing him before. He must be the doctor. As she pushed back a yawn, she looked him over. Not bad. She became suddenly disturbed by the paper-thin gown.

"I'm glad you're awake, Aisea," he said, tapping his pen against a metal clipboard.

"Taite. I prefer Taite."

"Well, Taite then. How are you feeling? Better?"

"Yeah, I guess. Sore. I don't remember much. Where am I?"

"Isn't it obvious? You're in the hospital."

"Yes. That much is obvious, but where? How did I get here?"

"The rescue team brought you here. It was unfortunate you were wounded, but you'll be as good as new soon."

"Rescue? No, there was no rescue. They were chasing us."

"Taite, sometimes the trauma involved with such a serious injury — you could have died — well, sometimes the mind gets confused. The facts blur. No, Taite, you were misled by dangerous criminals. Our men saved you. Look what they did to you."

"They? What are you talking about?"

"Aisea... er Taite," he said, "I wasn't there, but I have spoken to those who were — the men who brought you in bleeding and unconscious. Your companions ran off, leaving you to bleed to death. In fact, one of them shot you."

"That's not true. Why would you say that? They didn't shoot me."

"No need to get upset," he said in his smooth, superior voice. "It isn't good for you. You might injure yourself further."

"Why are you here?" she asked, determined to change the subject.

"Ah yes, just checking in. Is there anything you need, Taite?"

"Now that you mention it," she said, holding up her bound hands. "Can you do something about this?"

"Hmm... that's a possibility, Taite, but as I said, we rescued you from dangerous criminals. I need to be sure we can trust you."

"What? Like I can run away? There is nothing in this room. The door is locked. There are no windows. Trust me with what?"

"Yes, you've made your point." He dismissed her words with a wave. "I suppose I can remove those for now. If you try anything, we can always put them back on, can't we?" he asked with a smug smile.

Taite held her hands toward him. While he was somewhat handsome, she hated him already. He freed her hands in no time with dexterous, perfectly manicured fingers. Red marks encircled her joints, itchy raw skin that hadn't seen air for weeks.

"How long have I been here?" she asked as she inspected her wrists.

"I hardly see why that matters, but let me check." He flipped through the papers on his clipboard. "About four weeks. Besides the obvious wound, you suffered from dehydration and undernourishment. You had a nice bump on your head too. From when you fell, I assume. We had to keep you sedated for some time out of fear you would aggravate your injuries."

"Four weeks? That can't be right. I don't remember hitting my head. Are you sure those are the right records?"

He chuckled in his arrogant way, like he knew something she didn't. He most likely did. "No, Taite, this is your chart. Difficulty remembering a head injury is common enough. You needn't be concerned by that."

"But I am concerned by it," Taite said, rubbing her hands over her head. There seemed to be a sore spot over her ear.

"Nothing to worry about, I assure you. We ran a scan. There's no

94

internal bleeding, no signs of anything amiss. Trouble with your memory is expected, but not a definite sign of other problems," he said, studying her face.

"I'm relieved to see you're doing better. I will leave you to rest. If you need something, tell the nurse." He smiled, his teeth straight and gleaming white.

Then he hurried out the door. What did he know anyway? Baylin may have left her there, but he wouldn't have shot her. What reason did he have had to shoot her? She didn't quite recall everything that had happened. That much was true. Only brief recollections of running, pain, and Baylin disappearing seemed clear. Before that, it was a blur — a musty bus, Lanie, walking, lots of walking. Her memories swam like slippery fish in her head. She couldn't grasp them tight enough to piece it together.

She didn't remember why they were running. Something about a cave. She turned it over and around her mind, trying to get a firm hold, but it was useless. The memories remained locked away where she couldn't reach them.

A few hours later, another nurse and a tray of food. This nurse was younger with too much make-up and a head full of thick black hair. Taite thanked her with a smile and asked, "Is there a way I could get some paper and a pen, please? I need something to do."

With sympathy written on her face, the nurse said, "I don't see any harm in that. I'll see what I can do."

Moments later, she returned with a small black notebook and a fountain pen. "Here you are," she said, looking rather pleased with herself. "It must get dull stuck in here all day. I hope that helps. If you need anything else, just say so."

"Thanks."

As soon as the door locked behind the nurse, Taite opened the small notebook. It was comforting to hold something as familiar as a book, and she thumbed through the pages, inhaling the scent of paper and glue. Then Taite began to write everything she could remember; Baylin, Lanie, and everything they told her about what happened. If she recorded it all, she might remember.

Large chunks of time stayed missing. Her hand cramped, and she had filled several pages by the time a nurse returned.

The next day passed much the same. Fresh bandages, nurses coming and going, a visit from the same tall doctor. This time he said Baylin was some kind of wanted terrorist responsible for killing several people. He knew Baylin's name. He needed to find out where he might be.

Taite had a faint memory of Baylin telling her people were hunting him. He had never mentioned killing anyone. That didn't seem to fit. She didn't think he would do that, not without good reason. Then again, she didn't know him well.

Regardless, she had no idea where he was going and told the doctor as much. He frowned and crinkled his brow. Clearly, he thought she was lying, but he was the one saying memory loss was normal. When he left the room, he was agitated. Again, she wrote everything down in her book.

Several days went by like this. The doctor, his name was Dr. Fermin, though Taite thought of him as Dr. Vermin, would ask questions. Most centered on Baylin and how important it was they stop him. He rarely mentioned her wounds anymore or why she was still there.

TWELVE

Dr. Fermin had a small stack of papers in hand, photographs, as he walked into Taite's room.

"How are you doing this fine day, Taite?" he said in a cheerful tone.

She was having a bad day. "How would you be doing in my place? Why do I need to be here?"

"You can't rush healing. Besides Taite, where else would you go?"

His voice made her want to gag. The condescending calm was sickening. Standing up, she paced the floor and asked, "Well, why is the door locked? Why can't I go outside?"

"It's for your own safety, Taite."

She hated when he used her name. As she continued pacing, her bare feet made little sound. "Safety from what? If you would at least let me walk around the building. This is torture, staying in this one room for weeks on end."

He smiled a knowing smile. "You are ignorant of many things. Leaving isn't possible now."

She frowned across to where he sat on the edge of the bed. "Well, what do you have? Why are you here?"

"Ahh, yes. I have something to show you. Actually, I need your help, Taite."

"How can I possibly help you?" she asked, not bothering to mask the irritation in her voice.

"I've been given some photographs. The authorities have asked if you would help identify a few people."

"Right, 'cause I know so many people."

Without a trace of his usual arrogant grin, he said, "You may be familiar with these."

"Fine, let me see." But she immediately regretted taking the crinkled photograph from his fingers. There was a girl lying on the ground, loose golden curls flecked with blood. Her eyes were half-closed, her skin colorless. Lanie, and she was most-definitely dead. A profusion of dried blood caked her shirt, and crimson freckles adorned her face.

With a hand clamped over her mouth, Taite muffled a gasp. Tears sprang up and her stomach turned as she thrust the photo back to the doctor

"You've met her?" the doctor asked. His smugness had returned.

Taite nodded, her hand still on her mouth.

"Who is she?"

"What does it matter if she's dead?"

"Calm yourself, Taite," he said. "It does no harm to tell me her name, does it? A simple matter of identifying a body. A name to place on the grave. That's all."

"Lanie. That's all I can tell you."

"Lanie. That's what we suspected, but thank you for confirming it. Isn't — I'm sorry — wasn't she Baylin's sister? Horrible, how it happened. And him leaving her to die. Seems to be a habit."

Taite scowled and bit her tongue.

"We'll move on to the next image. Only a few more."

"I don't want to see more," she said, shaking her head.

"I'm afraid that doesn't matter," he said, pulling out another photograph. A man about twenty with crumpled dark hair looked past the camera, as if he hadn't seen it. While he was dressed much like she remembered Baylin, she didn't recognize him.

"All right. Let's go on," Fermin said as he flipped to another image and held it up for her to see.

She squinted at the small, distant figures.

"Have you met any of these men?"

Taite took the photo in her hand. Three male figures stood near an entrance. It seemed like a still from a security camera and was rather blurry. With a fierce expression and rifle at the ready, one of the men looked the same as the last photo. The second was shorter with a muscular frame. The third may have been Baylin. As he stood facing away from the camera, it was hard to tell. They shared the same build though. She studied it closer.

"I can't be sure," she finally said. "But I've never seen those two."

"And the third? Appears to be your Baylin, correct?"

Taite peered at him with suspicion. "It might be him, but that photo is terrible."

"I wish you could be more certain. This is a photo of a small team that infiltrated a warehouse a month or two ago. Stole weapons and murdered the old maintenance man who happened to be on duty. Terrible thing. Your friend wouldn't do something like that would he?"

"I barely knew him," she said and turned away.

"I didn't mean to imply you had anything to do with it. But sometimes people can be misleading. He's a criminal."

He shuffled through photos, then said, "There is something else,

Taite. Something you should know." He dropped his voice to a sympathetic tone. "The bullet recovered from your wound matches one found at the warehouse. I can only conclude Baylin shot both you and that poor old man. He shot you right in the back, Taite."

"He did not," she said, infuriated without knowing why. Baylin wouldn't have done that. Why did he insist on lying?

"You were an inconvenience, slowing him down. He left his own sister. What kind of person does that? Someone with no respect for human life. You can't remember the shooting. Or you don't wish to remember."

He paused and took a deep breath as Taite stared wide-eyed. "That's enough for today. You look tired. Get some sleep." He turned with a gleam in his eye.

"I don't believe you."

"Sometimes the truth is hard," he said as he slipped through the door and locked it tight behind him.

Taite picked up the remains of her last meal and threw it at the door with a shattering clang. Pacing back and forth in the tiny room, she recycled the conversation, the photographs. She couldn't fathom what they wanted with her or why the doctor said these things. But the notion that Baylin may have shot her made no sense.

And Lanie was dead.

She lowered herself back down, wanting to throw up. The rest of the day, not that she could tell if it was daytime, she alternated between pacing the floor and sitting agitated on the bed.

Each day became more challenging. It became difficult to sit still — hard to focus. As she sat on the thin mattress, she bounced her knees. Baylin wouldn't do that, but he did nothing to save Lanie. He might be capable of anything. She had chewed her nails down to the quick. She didn't remember starting that habit. Her hands clasped around her head, as if to squeeze the memory out like juice from an orange.

Still, only scattered fragments surfaced.

Taite grew impatient and irritable. When the nurses removed the bandages for the final time, Taite snapped. It wasn't the first time.

"Why am I here?"

Silence.

"Answer me!" She slammed her hands on the floor.

The nurses seldom acknowledged her, but they always, always remembered to lock the door.

Weeks before she made her way into the hall when a nurse left the door unlocked, but no more. It wasn't a pretty scene. She was a captive, not a patient. At least now that was clear. That's when she decided not to cooperate. In fact, she made things as difficult as possible.

Dr. Vermin waltzed in one morning, looking irritatingly chipper. He smiled at Taite, a big fake grin, and said, "I may be able to help clear your head."

"I don't want to take more pills." She suspected they had been slipping something into her food.

"No. That's not what I meant. Look," he said. He thrust a hand toward her. "See?" Two small misshapen chunks of metal sat in his palm. "These are the bullets I mentioned. They're from Baylin's gun." He picked one up to examine.

"This one was..." he placed it against her shoulder, "right there. Lodged against the bone. You're lucky it didn't do more damage."

She sat watching him, but something bothered her. Maybe it was just the knowledge that it might be true. The bullets looked identical. They were crumpled and scraped in all the same places. Did that mean it was true? She lowered her head. Fermin left the room, taking his prizes with him.

True or not, she despised that man.

Afterward, Taite brooded on the bed for hours before falling into a restless sleep where her boots slammed against the ground in a heavy, monotonous rhythm. She couldn't seem to run fast enough. Someone was chasing her. In an instant, her feet lost all traction, sending her whirling to the ground. It was slick with blood. Shots rang out. She struggled to her feet, but she failed. Everything went dark. Then she was drowning, fighting for the surface. Baylin appeared phantom-like above, hand outstretched as if to pull her up. Or had he pushed her down?

Taite began to have the same dream over and over. Feet drumming against loose gravel, heart thumping hard in her chest, and blood pouring down. Baylin ran ahead. She called out, but her words evaporated in a driving wind, and he kept running.

Every time, she woke in a cold sweat. In the gloom of the featureless room, she would lie in the narrow bed and stare at the emptiness of the ceiling. She imagined other people like her lived within the hospital — trapped, forced to survive while a world went on turning. Not even her world. Her world was light-years away.

No. That wasn't possible.

She was still on Earth. Except she had seen impossible things. Maybe she was losing her mind, hallucinating. She wanted to believe she was in her own room, dreaming it all up.

+++

The nurses had started giving her injections. She didn't know what they contained, and the nurses disregarded any questions. The first time came after she refused to eat. While she assumed it was a nutritional supplement or something, whatever it was made her groggy. Her vision wouldn't quite come into focus and her skull throbbed at the temples. There was a faint roar in her ears that never stopped.

The next morning, she was more herself and cleaned her plate. They came with the needle anyway. Her protests were to no avail. The third day, she kicked a tray out of the nurse's hands when she approached with the syringe. As she screamed, they held her down. The nurses had become heartless automatons.

Most of the day, every day, she sat in blank oblivion. Sometimes, the doctor would stop by with questions. Some were about her father.

"What does he have to do with this?" she tried to ask through the mental fog. One day, before the injection, Vermin entered the room as she paced in circles. He had another photograph.

"I'd like you to look at something, Taite. Have a seat," he said, gesturing to the bed as he looked over the image. He said nothing more but held out the photo.

Her jaw dropped as she lowered herself down. "What are you doing with that?" Taite asked, anger rising in her core. She was shouting before she realized. "What does my father have to do with this?"

Dressed in a lab coat, her father stood next to a military officer in uniform. Her father's hair had not yet started to gray, his smile broad and bright. She had never seen him smile like that.

"Your reaction tells me exactly what I wanted to know. You have no knowledge of it, do you?" he asked, placing the photograph in his coat pocket. "Perhaps it's time you did. Calm down and tell me what you can about your father's work."

Taite squirmed, but she answered in halting phrases. "Not much.

He's never talked about it. He's some sort of scientist. Conservation or something."

"That is true. Dr. Taite worked with conservation. Conserving humanity, that is. He helped develop the program years ago before you were alive. A brilliant man, your father. Your name, Aisea, was a little nod to his life's work, the project, AISES. Of course, it began long before I became involved."

"If that were all true, why are you telling me?"

"It is your father's fault you're here. Don't you think that's something you should hear? I would want to if I was in your shoes."

"What would you know about it?" Taite said with a snarl.

"I know you should watch your tone," he said, his jaw set as he spoke. "Your father, Baylin, and everyone you've relied on has let you down, Taite. I don't understand why you bother being so loyal."

"Leave me alone," she said, her voice dying to a whimper. At that moment, a nurse opened the door with the tray and needle. "I don't want it. Please, I don't want it."

"Be a good girl. Take your medicine," Dr. Fermin said, as he leaned over and gave her cheek a firm pat.

"No," Taite hissed through clenched teeth, as she grabbed his arm with both hands.

Vermin scowled and tried to wrestle his arm away. But without thinking, Taite lunged forward, and bit his forearm as he struggled.

It was a mistake; she knew as soon as her teeth met his skin. She would pay for it, but it was still satisfying to watch the shock on that usually unaffected face.

He shouted for the nurse, whom Taite kicked in the ribs. She let out a screech and seconds later, Taite was pinned by hands from every direction. Blood rushed through her ears. Fermin, breathless and rubbing his forearm, retreated to the doorway.

A pinch, and the injection would soon do its work. Taite relaxed in defeat and sank back into the pillow as the familiar surge of warmth overcame her. When she woke, her head was still heavy and spinning.

Day after day, it was like this, an endless blur of a drug-induced stupor. Some days, she attempted to scrawl a few jumbled words in her journal. Other days drifted by completely unaware.

A sailor lost at sea — that's how she considered herself. And she was sinking. Before, she assumed crazy people were simply crazy, but the scary thing is how blurred the line can be. Things had started to tilt, and then they spiraled out of control.

The nurse came, another injection, another plate of food she could barely taste. She pushed it to the tile and rolled over as the dish shattered to pieces.

Some days, all she did was sleep, but then she would have the dream again. Afterward, she fought sleep until exhaustion gave her no choice. It took her anyway. The dream was worse now, always worse than the time before. A river of blood. Her father with a disgusted look on his face. A gaping hole in her side.

One day, Taite was sitting up in bed when her father strolled into the room. Surprised, she tried a weak smile and felt upside down for a moment, but then he spoke. His voice was wrong, and he called her Taite. Her father never called her that. So she told him she was tired and curled up to sleep.

Burning pulsed through her head almost all the time now. Her once wavy hair had become a mass of tangles, but she didn't care. It was so pointless to go on existing like this. No one would care if she disappeared. These thoughts flitted through her mind when someone cleared their throat. She looked up from her hands to see Vermin sitting at the foot of the bed. How long had he been there?

"About five minutes."

Taite jumped in amazement to hear him answer. "Can you read my mind?" she asked, her voice catching.

"You said that out loud," he said with a chuckle.

"Oh. I don't like it here. I want to go home."

"That isn't possible. We need you here, Taite."

"Wha... Why do ya need me?" Taite asked, words slurring.

"Don't worry about that. You're safe. No one is out there for you. No one who cares. I care though, Taite. We'll take care of you."

THIRTEEN

Date: November 20th — So it's official, I turned seventeen last week. It still sucks to be younger than everyone else in the senior class, but I guess that's the unfortunate side effect of skipping a grade. Dad gave me this journal for the occasion. It's a far cry from the car I asked for, but it's pretty. At least he remembered I write. That's something I guess. Besides, he freaks out when I drive. "What if something happened to you, Aisea?" he always says. Is this because I'm an only child? I guess it's nice that he cares, but he can be a little overprotective. Like that time he threw a fit when Emmy lit up a cigarette in my presence. Went on for an hour about the damage to my lungs. Whoa, Dad, relax. I guess I shouldn't complain. He remembered my birthday this year and came home for it this time.

The pages were rough along the edges like they'd been torn by hand and were covered in the inclined script he now recognized at Taite's. Running a calloused finger down the ragged edges, Baylin continued to read, ignoring the notion that he shouldn't be prying. Anyway, he would probably never see her again.

She had filled less than half of the pages. As he turned it around in his hands, a few papers slipped from the journal and drifted down to settle on the sand. Though he hadn't seen one in a while, photos were common enough in the colony. Usually, they existed only as digital images. Hardly anyone printed them anymore. The colony considered it an unnecessary use of resources.

Taite stared back at him from the paper in his hand, a grin on her lips and one arm wrapped around a shorter girl with hair that appeared dark purple against Taite's brown. Taite looked younger than he remembered. Or perhaps it was the lack of worry on her face. There was not a trace of the scowl she often wore. Even as a child in the colony, he hadn't felt as free as Taite appeared in the picture.

Both girls wore short pants leaving their legs exposed most of the way up. Bare feet draped casually on the steps where they sat. Taite's hair just grazed her shoulders and fell in thick disheveled waves.

Behind the girls stood a doorway, carved and full of glass panes. From along either side of a walkway, sprang vegetation that spilled over its confines in green abundance he had only heard about. The house itself seemed to have a kind of life to it. It was painted a pale yellow, with pillars that must hold a porch roof. He suddenly wished he had taken time to ask her more about her life on Earth.

The second photograph showed Taite and the other girl again. This time, the girl's hair gleamed almost white. A tall boy, the sides of his head shaved, stood between the girls. Kinda looked like an asshole. Beside him, Taite wore a long red dress and her hair curled around her shoulders. He never bothered to notice if Taite was pretty or not, but here with the opportunity to look, he didn't have to question it.

The picture had little background, fragments of some interior room with walls about the same green as her backpack. It occurred to him he had put little thought into what Taite experienced here. She had a life before — a house, a father, friends, and now it was gone. The choice to leave his old life behind had been his. Taite was given no say in the matter. She handled it rather well.

Date: November 22ⁿᵈ — Thanksgiving is this week. I am not looking forward to it. Everyone else has big family dinners with turkey, and all that. Emily's mom will cook an enormous meal for the twenty people who come to her house. Me? If Dad is home, we go out to eat at some fancy restaurant... just him and me. I love him, but I can't help but be jealous of Emily. Even family arguments around a football game sound interesting by comparison.

Two years ago when Dad was out of town, Em's family invited me. It was great but depressing at the same time. Emily's mom is such a... mom. Like a blog-worthy, perfect mom. Makes me wish I knew my mother, or better yet, that she was still here. There are limits to what Dad can do, what I can talk to him about. Besides, he's always so busy. Sometimes I feel like an orphan. Wish I could skip the Holidays.

Gage called his name, and Baylin closed the book, sliding the photos between pages before tucking it into his pocket. They were only days away from Duratio's base, where Dakota and everyone else surely wondered where he was by now. Where Lanie was. Gage would be a pleasant surprise for them though. He hadn't been to the base in some time, preferring the solitude of his own little outpost. Guarding their self-defined border and relaying information, he still contributed in a big way.

"So far I've learned her father was overprotective and not around often. No mother for whatever reason. That doesn't explain much," Baylin said as Gage approached.

"No, no, it doesn't. If you ask me, you won't find anything in there that will answer any of our questions. Waste of time. Unless you're reading it for other reasons."

Baylin huffed. "What other reasons could I have, Gage?"

"Hmm, let me think... curiosity about a member of the opposite sex, perhaps?" he asked with a mischievous twinkle in his eye.

Baylin shook his head as he stood up and shouldered his gear.

+++

Date: December 1ˢᵗ — Thanksgiving turned out as I expected. Dad was called away at the last minute. I could have gone to Emmy's still, but I wasn't in a social mood. I stayed home and ate a microwave dinner and blared music in my room. The food sucked. Everything sucked. Dad apologized like he always does. Whatever.

Date: December 5ᵗʰ — I wish it would snow, Em, Jared and I planned on sledding on the big hill by the park, but there hasn't been a big snow yet. Life has just been uncooperative lately. Dad says I am too old for sledding anyway and reminded me how last year a kid fell off his sled and broke his leg against a fence post. Leave it to him to see the worst. I have a few more months to act like a kid. I'm going to do it! After that, college classes, studying... and maybe a party or two.

Date: December 7ᵗʰ — Emily and I snuck out the other night. Not something I usually do, but there was a party, and I really wanted to go for a change. It was on the other side of town, but Emily drives. Anyway, I didn't see the problem. And I didn't bother asking Dad, he would flip at the thought of me at a party with *gasp* smoking and possible drinking. He would say, 'Think what that would do to your liver, Aisea.' I don't drink, but he doesn't trust me. Emily said the last time she got drunk, she wound up throwing up all over

herself. This doesn't appeal to me for some reason. Oh wait, I remember...
'cause it's disgusting. Not to mention she isn't sure if she and Jared did
anything or not. Anyway, Dad was home for once. After he passed out with a
book on his lap, I met Emmy outside.

The party was all right, I guess. Music so loud my ears were ringing, people
I don't know, and yes, lots of smoke. I spent most of the time on the porch, so I
could breathe. Emily and Jared spent most of the time in a corner with their
faces plastered together. Why they went to a party to do that, I can't say.

When I was outside leaning on the railing, some guy grabs my butt. Hello? I
don't think so. After I threatened to knee him, I walked home. It was boring
anyway and my head hurt. Of course, with my luck, Dad waited like a Roman
sentry at the front door. I am pretty much forbidden to leave the house. As
usual, he completely freaked when he smelled smoke in my hair. What is he
planning on doing — keeping me a prisoner forever?

Date: December 10ᵗʰ — So here I sit, scarfing down some green concoction
Dad calls a smoothie as I write. They're supposed to be sooo good for you, he
says. He's crazy with this health stuff. I am still in solitary confinement. I'm
not even allowed to see Emily and Jared... 'bad influences' Dad called them.
This is so much B.S. I am sick of being alone. Even when Dad is here, it's the
same. The only time he talks to me is to lecture me or shove more of this green
shit down my throat.

Baylin turned the page to reveal a sketch of a bird in a tiny cage.
Black lines scrawled angrily across the spread, spilling over the
binding. He remembered Lanie had been impossible to live with
when she was a teenager — always moody. She threw things at him

from time to time. Of course, he hadn't lived with her long before they had been sent their separate ways.

The last few days at the base, he thought a lot about Lanie. Baylin wouldn't mourn her, not yet. He refused to acknowledge she was dead. It had been almost a year now since it had happened, but there was a chance they had saved her. That's all he saw. Until he knew otherwise, Lanie might be alive. He would do what he could to find her.

Taite was another story. Taite was definitely alive somewhere. Her wound was only in her shoulder. He scowled as he replayed the scene again in his mind; her knees crumbling beneath her as red drops sprayed across her horrified face. She wasn't like Lanie. And she didn't understand things here. Taite was just a kid really and his responsibility. He failed — failed them both. But mistakes can be corrected, and he would. He could still find them.

"How many times are you gonna read that damn thing?" Dakota asked as he walked up behind Baylin.

Baylin raised his eyebrows and snapped the book shut. "I don't know," he said. "It still seems like something's off."

"Yeah, something's off all right," Dakota said. He had been different before. He and Baylin had always been close, but since Lanie was gone, he was brooding and bitter.

"We have other things to do. Important things, I should say, and there you are reading your little book. It's an unhealthy obsession if you ask me."

"I didn't ask you," Baylin said as he rose and stalked down the hall. Dakota followed after.

"Do whatever you want in your spare time, but we have work to do. You're in charge now. Everyone looks up to you. You need to focus."

"Don't lecture me, Dakota."

Only a few months before, Duratio had lost its leader. They raided an outpost after hearing about a store of weapons and other supplies. As far as that goes, it was successful. But in the end, Baylin considered it a disaster. Samuel, who everyone looked up to and followed without question, was shot. Baylin and Dakota pulled him out, smearing blood all over the place. As soon as possible, Cy removed the bullet from his chest, but he died minutes later. They all knew the risks, but Baylin never got used to it.

Since then, he and Dakota had been trying to fill his shoes. It hadn't been easy. Baylin was tired of existing by stealing from their enemy. Tired of using all their energy on surviving when they should use it to make a difference. They had talked about leaving, starting their own colony of sorts far away. It never seemed to happen. An invisible umbilical cord attached them to the colony. A perpetual give and take. Baylin hated it.

FOURTEEN

Taite wanted to be free of her continual state of misery. There was nothing for her but numbing repetition, confusion, and pain. In her endless spare time, Taite thought about the solace of death more and more. By now she had given up on writing. She had filled her pages.

She remembered the doctor telling her he needed her, and she couldn't leave. But in her mind, his face twisted in surprise, and the nurses came running like frantic ninnies. Her body laid crumpled and bloody on the floor. What would that do to his plans? Whatever they were.

This was Taite's distorted fantasy world, but it seemed it would remain a fantasy. As she looked around and found no way to end her breath, to stop the drumming of her heart. Not even that. She couldn't even manage to die. Tears streamed down of their own accord. She didn't want to die, but this wasn't life. And it was hopeless.

As she sat fidgeting with the fountain pen, she twirled it in her fingers like a miniature baton. The light glinted off the metallic nib, old-fashioned and pointed. While she scribbled on her arm, she scratched the delicate skin of the underside of her wrist. It was an accident at first, then she scraped a harder line, her skin welting up in a reddened ridge. Odd that they used this kind of pen here. Fate. Another line, and drips of red wet the nib.

She stared at her blurry hands; pale, weak, and pathetic hands. Blue veins pulsing beneath her translucent skin. She was sick of everything. Of hearing the same phrases out of Vermin's mouth. Every time the nurses gave an injection, they said the same things too. Worse, Taite found the Doctor's words kept replaying in her head. She tried to ignore them, to shake them out, but nothing worked. And it was all true whether she wanted to admit it or not. She had no one.

Taite stood and began pacing like a caged animal, and the roaring in her ears grew louder. Was it only in her head? The room spun, and she couldn't breathe but in gasps. She couldn't hold herself together anymore, and she quivered and crumbled into tears. Her sobs built until they were uncontrollable. She slumped to her knees on the cold floor and choked for air between spasms of crying.

It had been a gradual decline, but there she was, torn apart at the seams. Then the nib of the fountain pen winked at her from the floor as if to say it had all answers. She glared back, scowling.

Without another thought, she snatched it up and thrust it with all her might into her wrist with a grating scream.

Like red ink, blood oozed up from the embedded pen. Taite slumped down on the floor, her forehead only inches from the tile. Still clutching the barrel of the pen, her right hand trembled hard. A burning sensation poured up her arm into her shoulder as she tried to yank it out. She didn't have the strength, and a moan was all she released. Red ink trickled down her arm and pooled on the tile.

She laid her head down, the coldness of the floor chilling her cheek like the snowy bus window in her memory. As she listened to her heartbeat, she shut her eyes. The pulse in her wrist pushed the ache and the flowing stream down her arm. Taite thought of her neighbor, Mrs. Dalton, washing her scraped knee. She would be so upset with her. Several faces crossed her mind. She would never see them again, but that was true regardless. Then Taite drifted off somewhere where sensations were extinguished.

+++

Her eyelids fluttered open to the same white ceiling she had seen for countless days. Tears began to slide down.

Taite tried to lift her hand to wipe them away, but she found her arms tight around her ribs. She couldn't move them. Terror gripped her, and she panted as she fought to pull her arms away. She struggled until she was spent. After, it occurred to her they had bound her in a straitjacket. Somehow that was even worse. Her breath quickened until she thought she might pass out. As she yelled for help, she tried to get on her feet.

She squirmed to the bedside and swung her legs over. "Get this thing off of me!" Taite shouted and kicked the door.

"You can't keep me in here!" She brought a knee toward her chest and slammed her bare foot into the door. Still reeling in pain, she rammed the door with her shoulder. "Let me out of this thing!"

Why didn't they just let her die? She slid down to the floor and curled into herself.

+++

"Taite, I am so disappointed in you. What a selfish thing to do," the rat of a doctor said, staring down like an executioner. "Didn't you

116

stop to think how this would affect everyone else? You've made this very difficult on us."

He reached down to release her arms from their hold, and a nurse finished unstrapping the back of the jacket. Taite breathed a deep sigh as the fabric pulled away. Her wrist was bandaged and ached up her arm into her left bicep. As she unwound the blood-soaked dressings, the nurse revealed a deep, oozing puncture near the fragile wrist bones. Taite snapped her face away.

"Look what you've done to yourself," Vermin said, shaking his head in disgust. "Stupid girl."

Taite's temples burned as she stared up at him, wishing he would fall over dead. "Screw you," she said through clenched teeth.

"That wasn't very nice," he said "Was it, Taite?" he asked much louder. His face had broken its cool composure, reddening along his cheekbones for a moment. But only a moment.

Calming himself on an inhale, he said, "Until you can be civilized, you must stay in your new jacket, I'm afraid."

"No. Please don't put me back in that thing," Taite said, jerking her arms close to her chest.

"You'll do as you're told. It can be easy, or it can be hard."

"Get away from me!"

"Nurse," he said, leaving the remainder of the sentence lost in silence. The nurse reached for the jacket, discarded on the foot of the bed.

"No," Taite said in desperation. "Please, no. I'll behave." The rest turned into a blur of shrieking and flailing, kicking. Hands like vises against her skin. Buckles tightened, her own arms wrapped around in a smothering embrace.

"It's for your own good. Someone has to teach you how to behave,"

Fermin said as he stomped out the door, his polished black shoes reflecting off the gloss of the tiled floor.

Days passed uncounted. Most hours Taite spent sleeping or rocking herself on the floor as she shivered and contemplated if it was possible to will her heart to stop beating.

The ambient roar in her ears faded to a painful silence. Silence from the surrounding room, silence from God who must see what was happening to her. She prayed for release, but it didn't come.

Her moods ebbed like a tide. In her more lucid moments, she was convinced something was wrong. Of course. Everything was wrong. But she couldn't shake the feeling she was overlooking something. Memories. Something didn't add up. As she ran a bare foot along the underside of the mattress, she pushed the black book from its hiding place.

She fumbled through the pages with her feet, giggling at how ridiculous she must look. Words ran crooked on the page, and some were very hard to read. She shuffled through the book at random, and it glared back at her. The something that didn't add up.

Vermin said Baylin's gun was used to shoot her and the guard at the warehouse. But wouldn't Baylin have defended his sister if he had had a gun? She didn't remember a gun.

This was all some kind of mind game, and she had to get better at playing it.

Taite was still analyzing the facts when the door cracked open, and a slim nurse slipped through. The same girl who had given Taite the pen. She had seen little of her in the last few weeks, but she was sane enough to remember that heavy eye liner. As Taite observed her, the girl's round face was apprehensive but full of pity.

"I've been wondering about you," the girl said. "Since your...

accident, I'm not supposed to be in here. If I'd known you'd do that, I would have never given that pen to you."

Taite had taken to refusing to speak to anyone except herself. As she stared, the nurse continued chatting. "It took me by surprise. A little word of advice though. If you ever want to get out of that jacket — or out of here — you need to learn to shape up."

Easy to say. What did she know about anything? Taite became lost in her own thoughts and heard little else the girl said, though she rambled on for several more minutes as she cleaned. The nurse was right though. Taite hated to admit it, but she would never get out of here unless she cooperated.

Two weeks later, when the doctor came to check on her wrist for the last time, she didn't struggle. Instead, she stretched her arms and accepted the personal penitentiary of the jacket. Actually, she felt rather exposed with it off. The nurse cinched the jacket's extra long sleeves tight around her — too tight.

"Ow," Taite said with a wince. "I don't want to cause any trouble, I swear. Please, loosen the jacket."

"Taite, Taite, Taite," Fermin said, "how do you expect me to believe that? You've caused one kind of trouble after another since you arrived."

"I know, but I can't breathe."

"Well, you have been acting more civilized these days. Let's just leave the sleeves loose, but if you try anything..." he said, an unspoken warning hanging in the air.

The nurse raised an astonished eyebrow, but he said, "Loosen the sleeves. Maybe she won't thrash around so much. I'm tired of this nonsense."

The nurse trailed after the doctor, her wavy hair bouncing as she balanced the metal tray in her hands. Then she whirled around and said, "I'll be back with your lunch shortly."

As she stepped back around, she slammed straight into the back of Dr. Fermin, who had stopped to mark the chart in his hands. Taite suppressed a smile as the tray dropped to the floor with a resounding clang.

Fermin whirled on his heel, scowling. He grabbed the arm of the nurse. "What do you think you're doing?"

"I'm so sorry, doctor," she said as she immediately dropped to the floor to retrieve the tray and bandages.

Taite didn't hear it though. She gawked in amazement. Instead of the doctor before her, she remembered Baylin.

Fermin told her Baylin had shot her from behind, but her only clear memory was of Baylin running ahead. She had dreamed it a hundred times. Twisting around, his empty fists clenched as he yelled. Gage forced him along, hands locked on his arm. He had been ahead of her. The gun still tucked into his belt, blood running down his leg, soaking his pant leg.

Further back, she remembered guns hanging like bats on the cave wall. Gage and Baylin grabbed them as they hurried to leave. It hadn't been Baylin's gun. Not until the cave was there any sign of a gun. And Gage's gun couldn't have been at the warehouse to shoot the old man.

Fermin was a liar.

FIFTEEN

Date: January 2nd — Things have been weird lately with Dad — worse than normal. He seems distracted, and he practically forgot Christmas altogether. Barely talks to me and when he does he snaps. Something is going on. As far as I know, I've done nothing wrong. I guess it's work, but it's hard to say. He's always stressed about his job, and he's never taken that out on me like this before. I don't know what's happening anymore.

Then last night, he gives me a hug, saying he was sorry. I can't remember the last time he hugged me. The only thing I can guess is he feels guilty because when he grounded me I missed Jared's New Year's Eve Party. He and Emmy are mad now... like it's my fault? Anyway, weird.

Despite being raised with a sister, it seemed Taite wrote in a foreign language. Sometimes, she used references he didn't comprehend, phrases he supposed were common for her. It was pointless, but it occupied his mind at least, kept him from wandering down the road of guilt and grief.

At present, he could do nothing to find Lanie... even if she survived. The sinking feeling in the pit of his stomach grew colder each day, warning him she hadn't. He was looking right at her when she fell.

The wound looked like they hit her square in the chest. It would've taken a miracle for her to have lived, but he refused to accept it. With a sigh, he turned a page.

Date: January 20th — I need to have some blood work done. I've been tired, but I figure it's cause I can't sleep. Dad worries about everything else — vitamin deficiencies, chemical imbalances, you name it. I don't like needles. Correction... I hate needles. Blood I can handle but watching it being sucked out of me with a syringe in my arm? No.

Baylin glanced down at the old pocket watch he kept wound at all times. "Oh, hell," he said out loud, realizing he had lost track of the time. He was supposed to meet the guys for a game of cards, though he secretly found it dull. While the idea was to relax, the conversation always turned to a raid or a piece of new information. Otherwise, they talked trash, which he found even worse.

He frowned as he ran a comb through his shaggy hair. Somebody was always bragging about what they'd been doing with one of the girls. Half of it wasn't even true. With a groan, he headed toward impending boredom, making a mental note to chop off his hair.

+++

Baylin sat at the table, propping his chin up with one fist. Dakota and Jeremy were arguing. Jeremy accused Dakota of cheating again, and Baylin knew he was. Dakota hated to lose. Of course, Baylin couldn't say it out loud. Minutes flew by, and they were still at it. Dakota was swearing, but Jeremy looked amused. When Baylin dropped his mediocre hand to the table and left the room, no one took much notice.

Lanie had owned little, none of them did, but the few things she possessed were now packed into a small box. Since Kassidy delivered it to him months ago, Baylin hadn't brought himself to touch it. The box still sat on the shelf, staring at him, collecting dust.

He stumbled over now without knowing why and pulled off the lid. On the top, a coil of emerald fabric spilled like liquid. She sometimes worn her hair back in the scarf. Years ago, their mother gave it to her, he didn't recall the occasion. The green always brought out the color of her eyes. Cloth poured through his fingers and fell back to the box.

Lanie's favorite childhood doll sat limp in the corner. She brought it when they left home, as a reminder of what the R.A. had done to her. Then he remembered her as a little girl; blond curls bouncing as he chased her, threatening to tear the doll to pieces.

As a child, she was one of those girls who always played with dolls — feeding them, wrapping them up in a blanket. When they sent her to the PRP, she was devastated. That was long before Duratio. Before their lives became so complicated.

He always blamed himself for getting her involved in all this. When he first learned about Duratio, he was seventeen and enrolled in the military training program, same as his friends. The government required two years of service, starting at fifteen. Of course, Duratio and other similar groups were the enemy. He almost believed it. After the mandatory service, he even went along with his father's insistence that he joined the Order.

At first, he tried to take the Order seriously, but the reality of the organization became clearer every day. Something in his thinking shifted like the sand beneath his feet. The planet Aises began to look like a contorted dream, twisted and disturbing. He never realized what happened until then. Until they asked him to take part.

During his first assignment as a guard in a re-education camp, he witnessed how they treated the inmates. Young and old, male and female, branded, worked, and force-fed the political agenda until they learned to choke it down. At the time, he always told Lanie everything He regretted that now.

When he left for Duratio, she insisted she wanted to go too. She was too young, only sixteen. But she experienced the cruelty of the government firsthand and would always have the scars. Her cheerful innocence evaporated after that. He couldn't protect her forever, and he couldn't choose for her. Baylin exhaled, staring into the past when a glint from the bottom of the box caught his eye.

+++

He spun the small ring on his little finger. It barely slid on. In the past, it belonged to his mother. She wore it on the index finger of her small hands until the day she passed it on to Lanie... the day they sent her away. Tarnished with age, the silver ring was patterned with delicate leaves among scrolling vines. Lanie valued it too much to wear it often. The band always had a habit of slipping from her thin fingers, falling with a faint clatter to the floor.

He hadn't spoken with his mother or father for years, not that he hadn't tried. Once he risked a visit to the colony, only to have his mother tell him to get out of her house. He still wanted to know what angered her more; the fact they fought on opposite sides or that he turned Lanie into a fugitive and a traitor with him. What did they think now? His mother would never forgive him. His father had long ago disowned him. He sighed and went back to reading.

Date: January 23rd — Passed out at the hospital. Good times! Nothing wrong with me. A waste of time and blood. There's finally snow on the ground, but now that it's here, I'm sick of the cold. I have so much to do anyway. Early next month, I'm supposed to go into the city to take a big exam to qualify for a college scholarship. Apparently, Dad doesn't want to pay my way through school. I'm already anxious.

Baylin flipped ahead, holding his place with his thumb as he reached to take a sip of his steaming mug. He had woken with another nightmare. It would be useless to sleep now. The dreams were often similar — he was always searching for someone. Lanie, he assumed. But the dreams were getting worse. Now, he would find her. Sometimes Lanie, often Taite or even Samuel. When he found them, he wished he hadn't. Death has many faces, and his dreams showed him many. None of them pretty.

He understood he felt guilty, he was failing everyone. After waking, he never gave the dreams much thought. This nightmare was different though. He couldn't shake the idea that it meant something.

Water extended as far as he could see. He had learned of Earth's oceans but had never seen so much as a picture. He thought they must be like this. The surface was steel gray, the color of a rolling thunderhead. Rough waves crashed all around her as Taite stood knee-deep in the water. She faced away, but it was her. She wore a silver dress that floated on the waves, spread out like a paper fan. The sky, glazed with pale blue, seemed faded on the edges as if it might wash away.

As he watched, red trickled down the shimmering folds of the dress. Taite didn't seem to notice the blood, or him for that matter. As if waiting for something, she only gazed at the horizon. Churning into a foaming pink froth, the water mixed with red. He jolted awake in a cold sweat.

+++

Date: February 3ʳᵈ — I've been studying like crazy. Two more days to cram, and I can put it behind me. I hope college is worth all the work. Dad insisted on taking me in for another medical test the other day. I tried to get out of it. Emmy and I made plans that day. We were gonna go ice skating — nope. Shocker. Dad ruins my plans... again. He is getting crazy with this stuff.

Date: February 6ᵗʰ — Today is the big day. I can't wait to be done. I am still not 100% sure what I will major in, but I'm thinking architecture. Or maybe marketing. Ugh... decisions!

OK, something's weird. Dad just came in — without knocking — looking all pale to say that if I don't want to go, I don't have to. How else can I get to college and away from here? I'm taking the freaking test. Besides, I'm not throwing all that studying away. I've got a backpack ready to go. Gonna be a stressful day.

"Don't you think this is a little suspicious?" Baylin had said, when he first read the page some time ago. "I'm guessing her father knew something."

Gage was half-listening as he walked a few steps ahead. They were nearing the base and had quickened their pace.

"Yes, it's odd. Makes you wonder."

"That's the last entry before Aises. The next one's from here."

"Oh? Anything about yours truly?" Gage asked, gesturing to himself with a broad hand.

"Just that you're extremely attractive."

"Why, I oughtta..." Gage raised an eyebrow and slammed a fist into the palm of his hand.

126

"No. Seems she hadn't written since we met up with you. Hadn't found the time maybe."

With mock sophistication, Gage said, "Too bad. I do tend to liven up the page."

Baylin smoothed down the leaf of the journal, recalling the conversation with a smile. He hadn't seen Gage in several months now.

When they reached the base after losing Taite, Gage stayed for a while. He was needed, but he was never comfortable around people. After a few weeks, he strolled out across the desert. Baylin hadn't seen him since then. Hadn't heard from him either. But that wasn't unusual for Gage.

Still, he worried. After they shot Taite, they had certainly discovered the cave and searched it. Baylin tried to convince Gage to stay, but he was set in his ways, and his ways were out in the wasteland. Baylin traced his index finger along the embossing on the cover. He had read it several times now. He had to admit it was a strange hobby, but he wouldn't call it an obsession.

The door latch clicked open, and he tossed the book to the couch. Dakota was already on his case about reading it. Baylin pushed a foot against the table it was resting on, spinning his chair around.

"There you are."

SIXTEEN

Days later, Taite relaxed on the bed with her legs folded before her. A lunch tray sat empty on her lap. People came and went with the daily routine, and no one gave her any notice. But she wasn't concerned by it. She remembered everything, though they had tried to make her forget. It was as if part of her mind had been dormant and was now waking. While it didn't come easy, she recalled the trees and running, falling. Sometimes, she had almost wanted to forget, to let it slip away like a fleeting dream. Pain is a powerful thing, but so is hope. She would get out of here.

Taite watched the door open, and the doctor once more entered her room. She scrambled to sit up, slinging the long sleeves of the jacket out of her way. The doctor insisted she wear it as a reminder. Taite pursed her lips, wondering what they would subject her to today.

"Well, Taite, it looks like you're leaving us," Vermin said with a satisfied sigh.

"What do you mean?"

Then Fermin's demeanor changed as he sloughed off his false face as a snake sheds its skin. "I'm done with you. You've caused me nothing but trouble in one way or another."

He creased his brow, as if he'd taken a bite of something sour.

Taite's jaw dropped, but words failed her. Was this a trick or another drug-induced hallucination? But they had stopped the injections weeks ago.

"Are you serious?" she asked, standing up to face him. "You're letting me go?"

"It was never a joy to have you here. My work is complete, and I don't care why they're moving you now. I'll be glad to be rid of you."

"Where will I go? What will happen to me?"

His eyes flashed with inexplicable anger, and he asked, "Didn't you hear me? I don't care."

Taking her by complete surprise, Fermin pushed her into the wall and leaned in — his breath laced with a hint of lemon. "I have no further use of you, but someone else does," he said, a soulless expression in his eyes.

He released her and stepped back. As he took a slow breath, he returned to his usual chilly self. "You will be turned over to a different department. I didn't bother to ask details, since..."

"You don't care." Taite finished the sentence in a whisper.

"That's right."

Only moments later, Taite was led through a sterile corridor with countless doors. The straps were again tight on her jacket, and firm hands griped her skeletal elbows. On either side, a man stood almost a head taller than her with an expressionless, vacuous face. Dressed in unfamiliar Prussian blue uniforms, low brims turned their eyes into shadowed pits.

After exiting the building, one of several low rectangles surrounded by dried grassland, they led Taite toward a canvas-covered truck. In place of tires it had rolling tracks like a tank. A flap was tacked up at the rear, and a guard shoved Taite inside.

Under the tarp was shade and shadows. As she sat on a bench that ran the length of the truck bed, she was surprised and relieved to see she was not traveling alone. An aging man slumped beside her, his head back and eyes closed. Sweat plastered his thinning hair to his forehead.

Across the aisle, a woman stared toward the back of the truck. Her auburn hair had been cropped short, making her look a younger than Taite suspected she was. Next to her, obscured by darkness, sat a lanky boy near Taite's age. He had one of those faces that made it difficult to guess with any accuracy.   black hair fell across his eyes, and he made no effort to control it.

Looking up as if he felt her glance, he lifted two fingers in a casual acknowledgment. He dropped his hand as his eyes swept over her. No doubt he noticed the jacket, the lovely parting gift the Doctor had given her. The others wore sleeveless gray shirts and loose charcoal-colored pants. No one bothered to make eye contact with Taite, except the boy with black hair.

On occasion, he glanced up as if he would like to ask her something. She guessed it was about the jacket. Taite suddenly realized what she must look like to these people and frowned. Her hair hadn't seen a brush in months, and well, she had on a straitjacket. She imagined them all guessing what she had done to be strapped to herself in the sweltering heat. After her unfortunate epiphany, she stared at her feet in shame. The floor beneath her boots was scuffed and dirty — a long gouge across the surface.

As the engine roared awake, the smell of exhaust filled the air. The other girl coughed and stretched on the bench. While the black-haired boy doodled on the painted surface of the seat. From where Taite sat, it appeared he had scratched out a thick outline of an abstracted bullet.

Wherever they were going, the drive was long, rough, and scorching. The straitjacket was perfectly suffocating in the heat, and perspiration soaked Taite through. She considered this another type of torture the son-of-a-bitch doctor had planned.

Once, the truck stopped, and someone brought water out to them. Taite's hands were useless, and the old man next to her tilted the canteen back for her to drink. As much water dribbled along her chin as slid down her throat.

+++

Hours later, the truck made a sharp turn, sending Taite crashing into the unlucky man beside her. And then they stopped. Taite was the first pulled off the truck, and another stoic soldier grabbed her arm and pulled her away. Her lips twitched in a suppressed sneer as she conjured up a twisted image of cattle being led to slaughter.

Around her, stood buildings placed in rows like a child's blocks. An unfamiliar flag fluttered and rippled from its pole, sending whispers into the wind. In the center of the flag was a single circle in a dark blue field. A thick white band ran across the bottom. Within the band, a scarlet double helix spanned the length. The banner was the only real color in the place. The landscape was a dry, barren, muted gold. At least that looked familiar now.

Far in the distance, rock formations towered, giving the appearance of petrified soldiers forever at their posts. While the sun looked down with glaring heat, a soldier pushed Taite along until they approached the one small shack that was out of line with the others.

A knock on the shabby door.

"Enter," said a voice from within.

Inside, a gruff man sat at a minuscule desk, writing with a black fountain pen. Taite glared at the pen, unaware the man was staring at her. What did they have against ball-point pens here? The door shut behind her, and she snapped alert.

The man's chair scraped backward across the wooden floorboards. As he walked toward her, Taite grew apprehensive. The temperature seemed to rise and blood rushed to her face. Not that his appearance alarmed her. In fact, he looked rather ordinary, wearing a casual uniform, his sleeves rolled to the elbows as he glared

She wanted to hide. His gaze was piercing, but not like the doctor. Fermin had been a weasel, taking orders from whoever gave them. This man was in charge here, and he was quite comfortable with it.

"Aisea Madeline Taite," he said, as if she didn't know her own name. But she nodded instead of smarting off.

"They tell me you're a handful. We aren't going to have any of that nonsense here."

Taite watched her feet, wiggling her toes in the too-big boots the nurse had brought her.

"You will work, but you can't do much with your hands strapped behind you."

He bellowed at the door. "Get back in here and get these straps off." As he rolled his shoulders, he muttered, "I ask for extra hands and they send 'em to me tied. Idiots."

Behind her, a soldier reappeared and began to unbuckled the straps. She stretched her arms, the extended sleeves swinging in front, stirring the still air. Her damp prison slid to the floor.

"You'll do what you're told here, and we'll all get along fine. Our work here is for the greater good. That's the focus. Otherwise, there's always your favorite fashion accessory."

Taite wasn't convinced he believed what he said himself.

"Take her to the others. Get orientation out of the way."

"Yes, sir," the voice said from behind.

Orientation they called it. Well, it was nothing like orientation freshman year. Her jacket draped over one arm, the weight of it was strangely comforting as she perched on a small folding chair waiting for her fate.

Another officer; the same uniform and same serious expression on a different face. The man in front of the group almost shouted as he explained they would help extend and improve the road. He didn't say why or where it went, but it was their job. They would work on it every day. He talked a great deal about the importance of the work. The road would allow supply trucks to bring vital weapons and food to fight the radicals who threatened the success of the colony. It was strange, and it seemed all wrong to Taite.

Then one by one, they were called out of the building. August, the girl from the truck, left first. About ten minutes later someone else. No one seemed to be coming back. Taite bounced her legs against the chair, picking at her nails — lines of black dirt beneath the white.

Until they called her name. A tall, lean guard escorted her to a small building down the lane. Taite didn't see the others anywhere outside, and she grew more tense by the minute.

Inside, she was forced into an empty chair across from a bald man wearing glasses and chewing on a pencil. The man didn't look up but continued making notes on the clipboard he held. As he paused to gnaw on the end of the black pencil, he glanced at Taite before rolling up his sleeves.

Taite's irises followed his tattooed arm to a nearby table. An assortment of objects sat in disarray; a comb, scissors, some type of pen and a pair of handcuffs. Her pulse jumped. The man raised his eyes again and said her name as a question.

Taite nodded and started to ask what was going on, but he stopped her. "First things first. Everyone gets a nice little haircut. In your case, a more substantial one."

Her hair had grown in her endless days at the hospital and trailed well past her shoulders. It now hung in a very knotted ponytail. She shrugged. Probably easier than combing it.

A few minutes later, tresses of light brown hair lay knotted on the floor. She reached a hand up to tug at a chin length strand. The bald man swept up the scattered bits of her from the floor and walked back around. But then he reached for the cuffs, and Taite bolted.

"What do you need those for?"

"Most don't enjoy this next part. Especially the girls," he said through a broken smile. "One of 'em punch me, knocked out a tooth. She was a feisty one. That's why we use the cuffs."

"What are you going to do to me?" she asked, her voice rising an octave.

"Now, don't worry your pretty little head. Only hurts a bit. Plenty of people volunteer for this sort of thing." He clamped the metal around Taite's wrist and directed her back to the chair.

"For what?" she asked as she grabbed the metal cuff around her scarred wrist.

"Gotta put your number on ya. Everybody has a number. No need for concern." He had the strange pen from the table, adjusting the tip.

She squinted closer and realized he planned to tattoo her. "No, I don't want a number," Taite said. "You're not going to touch me with that thing."

"See," he said and raised his dense, overgrown eyebrows. "This is exactly what I was talking about. Those guards outside say otherwise though. Sorry, miss."

He tilted the chair up at an odd angle, forcing Taite to stare up at the ceiling. Another pencil appeared from his shirt pocket. Pencil pressing the skin below her collarbone, he wrote out numbers that he would soon make permanent.

As he stood at her side working, her hands were clasped tight behind the chair and she could do nothing. It took longer for him to trace over the lines in ink, and Taite squirmed as the needle pierced her skin.

"Don't make me mess up, little lady. I am not kind to people who interfere with my art. Ya might want a nice butterfly later. Butterflies are popular with the girls, ya know. Been a while since I've inked something feminine."

"I don't want a freaking butterfly," she said through clenched teeth.

The man only chuckled.

The process was uncomfortable, painful, and she wondered how so many people could stand to be covered in tattoos. Taite winced but dared not move a muscle until the man stepped back and said, "Now, that wasn't so bad."

Taite curled her upper lip and stared.

Cuffs removed, he pushed the chair back to its original position. Taite craned her head down to see the inflamed black marks, upside down from her point of view. Random numbers that meant nothing to her, and now they were part of her for life.

SEVENTEEN

"That's how it all happened, the jacket, the bullet wound, everything. That's why I'm here I guess, but it still doesn't make much sense. I still don't know why," Taite said, finishing the long answer to a short question. It had taken her days to get through all of it during short breaks in the day or during meals.

"That's interesting. Very interesting," Xander said. Over the last few weeks at the camp, Taite slowly became friends with the raven-haired boy from the truck. It started with an explanation of Project AISES: an acronym for the Alliance for the Improvement and Survival of Earth Species. That's how the planet got its name. Then he told her about himself. Like Baylin, he was born in the colony. After his older cousin told him of the Duratio resistance, Xander grew curious.

Before too long, his parents sent him to the re-education camp, under the watchful eye of the Order of Atrox. Named after the system's star, most people just called it the Order. They called all the shots, including the gunshot aimed at her shoulder.

They were just awful. The whole thing was awful. To have parents so brainwashed they sold you out would really suck. Though in the pit of her stomach a knot warned her they might have more in common than she wanted to believe.

Xander's family had taken his interest in Duratio hard. His father saw him as disloyal. They weren't speaking before he sent Xander to the camp. Once, Taite asked him if they ever wrote to him. She thought the R.A. allowed that sometimes, although they read and inspected everything. Xander answered with a shake of his head and downcast eyes.

His mother came from a Korean ancestry and had lived on Earth as a child. While the bits and pieces she remembered contributed to Xander's interest in a better life, they did not persuade her to accept her son's decisions. So, Taite and Xander found themselves in similar situations, with no family to speak of anymore. Nothing but scattered memories and regrets.

Xander interrupted her thoughts. "What role did your father play? You said Dr. Fermin asked about him."

"He was involved somehow, but I didn't find out exactly. No clue why they sent me here either, but I'm glad to be out of that place."

"You must enjoy the work more than I do," he said as he snatched her water bottle away and took a long swig.

"No, but it's better than the hospital." As they talked, August, the girl who came with them on the truck, strolled up.

"Hey, slackers. Shouldn't you be working for the greater good or some such shit?" she asked, curving her fingers into quotation marks.

Taite only smirked. August's sense of dark humor often kept them company. While Taite made every effort to fade into obscurity, August acted tough and got into trouble more than once. August was a delinquent. She was twenty-two and claimed to have been a transplant from Earth. A claim never confirmed. Raised in an orphanage of sorts, she proved herself unwilling to bond with five different sets of foster parents. She was clever though, always planning schemes to escape. So far, she had been unsuccessful.

Last month, she stole a truck key by fooling around with a guard. In the dark when she made a run for it, the spot lights flipped on. Four guards came out of nowhere to surround her. She spent a week in isolation. She had an endless reserve of determination and schemes. Taite wished for half her energy.

Their conversation had dwindled, and Xander said, "Guess we better get back to work." He gave Taite a light slap on the back.

Taite sighed. "Only a few more hours."

Brushing a strand of deep red hair from her eyes, August nodded over to where a guard stood several yards away. "He looks half asleep," she said. "I wonder if he would even notice if we just walked out of here."

"Sure," Taite said. "Heck, let's ask him for a map."

August scowled and said, "Well, I wasn't actually gonna try it. Not today."

"Come on," Xander said. "There's work to do. Let's go."

They capped their canteens and resumed the tedious job of cutting out stubborn shrub roots. The things didn't need much to survive and spread like mad. While the day was hot and miserable, the shift flew by. After, the guard drove them back to camp along the road they were clearing. As they bumped along the half-formed road, Taite braced herself with calloused hands, new blisters stinging on the surface.

Every day it was the same. And every day, they came closer to the tall rock formations in the distance. For four months now, in the heat or the cold, they worked. When their 12-hour shift ended, they returned to camp for so-called 're-education' classes. Taite called it crap she only half-listened to, but some things sounded familiar. Both Baylin and Xander said this place, Aises, had been colonized to preserve the human species. The officers were certainly proud of that. They reminded them every five minutes.

Taite and the others heard all about the great things happening, but nothing of the bad. Nothing about kidnapping, torture, or forced population control. Taite may not have had every detail, but she didn't trust these people. The whole organization was full of two-faced creeps.

On the other side was Duratio. As she had learned more about Xander, Taite came to learn his ambition in life was to find Duratio and join up. He said she should come too, when they escaped. Because, he promised, they would get out. And where else could she go? But the thought made Taite uneasy. It had been so long since she'd seen Baylin. She didn't know him well and possessed even less knowledge of his little group. Maybe they were terrorists. But Xander was so enthusiastic.

In the months that followed at camp, Taite kept mentally comparing Xander and Baylin. It was odd that Xander wanted to join Duratio when he was so completely not like Baylin. Baylin seemed to have no allegiances to anything but his precious resistance. Then there was Xander, who always wore his grandfather's dog tags on a chain encircling his neck — a grandfather he had never even met. Who never said a negative word about the family who discarded him.

Ever the optimist, Xander was trying to recruit August into Duratio too, but her interest stopped at getting out of the camp, being free. Even Taite knew that idea was silly. She wouldn't be free anywhere on this forsaken planet. They wouldn't let anyone be.

EIGHTEEN

"We're missing something here," Anthony said after tracking Baylin though the hall. Anthony hated to admit when he couldn't quite solve a problem. He took pride in his work, and Anthony did a lot of work. Besides maintaining the computer system, he was the best code cracker Duratio had ever had. The last few weeks, had found him stumped on pages of encrypted communications they intercepted.

Baylin nodded in agreement, as he said, "You'll get it. Focus on what you can be sure of now." Baylin straightened up and rose from the table, thinking it was a good time to squeeze in a short workout.

"About that," Anthony said, "I am sure of a few things."

"Yeah? What have you got?"

"A new camp. The coordinates are in here and everything," he said, shuffling though his files. "Here ya go. See?"

He held out a sheet for Baylin, who skimmed through. His mind was not on this stuff right now. Re-education camps were always springing up or relocating to prevent interference and escapes. Though something was different about this one.

"This is fifty miles from here. That's the closest one so far," Baylin said, a note of concern in his voice.

"That's why I'm pointing it out. A new road is mentioned, but they don't say where it's headed."

"Good catch, Anthony," Baylin said, still studying the page. Anthony was back to his files, distracted by his own ideas. Baylin returned the paper to the table. "We'll definitely need to check that out sometime."

"Before you go, there's one more thing. It looks like registration paperwork from the camp. Just run-of-the-mill stuff. It wasn't even encoded."

Baylin was only half-listening as he kicked his boot up on the table to tighten the laces out of habit. "And?"

"I'm not aware of all the details, but Dakota mentioned Lanie and some other girl you were searching for."

Dropping his foot to the floor, Baylin sat back down with renewed interest. "Did you find something?"

"The records show a truckload of new recruits, as they call them. No names or details here, but two women are listed. The main subject of interest is one transferred from a base hospital. The other was recommended by her employer in the colony," Anthony said as he pointed to the records with his pen. "It isn't much. It might be a coincidence, and I'm not sure about the timing."

"You're right. It isn't much, but it is interesting. Thanks. Tell me if you get anything else."

"Sure thing."

As he considered the possibilities, Baylin made his way down the hall, hands buried in his pockets. It was odd enough for a camp to be established so close. How did he miss that? Could it be pure chance if Taite was there? The whole thing reeked of trouble.

+++

The world looked upside down, but Baylin often spent time hanging by his knees. He found the extra blood to his brain helped him think, and with the tug of gravity, he was becoming more and more convinced Taite might have been taken to the camp. Though he still had no explanation for her staying in the hospital for over a year. It might be wishful thinking altogether, but a raid on the camp was the only chance to find out for sure. Plus, it was the best shot at replenishing supplies before the storm hit.

A pair of boots and the legs to which they belonged marched toward him. When he realized it was Dakota, he pulled himself up, grabbing the metal bar to flip his legs down.

"I will never understand why you insist on doing that, Maras," Dakota said.

"It's good for the brain and the back. You should try," Baylin said as he righted himself to look Dakota in the eye.

"My brain is fine as is."

"That's debatable," Baylin said with a smirk. "Did you need something?"

"We need to talk."

"About?"

"I was talking to Anthony in the hall," Dakota said. "He mentioned a new camp, so I assume you'll wanna check it out?"

"We were talking about possibilities. That's all," Baylin said, sitting at a nearby table. "Here to convince me it's a bad idea?" Baylin drummed his fingers on the tabletop and prepared himself for another disagreement. "We'd be able to find supplies — even some equipment."

"Sure, but that isn't why you want to go."

"If I can kill two birds with one stone, then why shouldn't I?"

"You, huh?" Dakota asked. "Here, I thought we were all in this together."

"Well, you know what I meant."

"Of course, but it's a waste of time and resources. There are better places for supplies."

"This is closer, and they could have information, not only about Taite, but about Lanie too... or hell, they can at least tell us where that road is going." Baylin knew he had scored a point with Dakota by the pause that followed.

"Well, maybe that," Dakota said. "But I still don't like the idea. Sounds like a waste of time."

"The storm is coming soon, and we need to be sure we're ready. The camp will be stocked with fuel, food, ammunition. We should go while we can. The camp is just out of the storm's path, but they may move it later. This might be the only chance. You just don't like anything with a possible connection to Taite. I don't get it. You've never even met her."

"I don't give a shit about her one way or another," Dakota said. "I don't want anything distracting us from what we need to do. You're putting too much energy into this."

"Like I said, two birds with one stone. Besides, Lanie would have wanted me to try."

"Fine. Do what you want," Dakota said. "You always do anyway."

Date: How the hell would I know?

Anyway, I see three possibilities:

1. I've gone crazy

2. Everyone else has gone crazy

3. I am now on a planet I wasn't aware existed last week.

Not sure which option I prefer. But I just saw someone get shot, and that's a first I could have done without. Kinda hoping that wasn't real right now. While I hadn't known her long, I liked her. I keep seeing it over and over in my head. I can't seem to shut it out.

Now, I'm stuck with her brother, and I can't decide what to make of him at this point. After what happened to Lanie, I'm not sure what's happening here. I don't feel safe at all, and I miss my Dad and everyone. Unless it's option 1, I may never see any of them again. If it's option 1, would I ever really be able to tell?

NINETEEN

With sighs and grumbles, they sat down to a meal of re-hydrated lentil soup and bread. Over forty people filled the lantern-lit hall, most of whom Taite didn't know well. Like her, many still wore their heavy parkas. Even in the dark hours, the work didn't stop. And with the dark, came the cold.

While Taite sopped up the last drops of brown liquid with her stale bread, a tall man with broad shoulders walked over. He whispered to Xander in a thick accent from somewhere Taite would never have the chance to go. She wasn't able to make out his words or even form a guess. While Taite had seen him before, he didn't work in their group, and she knew nothing about him.

Without another glance, the man continued down the length of the room and sat at a table. Xander wore his best poker face, near unreadable. Taite had no clue what he was thinking and arched an eyebrow in a wordless interrogation. Shoveling a chunky spoonful of soup in his mouth, Xander let a brown drip escaped down his chin. He was stuffing his face to avoid her. An obvious move, but he was not going to by with it.

"What's that about?"

He usually told her everything. Why was he so mysterious now? As he chewed his over-sized bite laboriously, he raised an index finger. Taite watched the motion of his throat as he swallowed and wiped his mouth on the back of his hand.

All he relinquished were a few quiet words. "We'll talk about it later." His eyes darted over to the door where two armed guards stood at attention.

"We'd better."

+++

Xander, August, and Taite sat on the bunks lining the wall of the recruits' quarters, waiting until no one lurked outside the thin walls. Xander insisted on telling August his little secret too. Not that it mattered. August only cared about getting out, which Taite dismissed as impractical. This place was a prison as much as the hospital, but at least she could see the sky. This was real anyway. No doubt about that.

As she waited, she listened to the breathing of their bunkmates and the occasional sound of someone rolling over in a narrow bed. On the cold, dark nights, like this one, a stove in the center kept the space somewhat warm. Still, Taite shivered as she curled into her blanket.

"Taite," Xander whispered nearby.

"You still awake?"

"Yes. Now, what's going on?"

"Where's August?"

"Present," said August, sliding down from her bunk.

"Keep your voice down," Xander said as he crept across the aisle and knelt on the floor.

"OK. So, Zeke, the big guy — I worked with him once when you had both gotten yourselves in trouble. We can trust him. Anyway, he's got a group together. Just a few, but that's good."

"Get on with it, Xander. I would like to sleep," August said.

"They're planning to get out of here soon," he said and waited for a response.

"Another escape artist, huh?" Taite asked with a yawn.

"No, this could work. This is real," he said, the excitement rolling off him in waves.

"Hey," August said, "my plans were for real too. I resent that."

"Face it, August, your plans never had a chance. This one does."

"Sure, it does," Taite said. "And I bet I can guess how it ends. With you involved, Xander, we magically find Duratio out in the sand and live happily ever after, right?"

"Ah ha," August said. "Duratio — A bunch of wannabe saviors. What can they do? Don't be stupid. It's every man... or woman for themselves out here."

"You're such an optimist, August," Xander said. "Make fun all you want, but we can find them. Anyway, you want in or you prefer to continue your feeble attempts on your own? 'Course you just use escape as an excuse to hit on the guards."

"You're such an ass, Xander," August said. "Of course, I want in."

"Taite?"

She sighed and asked unknowingly, "What have I got to lose?"

"I thought you'd say something like that. I'll find out the details in the next couple days. Anyway, keep this quiet."

+++

The early hours crept by as they woke up ten days later to blazing heat and an eerie silence. The small disk of the sun sat low in the sky, casting long shadows along the ground. It was the last day of light

147

until the next sunrise in eight days. Taite had barely slept at all, so much weighed on her mind. And then there was August, still snoring. That girl slept like a rock. Nothing seemed to bother her.

Today was the day, and her mind raced through the plan half of the night. Even when she drifted off, dreams of running disturbed her sleep... always running. Then, for reasons unknown to her, Baylin appeared — watching without saying a word. She hadn't had a nightmare in months and refused to think about him at all. She shook it away, but today's worry remained. The air was thick with it.

Nothing would happen for a while yet. If all had gone as planned, Zeke had a key to the armory shed. They had some time before the theft was noticed. When the sun sank to the horizon, and the work teams neared the end of the shift, they would run. At least that was the plan. Xander had gone over and over it until Taite could almost recite it word for word.

All day, dirt and sand drifted by on the occasional gust. It was stinging in her eyes and making work difficult. With the sand, flowed tension and anxiety, and everyone was unusually quiet and focused. Despite the sweat that clung to her skin, a cold chill made Taite shudder. Tucked into her belt beneath her shirt and vest, the butt of a pistol, jabbed her ribcage. It was another reminder this day would end differently. They each had one — hidden under shirts, down boot legs. Zeke had distributed them one by one. She hoped they would not have to use them, though Xander had shown her how.

The day wore on and her anxiety grew to a palpable knot in her stomach. Atrox hovered at the horizon, restless in its descent. Figures around her darkened into shadows in the fading light. Only eight of them worked this stretch of road, eight of them planning to run. Nearby, Xander caught her eye and raised his eyebrows, as if to ask if she still wanted to do this. It didn't matter what she wanted now. The ball was rolling, and forward momentum would carry them all with it.

August looked jittery with eager anticipation like a kid waiting to unwrap the birthday presents. Taite watched her as her fingers tapped against the shovel she carried. Odd that August seemed to be looking forward to this. Taite wanted out as much as any of them, but didn't August understand the risks?

A guard, the watcher, as they called them, yelled out the end of the work day and signaled the team to the truck. Taite trembled and reminded herself to breathe. Falling in step beside her, Xander offered his coat. Though the sleeves swallowed her hands, and she needed to roll them up, she pulled the jacket close around her. Drowned in waves of silent tension, they started toward the truck. Time slowed, and the last sliver of sun dipped into the distant stretch of horizon. Before it even began, Taite wanted it to stop.

Two guards came with them today, but they had rifles and radios with backup only twelve miles away. She glanced at Xander beside her. He gazed around, but he turned to give her a reassuring smile in the fading light. As she forced up the corners of her mouth, she struggled to put her thoughts into a sentence. She didn't pull it off before the moment erupted, and there was no going back.

Raised voices all around. Black shapes in shaking hands. The watcher yelled, his rifle at his shoulder. Then Taite turned, and the man was gone.

A shot rang out, but from where wasn't clear. Another shot — a silhouetted form fell in the distance. With the watcher lost in the pandemonium, Taite focused on the bent form of the other guard in the nearby truck, reaching for his radio. They were all dead if he succeeded.

Pistol in hand, Taite didn't think to use it. Instead, a voice rose from her chest. "In the truck!" Shots fired from her right, flashes of light against the warm air. In the glow of the cab, the guard slumped over the wheel. The whereabouts of the second guard remained a mystery in the chaos.

Taite ran towards Xander's voice, calling her name. Light leached from the clouded sky, the moons would offer little except concealment tonight. Against the fading glow, August's athletic figure sprinted to the truck. Close behind her, followed the towering shadow of Zeke.

"Wait for us!" Taite shouted, her voice clawing at her throat.

Xander grabbed her hand as they rushed forward together. They needed to reach the shelter of the guard's vehicle. No chance to worry about the others until they did.

As fast as they dared, they ran on the uneven, sandy ground, irises trained on August and Zeke as they pulled the body of the guard to the ground. The weight of the guard's body pulled August down with him, and the light of the truck cab created a halo around the bloody scene, an unholy Pietà. Taite was momentarily mesmerized, while her feet continued to pound the ground with their own will. But then the spell burst wide open.

A blinding flash, the familiar burst of gunfire broke the silence, and the smell of gunpowder filled the air. Xander yanked her back by one arm, as he spun around and fired into the dark. The truck forgotten as another bullet whizzed by Taite's head. With a shift of direction, Xander and Taite sprinted to get out of range. On the ground a few feet away sprawled the lifeless form of one of their friends. No time to dwell on it.

Already, Taite smoldered with panic, and then a gloved hand grabbed for her arm. She pivoted on instinct, slamming her pistol into the guard's face with all her strength. Crunch. Blood on her hands.

Xander yelled for her to get down, and a shot thundered in the air. Seconds later, a second shot rang in her ears and a voice cried out.

Taite whirled around, but it was already too late. Behind her, Xander stumbled and fell forward into her arms, knocking her gun from her grip. Crimson smeared his face — eyes wide and lips open. A trickle oozed from the corner of his mouth, leaving a red trail as it traveled along his chin. He collapsed, sinking into her, sending her teetering off balance.

"Get out of here," he muttered in a gurgling whisper. "Find them."

Spreading wide from the open wound, a dark stain escaped from his gray shirt and onto the jacket Taite wore. Together, they fell in a heap to the sand, his slack weight making it difficult for Taite to breathe.

In the dim glow of the clouded moons, his near-black eyes were still open. But Taite wasn't sure he saw the terror on her face. He gasped against her, his heartbeat a slowing rhythm. While blood continued to flow from his mouth onto her shoulder, she tried to tell him to hold on and she would get help. But the words dissolved in her throat. Xander only smiled and faded away.

Tears burned her eyes, and the knot in her throat burned like rage, but she could do nothing.

August, Zeke and two others rattled away in the truck without a glance backward. Taite lay in the dirt, Xander's body heavy on her chest, and she was unable to bring herself to move. Surrounded by silence, she listened for footsteps. Listened for the rustling of movement, but only the wind filled her ears.

Minutes passed. Nothing more. It seemed Xander's last shot hit its target. Hot tears coursed down her face, but she still dared not make a sound. She needed to keep it together. Because the Order would send someone for them soon, and she couldn't let this be for nothing.

Taite struggled out from beneath Xander's broken body and slipped the chain from his neck. She paused for a silent prayer and a goodbye before sprinting toward the far-off rock formations. As she ran harder than her tired legs should be able, she let her anger feed the fire in her feet.

+++

All around her, tall monuments of solid rock jutted up into the night air, and only then did she stop running. While breathing in sputtering gasps and sobs, Taite threw herself to her knees with a sharp pain in her side. The small lunch she had eaten on break, she lost on the ground. In its place, flooded grief and fear.

Nearby she discovered a small hollow, a little den made when a giant rock tower had come crashing down onto another long ago. On hands and knees, Taite crawled into the tight space and stayed there until the clouds traveled across the sky.

When the temperature began to further decline, she slithered from her secret niche like a nocturnal desert lizard. The ends of her hair whipped into her swollen eyes as she studied the horizon. Xander had been so sure Duratio was out there somewhere, past the rock formations in the emptiness of the desert.

The land beyond the formations wasn't like the shrub lands they had been clearing. It looked more like the Sahara. She doubted even an animal could survive out there, let alone a whole resistance.

As she blocked the flying sand as best she could, she questioned if she could manage it and if she wanted to try. Perhaps this was one more horror that would pass. She clutched the chain she took from

Xander and checked for signs she was being followed. There were none, so she stepped out into the open desert air.

If August came this way, any tracks they left were long gone. It was hard to say where she and the others would have gone. Not to Duratio. Well, Taite had to find somewhere to go. To travel on foot was never part of the plan, not in these conditions.

As Taite made her way across the sand, the night wind grew unpredictable and more forceful. The rocks soon vanished behind her, and nothingness surrounded her. With little to go on but a vague notion of the direction from her talks with Xander, she kept walking anyway.

She tried not to think of Xander as she plodded along, but every step made her think of him, every jingle of his tags. He had wanted to charge into the desert, but what waited there for her? She wasn't interested in joining any group. She wanted to go home. Would Duratio or Baylin make that happen? Not likely.

Baylin — would he be there? Was he even alive? Heck, he probably wouldn't even remember her. She didn't know what to believe of him. It was possible he had no choice but to leave her. And she might never know.

Confusion and regret clouded her mind as she trudged through the sand. Light from the brightest of the moons shone through, but the others were barely noticeable. The wind grew colder and stronger, throwing grit hard against her face. Uncertain how long she walked, her lips were dry and cracking. And she had no saliva left to wet them.

Taite pulled Xander's blood-stained jacket over her head to block the angry gusts of whirling sand. Her legs struggled for solid footing, feet sinking and sliding with every step.

Along the skyline, a heavy bank of clouds rolled and threatened.

Whatever storm approached would not be something she cared to experience. The wind continued to howl by, threatening to topple her over. So much sand and dirt flew though the air that Taite couldn't stand to open her eyes anymore. She stumbled, and the frigid wind buckled her knees and sent her to the sand. Choked for breath, Taite tucked herself into a ball, defeated.

Xander's jacket made for a poor shelter against the driving sand. Even now, the weather was unforgiving, and it would only get worse. With the wind screaming louder and louder, Taite knew she would die, a skeleton buried in the desert. Alone on a planet most people didn't know existed.

TWENTY

Baylin told himself he should try to sleep, but he was always a little restless the day before a raid. While he never enjoyed it, this time was different. As he stared at the ceiling, he visualized every second, every move. There were more variables this time — too many. Though at least they had some luck on their side. They were able to time it so darkness would provide plenty of cover. Baylin's team would clear any guards and check for prisoners, while Dakota led the others to empty the supply cache. Dakota would have preferred it the other way around. And that's why it wasn't.

The thing that really kept Baylin awake was what he would do if Lanie and Taite were there. And what he would do if they weren't. He wanted to find them, but in his more realistic moments, he didn't think it was likely. In all his planning, he couldn't be sure how he would react in either case.

Dakota criticized him for his so-called obsession with the whole thing. Cy said he was using Taite as a mental distraction to maintain his state of denial about Lanie. And Gage had held his own opinions on the matter. Baylin didn't understand it himself. It might be none of those things, or it could be all.

As the bay doors opened, and the truck rolled out, Baylin looked over the horizon at the rising moons. He had worked himself up into an ominous mood. Somber and agitated. Dakota was different. Once he was ready to go, it was hard to hold him back. His eyes full of a ferocious energy that always made Baylin a little uncomfortable. People shouldn't look forward to this kind of thing, but Dakota did... once his mind was set. He had always been that way. Even as a kid, he seemed to get a high from danger.

When possible, Baylin avoided confrontation. The first time he had seen someone shot — the spray of red and the gushing wound, he had looked away. Beside him, Dakota had gawked in grim fascination until the man had breathed his last.

"You ready for this?" Dakota asked with a hard bump against Baylin's shoulder.

"Yeah, of course," Baylin said, as he tightened his boot laces for the third time. The truck had been making steady progress as the moons trekked across the sky. Soon, the clouds would thicken to block out even the brightest.

A short time later, when the truck stopped within sight of the camp, Baylin jumped to the sand. With anticipation of the task ahead, he was now fueled by a surge of adrenaline. It was always like this. First, it was anxiety that almost made him nauseous. Then it faded into stoic determination. His senses seemed sharper, his mind alert.

Through the scope, the camp looked deserted. He tossed the scope to Dakota, leaning against the truck.

Dakota said, "Looks like nobody's home."

"That's what I thought," Baylin said, relieved and disappointed.

"Man, Maras, if we came out here for nothing, I'm gonna kick your ass," Dakota said, peering through the scope again. He held up his free hand as if to silence Baylin who hadn't made a sound.

"I'm getting a heat signature. Just one."

"Really? That's strange, but we should have a look."

"Sure," Dakota said, as he pocketed the scope and gestured to the remaining men in the truck. "Brody and Josh, back us up. The rest of you stay with the truck."

Baylin moved the strap of his rifle to his shoulder as he tucked a pistol in his belt. Dakota was enjoying this a little too much, but that would take some pressure off himself. "Change of plans. I'll check the supplies. You investigate that heat signature, Dakota," he said, just to make sure it was clear who was running the show.

"That's was I was planning," Dakota muttered, storming ahead of Baylin and the others.

Cautious as they approached, nearing the camp, it seemed unnecessary. The place was deserted. The ramshackle buildings stood pale, reflective in the dim moonlight. On occasion, the wind rattled debris, but otherwise, the only sounds they made themselves.

Dakota and Brody crept toward the lone heat signature on the scope, leaving Baylin and Josh to locate any supplies. Baylin knew already they wouldn't find any camp inmates, not Taite and not anyone else. He had noticed right away the flag wasn't flying. They had missed them. The camp must have evacuated ahead of the storm. Still, he was compelled to be sure.

As they passed each building, pistol in hand, he pushed the door open with one foot. Nothing remained but empty bunks. He muttered a cursed under his breath. At least let the storage room be full. Then with a gesture for Josh to follow, he made his way to the storage cache. It was the only windowless building, so it wasn't hard to identify. It was also the only building that was locked.

"On the count of three," Baylin said. Josh only nodded, his eyes twinkling beneath the veiled moons.

"One... two... three!"

With a kick, the door crashed inward. Baylin, his gun in one hand and a light in the other, pushed through the broken door and stepped forward. With the sweep of the flashlight beam, he revealed shelves along the walls, a few of which still contained boxes. The trip hadn't been a total waste. He gestured to Josh who still lingered outside.

"Get in here. You start hauling boxes off the shelves. I'll go find Dakota. We'll bring the truck up to load."

After stepping inside, Josh got to work immediately while Baylin turned and headed to the other end of the encampment. He hadn't heard shots, so he supposed that meant everything was fine.

But as Baylin neared the building, a low groan met his ears. With it, his pulse quickened, skipping a beat as he broke into a run. From his vantage point, he saw the door was ajar, a stream of yellow light pouring through. Rushing forward, his firearm in his hand, Baylin listened outside for a split second. With the silence, he forced the door open and froze in his steps.

+++

"What the — what's going on here?" Baylin asked, lowering his gun as he looked at Dakota.

But was obvious what was going on there. Hunkered on the floor, was a man with his hands and ankles tied, a red gash split his forehead. The man's eyes wide, and his respiration quick as Dakota stood over him.

As Dakota lifted his gaze to Baylin, he kicked the man in the ribs and said, "I'm taking care of the heat signature."

"It looks like you've been a little too enthusiastic," Baylin said, returning the gun to his belt.

"Hey, you wanted information. I'm getting information."

"This is not what I had in mind. And what the hell are you doing back there, Brody? We're on a tight schedule here."

"He's doing what I told him to do — searching the place for records. Anything we can use."

"Fine, but what did you do to this guy?" Baylin asked, gesturing to the bloodied man nearby. "This is unnecessary. We don't do this."

"I do. You might be interested in what I've already gotten out of him."

"What? What did he say?"

"Some prisoners escaped the other day. A few made it. A few killed. They trucked the rest to a different location. He said he doesn't know where, but I've been trying to jog his memory."

"Enough jogging," Baylin said, rubbing a hand over his eyes as he exhaled.

"Did he say who escaped... anything?"

"No, he wasn't here," Dakota said. "They sent him to clean up the mess."

"Where are the bodies?"

"Out back in a pit. I haven't gone to check yet."

"I'll go have a quick look. You stay here. Watch him. Just watch him. I mean it," Baylin said. "Then we go help load the supplies."

Baylin's shoulders slumped as he walked around the small building, and the beginning of a headache crept behind his eyes. While it was his idea, he wanted out of this place.

As his light scanned ahead, what looked like a large shadow stretched across the ground — the pit, and he trudged toward it. Since joining Duratio, he had witnessed a lot of things: injuries, death, bodies, everything. He couldn't get rid of the revulsion that went with them.

Baylin looked back toward the building, almost hoping to hear something that would require him to go scrambling back. In the stillness, he sighed, breath rushing past his lips with a cloud of vapor.

Conscious of his heart pounding against his ribs, he inched to the edge of the pit. His light shone down to reveal a pair of heavy boots covered in dirt. They were far too big to belong to a woman, and he scanned the light upward.

All men. A rather large guard sprawled face-down, a bloody bullet wound visible above his ear. No special burials in the desert. Not here. A camp inmate was tossed nearby — a bullet wound and a stab wound. Went down fighting. Well, that's something.

The other looked young, younger than Baylin by a few years. Coal black hair and a strong face. Blood had soaked and caked his gray shirt. The exit wound had torn through from behind. It was a shame someone so young wound up dead in a hole.

Any other face he couldn't see, but he found no Lanie or Taite. He flicked his light away, wishing he had a way to erase the memory from his mind. Death was so severe and final. Unyielding in its cruelty. While, he didn't like to admit it, his sister may have met a similar end. Discarded into the ground in some other pit.

He should have stopped it from happening. Pressure built in his chest and climbed his throat. But he pushed it back down like he always did. Lowering the light once more, he imagined himself lying in the ground someday. Was there something more after that? He wanted to believe so. The corporeal relinquishing itself to the divine.

By the time Baylin walked back around, his mood had grown worse.

"So, is she dead?" Dakota asked. He had wrapped a strip of cloth around the man's blood-smudged mouth.

"Shut up," Baylin said. "And no. All men."

"Huh," Dakota said. "So, let's go."

"What are you planning to do with your pal there?"

"I thought you'd make me leave him."

Baylin nodded. "Yeah, but leave him tied. We can't have him following us. They'll send someone else when they can't reach him." He interrupted himself, "That reminds me. He has to have a vehicle somewhere."

"Yeah, he does," Dakota said. "I planned on driving it back."

"Good," Baylin said before he stepped down to the ground.

"Let's get loaded up," he said over his shoulder as he hurried away.

"Be right there," Dakota said. He lifted the butt of his rifle and in one swift motion, slammed it into the man's head with a thud.

Brody's eyes widened.

"What?" Dakota asked him.

With a shake of his head, Brody carried an armload of papers out the door.

In a matter of minutes, they loaded most of the supplies into one truck. Dakota climbed into the driver's seat of the newly acquired vehicle. A big grin narrowed his eyes.

"What are you so happy about?" Baylin asked.

"Well, I was thinking."

"This can't be good."

"No, really. I was thinking now that we've got the supplies and another truck, we can send the others back to base."

"And go where? What exactly do you have in mind?"

"It's a good opportunity to get away for a while. We can go harass Gage. I know you're worried about him."

Baylin had mixed feelings about seeing Gage again, knowing it would stir memories he wanted to forget. He had felt uneasy about him though.

Baylin nodded and said, "OK, I guess we could try to find him. We'll take him a few supplies. We can hang out till there's a break in the storm. By the looks of that sky, we'd be driving back through the edge anyway."

Besides, he could tell Dakota needed to get away too, he'd been acting awfully harsh for the last few months. Like a gun waiting to fire.

+++

Dawn was days away when Josh and Brody drove off from the camp with the others and a truck full of supplies. They had orders to inform everyone that Baylin and Dakota would return whenever the storm let up. Until then, Jeremy and Cy would be in charge. It wasn't unusual for Duratio to be missing its leaders at the base. With the storm approaching, things were bound to be slow.

Josh and Brody's truck rattled along for several miles before the wind started to pick up, sand flying violently across the windows. While the vehicles were engineered to handle high winds and the sand of the desert, they would still have to make it back before the main storm wall hit.

Brody shouted over the noise of the truck and the strengthening gusts, "I need to take a break. Stop the truck."

"What?" Josh asked over the engine.

"I said I gotta take a leak!" Brody yelled again.

As he killed the engine, Josh said, "No need to scream about it."

162

Bracing themselves against the wind, they jumped from the truck. Brody moved to take care of his business in the sand, using the truck to block the gusts. Josh walked around to the back, stretching his legs as sand pummeled his face. For all the good it did, he put his glasses on and pulled his collar up over his mouth.

Brody yelled over the wind. "Dakota is a little crazy. Don't you think?"

Josh only half-listened, but he shouted back. "Nah, just more extreme if you compare him to Baylin. I kinda like that about him."

"I dunno. You didn't see him pounding on that guy back there," Brody said as he came around to sit on the back of the truck.

Wind pulling at his coppery hair, Josh stared off into the sand until he finally asked, "You see that out there?"

"What?"

"Right there."

"Yeah. What do you think it is?"

"I don't know, but we should check it out. Almost looks like a body."

TWENTY-ONE

Dirty boots. Through eyes veiled in her own sand-encrusted eyelashes, Taite remembered dirty boots in the sand. The rest was a blur of scouring particles blowing in a savage wind. Then a vague recollection of being pulled to her feet, stumbling, dragged along by faceless forms.

When she came to again, she was in a dim room, cool and quiet. The sound of the roaring wind still filled her head. Her initial relief began to evaporate, replaced by apprehension as she questioned where she could be. As she forced herself upright, the bones in her back popped. Scrapes, bruises, and filth covered her arms. Overall, she was disgusting. Plastic tubes trailed from her hand up to a half-empty IV bag hanging from a hook on the wall.

As she swept the hair from her eyes, a handful of sand flew around. She was still caked with it. Her hair hung in twisted, matted clumps. A layer covered sections of her skin, and more was down her shirt, and in her pockets. She was certain it was in her underwear. After brushing off, she felt her chafed face with her free hand. The sand must have almost buried her. Without thinking, she ran her fingertips across the stiffening dried blood on Xander's jacket. But she let her hand drop and turned her attention to the room.

With no windows, the only light came from a single flickering bulb hanging bare from the ceiling. Besides the low green cot where she sat, there stood a small metal table and a few boxes in the corner... and a bucket. She didn't care to know what that was for. This represented the extreme opposite of the sterile government hospital. The room contained a mishmash of found objects and outdated equipment. Dank and rather dirty, she hoped it was more sanitary than it looked for the sake of the IV in her hand.

Sometime later, as she sat aching, a knock echoed off the bare metal door. Without waiting for an answer, it creaked opened. An average-sized man, somewhere in his thirties, walked in the room. He had an open, friendly face surrounded by brown curly hair.

His mouth turned up in a small but toothy smile as he said, "You're finally awake! That's a good sign."

Taite stared. "Who are you?"

"I always forget the introductions," he said under his breath. "I'm the medic here. Not an official physician, but I fill the role. You can call me, Cy. That's my name, or you can call me Doc, some people do. You can even call me, 'Hey you', though that has the potential to be confusing."

"Fine, but where am I?"

"Before I can tell you, I need to know who you are and why you were in the desert."

"Hmm," she said, "If you worked for them, you would already know who I am. I was in a re-education camp, but a few of us escaped. I wandered out here."

"Do you have any idea where you are?"

"Maybe. A friend told me about it once. I thought I might be safe here. Anyway, I had nowhere else to go."

"If you escaped from a camp. Then, yes, you're safe here," he said with a grin. "I'll have somebody bring clean clothes. You can toss that jacket and wash up. A lot of blood there, but you didn't seem to be wounded."

"I want to keep it," she said, her fingers fumbling with a button as she spoke.

"Well... suit yourself," he said as he stood up. "I'll get you something to eat and drink." He walked out, closing the door behind him.

Taite didn't hear the click of a lock.

Hours later, she relaxed on the cot, free from the IV and the sand. Earlier, she nibbled on dried fruit she didn't recognize and sipped on a glass of water. Cy had advised her to go slow, so she didn't get sick.

Xander's jacket, still blood-stained and dirty, sat folded on a box. As she stared at the deep, rust-colored spot, she remembered the slow spread of blood as it poured out of her friend. It made no sense, but she wanted to keep the jacket. To keep that piece of Xander with her, to remember that he didn't die in vain. She ran a finger along the dog tags at her neck. The name of Xander's American grandfather, Tanner Owens, stamped into the metal.

Dr. Cy had told her that a small patrol had been returning to Duratio's base when they stumbled across a body in the sand. Assuming she was dead, they had almost left her there. By chance, someone decided to check and found a faint pulse. Once they brought her here, Cy treated her for dehydration and exposure.

Her arms and legs looked skeletal. She hadn't eaten well for a while.

Camp meals had done little to keep flesh on her bones. But at least she was clean now.

At first, Taite spent most of her time sequestered in the same little room where she first opened her eyes. It was part of the infirmary, but not much of one. The next day, Cy took some blood, testing her iron levels and cell counts. She was getting used to needles, though she still looked away.

In the following week, boredom overcame any hesitation to explore outside the room. Cy needed her to clear out for another patient, so he introduced Taite to Kassidy, a sturdy girl who looked like she could kick Taite's ass if she wanted.

Kassidy led her down a dim, narrow corridor with several doors along the way. Some, Kassidy explained; to the right was a meeting room, further down on the left she would find food. Through a maze of vertically challenged halls, they came to the women's quarters. A few bunks and hammocks lined the walls of a large room. A washroom opened up on one side.

Over the next few days, Taite settled into what would be her new home. Only about twenty other women occupied the room, and she didn't see them at all until evening when heads hit pillows.

For the most part, she kept to herself, venturing out into the halls when she was hungry or needed to walk off tension or boredom. She couldn't go outside. It wasn't safe for anyone now. The storm had hit full force and ravaged the surrounding area for miles in all directions. It would be weeks before it passed. Taite had never known a storm to last so long, but she had never experienced many things about this place.

Nerves sat on edge, and restlessness settled in with everyone.

Sometimes, the others stared at her in the blood-stained jacket. Taite didn't care, and it became a game to stare back until they lowered their eyes and looked away. She didn't always wear it, only when she felt lonely and lost. When she needed to remember.

Her old life seemed so far away. She still recalled the sound of her father's voice, the smell of the lilac that grew in their yard. Other things slipped away. It was like her old self had died like Xander and Lanie, and she finally had a chance to grieve them all. But with grief came a sense of hopelessness. Sometimes she would dream that she ran through the hospital, the corridors full of sand. She was forever running, but never getting anywhere.

TWENTY-TWO

It had been about three weeks, more precisely twenty-three consecutive days of monotony. Taite kept track on the wall by her hammock. She rolled out of the sagging fabric, slapping bare feet against the cold concrete floor. Though it was early, everyone else had already left. A few days ago when she bumped into Dr. Cy, he enlisted her to learn basic first aid. It wasn't something she pictured herself doing, but it had to be better than sitting around staring at the walls.

As she pulled on her boots and tightened the laces, for the first time in a long time, Taite did so with purpose. She had somewhere to be. Her bloodied jacket, she left behind. The red stain had turned a deep rusty brown. Dr. Cy had barred it from the infirmary — his slightly unsanitary sanctuary.

When Taite arrived, Cy was busy in the front room of the infirmary, sorting through a large cardboard box.

"Good morning," she said before asking. "What are we doing today?"

"Glad you asked. Today, we get the unusual treat of new supplies. We'll be sorting through to see exactly what we have to work with and to find a place for everything."

"That's good," she said, picking up a glass bottle of Penicillin.

"Where did all this stuff come from?"

"Ahh, I was afraid you'd ask that one," he said. "We don't always get to stick to the high road, Taite. Most of our supplies, including what we have before us, are actually stolen. They're R.A. issue supplies, but it's the only choice. It's steal or die sometimes. Or watch others die."

"I can't say I care if you're only stealing from them."

"We do what we must. They take us for bandits and terrorists, but that isn't the case. We've never intentionally killed to make a point. Sometimes people die, but we always avoid it when we can. That's always been a goal here."

"Really?" she asked with genuine interest. "I assumed it was every man for himself."

"Not at all," he said, almost offended. "If you don't start with a respect for life and liberty, then you won't go far to inspire change. People need to care about what they're doing and be confident everyone else feels the same."

"That makes sense, but I'm afraid that might be a little too idealistic," Taite said. "Unfortunately, I've seen that that isn't always true. Sometimes, people do what's necessary to save their own skin."

"I don't know about what you've seen or experienced, but sometimes things are not what they appear to be."

"Maybe," she said with a shrug. As she unpacked several delicate glass vials from the carton, she let the subject drop.

After they sorted everything into the proper places, Dr. Cy reviewed proper suturing techniques for closing wounds and instructed Taite to practice on a worn leather jacket. A straight slice, around four inches long, ran through the back. This would not be the coat's first repair. Another stitched opening ran along the sleeve, and the lower hem had been resown as well. Taite threaded the needle and stabbed it through. A few minutes later, she stepped back to double check the straight lines of the black stitches against the rich brown of the leather.

"Fantastic!" Dr. Cy said. "Nice and straight. That should satisfy him. Tie it off and you're all done."

"Satisfy who?" she asked as she pushed the thick needle through to the back of the leather.

"Baylin. It's his jacket. Have you met Baylin?"

Taite's hand jerked, and she jabbed the needle into her finger with a curse. The medic continued on without noticing and answered himself before she could respond. "Of course, you haven't. I forgot he left before we found you and only returned today."

She looked up, sucking the blood from her finger as she listened. So, Baylin was alive. Dread, confusion, and fury washed over her. Part of her hated him, but far away something else stirred.

As Cy told her, Baylin and a few others had been absent for quite some time. She didn't hear where they had been, but along the way they collected supplies of various kinds: medicine, clothes, food. Around here, that served as a special occasion. Rumor had it, they traveled through the edge of the storm, so everyone was even more impressed with the haul.

The storm, or derecho, as Lanie had once explained, took shape as a giant wall cloud that swept over on a routine schedule. It was far from over and usually all travel was avoided, but Baylin had also come into possession of a desert truck. Though still dangerous, this made it possible to reach the base during a lull in the winds.

Regardless of her confused thoughts about Baylin himself, his arrival turned out to be a good thing. The general mood lightened, and the stress of the depleting supplies evaporated. But Taite didn't see Baylin all that day or even that week.

For unclear reasons, Taite found herself avoiding places where he might be. Pathetic. Anyway, he might not even recognize her. But had anyone mentioned her? She shouldn't care anyway. The asshole left her to die. Because of him, almost two years of her life had been a nightmare.

People here seemed to like him though. The surrounding conversations were filled with 'Baylin this' and 'Baylin that'. By the second week since his return, Taite grew sick of hearing his name.

She spent most of her time isolated in the infirmary, learning new skills and reading. Cy provided several books and first aide pamphlets. Most of what they treated here would be dehydration, puncture wounds, and lacerations. Sometimes people came down with various illnesses too. Lately, there had been little medical activity, but Taite did stitch up a wounded hand. It proved far more complicated than the jacket.

The guy sliced his hand while making repairs to the new truck. Taite found it tricky to sew a patient who was squirmy and talking and bleeding all over everywhere. When she taped a square of gauze over the new stitches, it neared lunchtime. Despite the bloody bandages around her, her stomach growled with hunger.

Cy nodded at the work in approval and gave the patient some instructions. He smiled and said, "That deserves a break. Come on, Taite. Over lunch we can discuss myorrhaphy. That's suturing the muscle tissue."

"Um… awesome. That sounds fascinating." It might be fascinating for real, but over lunch? Nasty.

As people came and went in the hall, noise was not unusual, but lately, it was more active since the storm provided a forced vacation for most. Even the techies were spotted more often as communications were often down. The power sometimes flickered too as the generator sputtered. But today, a blaring commotion filled the corridor. Loud but playful voices rang through the underground hall.

Cy raised his eyebrows at Taite and said, "What that's about? Guess we'll find out."

She didn't need to find out. She didn't care. Taite wanted to be left in peace, but they walked forward anyway. As long as she could still get something to eat. Rounding a corner, before them was the source of the disruption. She should have known he would have something to do with it.

Down the corridor, right past the mess hall entrance, loitered a small, boisterous group. In the center, a tall figure stooped in a familiar brown jacket. His arm cinched around the neck of a stooped body, twisted back in a wrestling hold. Around them, everyone laughed and cheered on their favorite. The whole thing was very junior high, and Taite rolled her eyes. She had been curious if she would recognize Baylin when she saw him. At least she had that answer.

Though his hair was shorter and his face thinner than she remembered, he was still Baylin. As he told his captive to beg for mercy, she let Cy walk in front and did her best to disappear behind him. The victim was laughing for some reason, his face red and eyes teary. Such nonsense, but she bit her lip to stop a smile. Then Cy spoke, ruining everything.

"Baylin, he probably deserves it, but don't send him to the infirmary. I'm too hungry to deal with it," he said with a laugh.

Baylin looked up and smiled. "Don't worry. I won't spoil your lunch."

Baylin's arm still ensnared his squirming prisoner. When his eyes darted from the doctor to Taite, his brow crinkled for a moment in confusion.

Taite scowled and hurried on, disappearing through the doors to safety. After flopping onto a rusty folding chair, she tapped out a nervous rhythm with her foot. Her stomach was too knotted to eat now, and she didn't even want to talk to Cy. He would want to hear why she didn't wait for introductions or something. She didn't want to explain and wasn't sure if she even understood it herself.

A short while later, Cy, alone to Taite's relief, shuffled over to the table. "Why d'you rush off, Taite? I could have introduced you to Baylin."

"Oh," she said. "I'm just starving." She should have devised a better excuse.

"Taite, you aren't actually eating," he pointed out, as if she didn't realize.

She smiled. "Nothing gets by you."

"Is there something bothering you?"

"I'm not sure if I'm up to that muscle suturing discussion you mentioned."

"Oh," he said with genuine disappointment. "Some other time then?"

Taite nodded. "I'm a little worn out today." After collecting their lunch, they ate in awkward silence before Taite excused herself to her hammock for a nap.

In the hall, the crowd had cleared, but she passed Kassidy who gave a friendly shove that threatened to send Taite flying. She remained one of the few girls who didn't turn her nose up at Taite. Once in a while, she would even drag her into a conversation.

It was Kassidy who had explained that Aises and the star it orbits had been a secret for years. Proxima Centauri was always thought to be the closest star to Earth, but it wasn't. The star, named Atrox Fortuna after the Roman Goddesses of Fate, was first considered insignificant. Then they found water and oxygen on one of the four orbiting planets. That's when the government took an interest.

Amid fears of disasters ranging from volcanic activity, earthquakes, asteroids, climate change — you name it — the twinkling of an idea formed. The idea blossomed into a detailed plan. That plan was enacted before anyone at the base was born. In secret, engineers developed a Nuclear Pulse Propulsion engine, bringing more distant planets within reach.

The theory went back to the 1940s when the atomic bomb was created. Its intention was to harness the power of the atom for interplanetary travel. Known as Project Orion, The Partial Test Ban Treaty of 1963 brought it to a quick halt, or so the mainstream scientific community had been led to believe.

With the planet Aises in their grasp, a colony was soon within the realm of possibility. Over the span of almost a century, it had become a viable self-sustained reality. Taite wondered if it had all been necessary in the end. Did the Earth she remembered survive? Add that to her list of worries.

Taite threw herself at her hammock, but she couldn't sleep. She couldn't even sit still. If Baylin had said anything to Cy, Cy hadn't hinted at it. He probably hadn't recognize her. It wouldn't surprise her, the S.O.B.. What did she expect — for him to throw himself at her feet and beg for forgiveness? Something would have been nice, but the jerk didn't even acknowledge her existence and wouldn't until days later.

+++

Stalking down the hall, Taite was irritated from spilling a bottle of antibiotics. Focused on her self-reproaching thoughts, she was barely aware of the few lingering figures around her. Unconscious of the footfalls behind her, she jumped in surprise at the sound of her name.

"Taite, is that you?"

She sighed, she remembered that voice. And she was in no mood for it today. "Yes?" she asked, continuing her rhythmic march.

"Can I talk to you for a minute? Cy told me how they found you. You were at the camp then?" Baylin asked.

"I don't want to talk," she said as she stomped down the hall.

"Please."

"No, I don't think so." She was too tired for this.

"Stop."

That one word was enough to send her reeling. He had picked the wrong time and the wrong words, and she exploded, surprising even herself. Taite whirled around, blood boiling as it rushed to her brain.

"Don't tell me what to do!"

He smiled, rather arrogantly in her opinion, as he said, "I just want to explain."

He reached for her arm.

She wanted to smack the smile off his pompous face. As if flashing his best smile washed away everything she'd experienced. Repressed memories and concealed emotions came flooding forward. "No! You want to tell me what to think and what to feel. I don't need to hear it!" she said, stepping out of his reach.

"It isn't like that, Taite. If you would listen."

"It is like that. You wait until now when you think I've gotten over it. When it should be safe. Well, it isn't."

176

"I just thought you should know—"

"It doesn't matter. So many people have told me what they thought I should know or what I should think that I can't tell what I think anymore. Well, I don't need it."

When she stopped, she realized she had been shouting. People were staring, including Baylin, who looked a little shell-shocked. Oh, poor boy. He had expected her to be the same silly girl as when he saw her last. He looked around. Looked at Taite. Then looked at his feet.

As he shifted his weight to one foot, he said, "OK, Taite. Have it your way." He marched off, adding with a dismissive wave, "See ya."

Fists clenched, Taite still stood in the middle of the hall. It was rather satisfying to see him sulk away, and she felt a surge of triumph. But it lingered only a moment, and as it faded, a bit of regret took its place. She exhaled to calm her nerves. Then she shot a deadly look over to a girl staring at her with an expression that seemed to say nobody talked to Baylin that way.

And the rest of the day sucked. But she would do nothing different because of him.

+++

Another week passed. Taite didn't see more than a glimpse of Baylin here and there, usually as they passed each other in the halls. She was confident he was now furious with her and was happy to pretend she didn't exist. Since her blow up with Baylin, she had started skipping lessons with Cy. She didn't have an explanation, but Cy was irritated. While he didn't like to show it, she could tell he missed the opportunity to show off what he knew.

Every day, the wind was growing louder as the storm neared the peak of its crescendo. No one would even think of going out now. The winds were powerful enough to flatten anything in their path. Below, the electric generator which ran off both solar and wind energy, was sputtering. The massive storm wall blocked much of the sun, and the gusts were too much for the turbine to handle. They would have to shut it down. For the next week or two until the storm passed, the backup battery would have to supply the base. It meant low lights and no extra electronics of any kind. And conserving electricity at every turn. That's all Taite knew about it. That's what Cy said one day as he turned off an extra overhead light in the front room.

The good mood that Baylin's return brought began to dim like the lights. Taite would've preferred to sleep the days away. It was difficult to be trapped in the giant underground bunker that was the base, but she wanted to contribute. She returned to assisting Cy in the infirmary. Besides, keeping busy seemed the best way to stay sane.

Because of the storm and low lights, people were getting depressed. Cabin fever. It made their work sloppy. Taite and Cy saw several small injuries every week. Once or twice, something worse happened, like a broken bone. When that happened, Cy would splint it, and Taite would offer an extra pair of hands by injecting the dwindling pain killer or holding a hand as Cy set a bone.

She didn't mind the work anymore. And though she still didn't fully understand everything that was going on, she didn't seem to have many paths open to her. She started to fit in little by little, even recognizing a few of the people who came through. Her life still made no sense, but it finally seemed to have a direction.

TWENTY-THREE

The light bothered her eyes as it pulsed, threatening to leave her in darkness at any minute. She was reading a manual about treating burns, but she was getting a headache that made it nearly impossible to concentrate. The wind was lessening now, but so was the power in the backup system. In resignation, she closed her eyes and sat soaking up the silence.

Then it was broken by a low rumbling deep within the ground. The walls shook and a thunderous roar echoed through the walls. In an instant, she flew to her feet, her first thought to find Cy. The whole place could be collapsing. As she raced down the hall, she almost crashed into the head medic as he sprinted around a corner.

"Taite," he said, grabbing her arm as he pulled her back the way she'd come. "There's been an explosion below. I have to go help. You stay here. Do your best with whoever comes up. I'll be back as soon as I can, but there may be injuries that need treated before we can move them. Got it?"

Taite's eyes went wide as she nodded, "Yes, but- " she said in protest. She couldn't handle this on her own.

"You'll be fine. You can expect lacerations and burns. Do what you can to stop any bleeding and ease the pain. Taite, you know what to do," he said as he shoved bandages in an already overstuffed bag and flipped on the overhead lights. Then he was gone.

Taite stood dumbfounded, clutching her pathetic pamphlet on burn treatment. A short time later, her first patient arrived from the accident. There was gash down his arm, and he was loosing blood and turning white as a sheet. Forcing herself to concentrate, she led him over to a chair.

Cy had trained her to encourage people to talk, to keep their mind off their injury and pain. As she asked him about himself, she hurried to wash his wound and began to close it. While she worked, Taite learned the man's name was Brody. He had been one of the guys who had found her in the sand.

"Glad to see you're doin' better," he said, watching her work. Taite didn't remember him, and he seemed rather disappointed. Before she knew it, there was a line of neat black stitches running through the fine blond hair on his arm. He still looked pale though. He had told her they had been working on the main generator when the accident happened. A fire was burning now. Baylin and the others were struggling to put it out.

After sending Brody on his way with antibiotics and instructions, Taite made way for the next patient. This time, Taite worked faster, suppressing a building urge to see what was happening. There was a steady stream of cuts and burns, but she handled them all without major problems. Seven people, a few had multiple wounds, but she had found her rhythm. Cy was right. She could do this.

The last patient was out the door, and no sooner had Taite slipped into a chair than the door flew open again. She braced herself for whatever it might be, as two figures appeared in the doorway. Despite his head drooping downward and his whole body slumping, she knew immediately it was Baylin. He slumped into the other man who Taite recognized as Dakota. He had always looked familiar, but Taite wasn't sure why.

Unsteady on his feet, Baylin had blood running down his forehead into his face. Taite snapped from her semi-frozen state and gestured for Dakota to bring him over to a nearby chair.

While Baylin was conscious, he was not very alert. He must have had a hard knock on the head. There was a wound across his forehead — not too deep, but head lesions always bleed so much.

Dakota asked, "You got this?" He seemed doubtful she could handle it. Taite wasn't confident, but he wasn't going to know that.

"Of course," she said, as if he had asked the dumbest question imaginable. While pressing a cloth to Baylin's skull, she took a quick look to see his other wounds. There was a bad burn on his left palm. Other than that and a few minor scrapes, the main concern was his bleeding forehead.

Eyelids struggling to stay open, Baylin remained in a bit of a stupor as Taite fumbled with her free hand for a fresh needle. She wished Cy would come back to take over, but it seemed she was on her own. She washed the wound out and pinched the skin together with one hand. With the other, she pressed the curved needle through his skin. It felt different to stitch so close to the skull, and the slick blood on his forehead, still trickling down in a continuous stream, made the tight skin more difficult still.

As Taite added stitch after stitch, people came and went looking for bandages for smaller scrapes. It was distracting, but the company was not unwelcome. When she was nearly done, she noticed Baylin watching her work through one glazed-over eye. It had to be her imagination, but she could have sworn he was looking down her shirt. Surely not. He was probably too dazed to realize what he was seeing.

Scarlet streaks followed his angular jaw, but the flow ebbed and stopped as she closed the gash. With a sigh, she leaned in to tie the last stitch.

Now, Baylin's gaze seemed to be zeroed in on the scar on her wrist. Taite frowned and turned it away. In the next second, he pulled her down by her arm, warm blood in his hair smearing her cheek. The stirring of his breath brushed against her ear. "Thanks, Taite."

The door creaked on its hinges, and Taite jerked away, spinning to see Cy rush through the door.

Cy looked solemn as he asked, "How's it going? Looks like you've kept up just fine. Things have relaxed, so I can take over with his burns. You did good. Go take a break and clean up. You have some blood on your face there."

"OK," she said before asking, "Were there any major injuries? Is everyone gonna be all right?"

"A couple serious wounds, but they'll be fine. Dakota and Aiden are bringing 'em up. So we need to clear everyone outta here."

He clapped Baylin on the back, then lifted his chin to shine a light in his eyes. "That includes you, Baylin, so lets see what else you need."

Baylin only blinked.

Taite curved a corner of her mouth into a forced smile and changed the subject. "Are you sure you don't need me for anything else?" She wanted nothing more than to get out of there.

"No, Taite. Take a break. Aiden will stay and help. Most of the work is done. Need to get them settled in here and do the more delicate work. You go," he said, as he finished bandaging Baylin's burned hand.

Taite wasn't familiar with Aiden, but she nodded. "OK. Send for me if you need me."

She hurried out the door, as Cy told Baylin to stay off his feet for a few days.

+++

Safe in the women's quarters, Taite stripped off her blood-splotched shirt and locked herself in the small bathroom. Her face reflected off the old broken mirror. The image was shattered and distorted in the faint, intermittent light. A lock of hair stuck in the smear of blood on her cheek — Baylin's blood. Her face looked thinner than she remembered, and all minor traces of sun had vanished. Ink numbers stared back at her in the mirror, black against her pale skin. The ugly scar on her wrist and other smaller marks decorated her surface. She sighed. They made it impossible to forget. She looked like a living ghost.

With her dirty shirt, she scrubbed off the blood and turned away. She dressed and moped toward her hammock. Xander's stained jacket waited to comfort her like an old friend. Everything disappeared when she wore it — her scars, the tattooed numbers, the confusion. It was strange that it made her feel safe when it should make her sad. But she refused to give into it today and left it draped on the floor. Rolling into the fabric of the hammock, she thought of nothing and slept.

When she woke, the lights were out. She must have slept through the rest of the day and into the night. The long room was quiet except for the occasional creak of bunk springs. How she would have killed for one of those shitty bunks. As she closed her eyes, she willed herself back to the solitude of sleep, but it was useless. In the hospital when insomnia plagued her, she paced the floor, but there she had been alone. Here, she didn't want to disturb anyone.

She threw off the worn gray blanket and draped her bare legs over the edge of the teetering hammock. A faint smell of smoke and burning oil hung in the air, though the fire had been extinguished hours ago. With a slight groan, she slapped bare feet onto the floor and crept to the door. Her senses began to wake, her pupils dilating in the dark. Forms of beds and hammocks emerged from the blackness.

In the hall, someone had further dimmed the weak lights. Occasional air currents from the ventilation shafts chilled her bare arms. She didn't know how much longer they could last down here. Now that the main generator was off, the small auxiliary units were not very reliable. They wouldn't be able to keep up with the continuous drain.

Until now, she had limited herself to the few areas that she frequented in her daily routine. But tonight, she had the whole place to herself. No questions to answer, no curious glances. At first, the tug of the familiar had pulled her to the mess hall, but curiosity got the better of her. No time would be better to go exploring uninterrupted.

Through various sprawling directions, she wandered the halls. She tried a few doors only to find a storage closet full of cleaning supplies and a ratty old couch. Another room sat empty except for a long table. The third was locked.

On the opposite side of the hall, she found a room that proved more interesting. As she clicked the latch open, a faint humming filled her ears. Like everywhere else, darkness filled the room, but three small screens emitted a faint glow from the center. All around, small pinpoints of light speckled like artificial stars.

The air temperature increased as she walked through the threshold and shuffled toward the flickering screens of the computers. Bare feet crashed into a rolling chair, and she stifled a squeal as she hopped back on one foot. After she recovered and found the seat, she slid down and searched unsuccessfully for a keyboard.

"Boring," she said to herself and leaned back in the chair, propping her feet onto the shadowed desk. As she listened to the gentle hum of electronics and let her mind roam, she thought of her father. Had he really been involved in all this? Or had he worried when she never returned home?

Then Baylin came intruding into her thoughts again. Viscous drying blood on her face, words in her ear. *Leave me alone.* She forced herself to remember him running away as she bled on the ground. But he wasn't all bad, and the crooked grin flashed before her eyes.

Footsteps broke her quiet rumination, and she held her breath.

"Who's in here?" a voice asked from the doorway.

Well, speak of the devil. As she turned around, Baylin's tall silhouette stood blocking the doorway. Great.

There was no getting around it, so she asked, "Aren't you supposed to be getting some rest? And staying off your feet?"

A clumsy pause, as he decided which direction to take the conversation.

"Nurse Taite. What might you being doing here?"

"I couldn't sleep," she said with a chill in her voice as she got to her feet. "Anyway, I probably shouldn't be in here. I'll be going."

"You don't have to go. I can't sleep either. Maybe we can not sleep together."

"Excuse me?"

"Er... that sounded different than I expected," he said with an awkward chuckle.

"I'd say so," she said with an unseen eye roll. "I gotta go."

"Taite, we should talk."

"Talk about what?"

"Look, I didn't want to leave you there."

"Fine. But I want to leave now." She walked over to the door he still blocked. "Please let me through."

He sighed and turned on a dim light. "All right, but I need to check something."

"What are you talking about?"

"I need to see your I.D."

"My I.D.? What? Am I out past curfew?"

"Taite, this is serious. I need to see your numbers."

"Why?" she asked, stretching the word out and folding her arms across her chest.

"I think I've seen those numbers before. Let me double check."

"Fine, whatever," she said, not moving an inch. "If that's some kind of pickup line, you are barking up the wrong tree."

As he squinted one eye, he tilted his head like a dog. "I'm not sure what you're trying to say. I need to know your number to confirm information."

She rolled her eyes again. "Just get on with it," she said as she glared. He picked up one of Xander's tags, and the warmth of his fingertips sent a chill up the base of her spine.

"Who's Owens?"

"Just some old dead guy I've never met, OK? The tags belonged to a friend at the camp."

"Hmm." He muttered something, dropped the tag and pushed her shirt collar below her clavicle. Through a locked jaw, she told him to hurry up. The light was weak, but the black characters would stand out like a street sign. She glared as his mouth moved, reading the numbers that scarred her skin.

"Got it?" she asked. "Do you need to write it down? I do not want to repeat this little peep show."

"I got it," he said, lifting the fingers on his good hand and letting her crew neck collar slide back into place.

"Fine, then let me through."

"I don't understand why you're in such a hurry," he said, his hand on the door frame.

"Isn't that obvious?"

"You would have bled to death or died of infection. A healthy person can die out there. You've seen how it is."

Her chin sank, but she stared past him as she said, "Maybe that would have been better."

"Taite—" he said, his voice low, but she didn't let him finish. She ducked under his outstretched arm and rushed down the hall. From behind her, he asked. "I'll let you know if I find anything, OK?"

Taite hadn't cried since Xander died, but silent tears escaped as she lay curled in her hammock. It seemed seeing Baylin again had forced out buried memories and emotions. No matter how she pretended to be fine, nothing was fine. She was a spectator to her own life. Helpless to change the course of events, carried away in a current that might drown her. Taite wanted to go home. She wanted the impossible.

TWENTY-FOUR

Taite watched from across the room, as Baylin and Anthony poured over a stack of papers while drinking coffee and talking in hushed voices. As she finished lunch, she couldn't help but be interested in what they were so busy with over there. She wished she could read lips. Two days had passed since the generator accident. Two days since Baylin's interest in her tattoo, and she had learned nothing more. He said he would tell her, but would he? At the time, she hadn't cared, but now curiosity burned in her brain.

With intense interest, she observed and chewed on a fingernail. Anthony looked rather tired around the eyes and rose to refill his cup. Baylin sat there, tapping a pen as he examined a page. A bandage still covered the stitches on his forehead, and his burned hand was completely wrapped. His eyes darted over to Taite, and she didn't bother looking away.

When Anthony returned with a steaming mug, Baylin pushed back the chair. As he handed the page to Anthony, he said something and then stood to go, leaving the code cracker to focus. As he walked to the door, Taite debated strolling over to Anthony to see what he was up to or chasing after Baylin to demand answers.

In a second, she was on her feet. Taite hurried forward, giving Anthony a passing glance. Once in the hall, Baylin made fast progress, and Taite had to quicken her pace to keep sight of him.

"Baylin, wait," she said from several feet away.

He tossed an annoyed look over his shoulder and said with a smirk, "I don't take orders. Sorry."

While he continued walking, he shortened his long stride. As she caught up and fell in step, she asked, "Are you going to tell me what that was about? The other night with my tat, I mean."

"Your tat?" he asked with a raised eyebrow.

"You know what I'm talking about."

"OK, OK," he said, stopping to turn toward her. "Last summer — you weren't even here yet — we intercepted a series of encrypted communications. Anthony has been trying to crack them ever since with no real luck."

"And?"

"He noticed a repeating string of numbers. We didn't understand what it meant, and it threw everything else off too. Well, now we know what the string of numbers is."

"What?" Taite asked before it clicked. "Me? It's my number. 242911? Is that what you're saying?"

"That's what I'm saying."

"What does it say about me?"

He held up a hand to stop further questions. "Anthony is still working. We're not sure what it all means yet."

"When will he know?"

"I'm not sure, but I'll tell you as soon as I hear something. OK?"

She sighed. "All right, but you'd better tell me."

"Of course. Anyway, I still owe you." He gestured to the bandage on his brow.

With a puff of air, she crossed her arms and flung a hip out with the shifting of weight. "No, you don't owe me for that, but you owe me."

His mouth turned up in acknowledgment as he said, "I owe you pretty big, don't I?"

"That's an understatement," she said, and a bit of the bitter fell away.

"Yeah, I guess so," he said, running his good hand through his short hair, as if a strand had been in his eyes. A silver band he now wore winked at her from his little finger.

"Well, I have to go. Cy's expecting me," she said, hanging on to a thread of her anger. If not Baylin, who could she blame?

"Yeah, me too."

"Cy's expecting you?"

"No, but I have to get going," Baylin said with his crooked grin.

"Let me know what you find out." With a step backwards, Taite spun on her heel.

"I will," he said to her back. Taite sauntered toward her hammock to get off her feet. In truth, Cy had given her the rest of the day off, and she was completely spent.

Ahead, her hammock waited, and she was almost to the women's dorm when someone said, "Hey, wait up."

To her surprise, Dakota was walking toward her. As far as Taite was aware, he had no idea who she was. Other than when Baylin hit his head, they had never spoken. Taite had seen him walking with Baylin before, and he always seemed gruff and bad-tempered. Something about him made her uneasy, and she was immediately on guard. Even now, he glared with his deep-set eyes. The line of his jaw hard and resentful.

"Yes?" she asked with trepidation.

"We haven't been introduced," he said, his hands firmly in his pockets.

"No, we haven't. I'm Taite. You're Dakota, right?"

As he nodded, he looked her over with scrutinizing eyes. "Yeah. And you're the little refugee Lanie picked up before you got her shot."

Taite's jaw dropped at his open hostility, and she stammered for words. When she found them, they came rushing out.

"I saw it happen if that's what you mean, but I did nothing to cause it, jackass. Look, I may not be one of you, and I don't even want to be on this miserable excuse for a planet, but I would have helped her if I could. You can ask Baylin."

"I might do that. But you better stay out of the way. Baylin doesn't need more trouble, and neither do I."

"That's what I've been doing, but I have to put up with this crap."

"If you want to stay here, you'll put up with whatever I say."

"Somehow, I doubt Baylin will agree," she said with equal contempt.

"You'll stay out of the way, or I'll hand you over to the highest bidder."

Threats had never gone over well with Taite, but she'd never had much to lose. While she saw no reason for Dakota to be such a jerk, there was nothing to be done about that. Still, afterward, she often ducked out of sight when Dakota or Baylin came through the corridors.

One morning, long after finishing chores for Cy, Taite lingered in the infirmary. She could tell Cy was curious why she was still there but knew he wouldn't ask. They didn't discuss personal issues. So, she kicked her feet up and pretended to read a manual on proper CPR that she had already read weeks ago.

"Hey," Cy said from behind, as the door pushed open. "What brings you here today? Nothing bad, I hope."

"No medical emergencies if that's what worries you."

With a shift of her eyes, Taite glanced up, recognizing Baylin's voice.

"That's good," Cy said in his cheerful tone. "What can I help you with then?"

"I need to talk to Taite," he said as their eyes met. She raised an eyebrow.

Cy said, "Well, she's all yours."

"Can we go in the hall?" he asked, addressing Taite for the first time since entering the room.

"I'm reading, but I guess so," she said, trying to appear busier than she was.

As she followed into the corridor, she asked, "So, what did you want to talk about?" Only then she saw the papers in his hand and remember the code. As she pulled herself up straight, she snapped from a gloomy fog to an alert and angry storm. "Did you find something? What does it say?"

"One thing at a time, Taite. Let's go sit somewhere."

"Don't use that tone like I'm so freaking fragile."

"OK," he said with a subtle shake of his head. "There's a lot to go over, and I'd rather not stand here the whole time."

"Fine. Sorry," she said, stalking after Baylin who was already headed down the hall. They stepped into an empty room with a table and a few scattered chairs. One sat toppled over, missing a leg.

"Who else knows about this?" Taite asked, flopping down in a wobbly chair. Baylin sat beside her and spread papers out on the table.

"Anthony, he's the only one who worked on these transmissions. Cy was told a little. I just had a few questions for him."

"Cy? Fabulous. You didn't tell your best bud Dakota?"

"No, I didn't think that was a good idea."

"Agreed. OK, so what's this about?"

"Taite, all of it's about you."

"What do you mean? There's close to thirty pages there. That can't all be about me."

"There's forty-two pages. We've had a lot more, but these are the pages that mention you."

Taite sat up straighter, sliding toward the table to see for herself. Baylin collected and stacked the papers again.

"Wait a minute! If that stuff concerns me, I want to freaking see."

"Let me explain first, Taite. It's complicated."

She glared, his eyes concealing an indistinguishable expression.

"Get on with it then."

"I'll go through backwards. That'll be easier."

"Whatever. Just tell me something."

"When you were at the camp and escaped, first, they thought they had killed you along with a few others." He pointed out a series of numbers. "I saw 'em later when we went to the camp."

"Xander." She nodded, reaching for the chain around her neck. "You went to the camp?"

"A few days later, but that's not important," he said before continuing. "When they believed you were dead, they were furious. But then your body didn't turn up. They're aware you survived."

"Why do they even care about me anyway?"

"We'll get to that."

He handed a few papers to her. And there it was in black and white. Even the report where they tattooed her numbers.

"Your number, 242911, your 'tat', as you called it. That's your code, even before the camp. It's just not the same pattern as a normal camp number. Anthony and I didn't recognize it."

"Before the camp? What's in there about that?"

Looking back at the paper, he said, "Well, there's a report on your... progress at the hospital and what happened there." His eyes remained fixed on the papers before him.

Taite could guess the rest. Obviously, they had left nothing out. She snatched the paper away and scanned over it. Everything was there, things she had forgotten about, and things she wished to forget. Blood rose in her face, and she wasn't sure if it was anger or embarrassment. Possibly both. Baylin had read things that made her want to crawl under the table. As she put on an unaffected mask, she cleared her throat to break the horrible silence.

"Besides reviewing what I already remember, I don't see much here. This may have been educational for you, but I lived it, so it isn't news. I see what they did, but not why. Anything else?" she asked, forcing her voice to stay calm, as if none of it bothered her.

He stared and said nothing. Was he assuming it was all lies, and she would clear everything up? She waited for him to speak, but he lifted his hand and tapped a finger on the scar on her wrist. She jerked back in surprise, and he asked, "Did you really do that?"

"Guess so," she said, looking away.

"Why?"

Amazed at the question, she turned back to him, "You read all that, right?"

He nodded.

"Well, there ya go. What else do you need to hear?"

"Seems extreme. They must have been upset when they found out."

"Yes, extreme is a good word, since I was trying to kill myself, Baylin. That is extreme, isn't it? When you're on the verge of insanity, and life is one wretched day after another, things are extreme." Her voice was rising, but she stopped herself to avoid outright shouting again.

"OK, Taite," he said in his best imitation of a psychiatrist. Taite found it both amusing and irritating. "I didn't mean anything, but I don't like to imagine it."

"Oh gee, sorry for making you uncomfortable. I didn't enjoy living it, but I didn't have a choice in the matter. You kinda made that choice when you get down to it, so thanks. That was great."

While he chewed his inner cheek, Baylin looked at her in silence. He inhaled and said, "Maybe I deserve that Taite, or maybe I don't. It doesn't matter. I can't change it, but I wanted to go back for you. After what happened with... with Lanie, I didn't want to leave."

"Aww," she said, her next words soaked with sarcasm. "I guess that should make it all better, but it doesn't."

"Taite," he said, with increasing agitation. "You aren't being fair. Aren't we were past this? I couldn't do anything else. I tried."

"Whatever. I know," she said and shook her head clear. "What else is in this paper? Still a lot of pages there."

He paused, shuffling the papers and avoiding eye contact. So mature. Jerk.

"There is more, Taite. A lot more."

"Well?"

"I'm not sure how you'll take it. After your reaction so far, I don't want to tell you the rest right now."

"Baylin, stop playing games. Tell me. I'll behave." A relapse into the submissive attitude of the hospital, and she regretted the words as they left her lips.

"I'm not playing games." He looked up, his mouth drawn tight.

"What?" she asked, as the edge of her anger dulled. She grew more concerned by the minute. "What could be in there?"

Baylin sat the papers down, his chest expanding with a deep breath. "There's no good way to say this. Your father's in there."

Taite drew back, recalling the photograph that Dr. Fermin had shown her. It shouldn't be so surprising, but she still felt sick.

"What about him?"

"Some of this stuff is actually from him, Taite. Communications back and forth."

"From when?" she asked, as she focused on controlling the emotion in her voice.

"We've had these for a while and didn't realize what they were. Anthony saves everything though. He remembers most of it too."

"What's it about?"

"It's still incomplete information, but it appears an arrangement was made between your father and the head of the R.A. at some point." He paused for so long she questioned if he would finish.

"He agreed to turn you over to them."

For long seconds, Taite said nothing. The taste of blood was in her mouth as she chewed her lip into a bloody pulp. Baylin was silent, waiting for her to say something. But she stalled until she choked down the burning lump in her throat.

"That can't be right." Her voice came out heavy and broken.

"I'm sorry, Taite."

"He wouldn't do that. He's my father."

"There's more. Should I go on?"

Taite held her head in her hands as she leaned on the table and nodded.

"Dr. Jackson Taite is not your father."

Her head shot up as if he had thrown ice water in her face.

"What do you mean? Of course he is," she said through shocked incredulity. "That whole paper has to be wrong."

Baylin's eyebrows crinkled sympathetically. He pushed a sheet of paper across the table. "I'm only telling you what it says here."

With a quick scan, it was clear that was exactly what it said. Since she was of sufficient age, he was thanked for years of service in the upbringing of the 'subject' and released from further responsibility.

"This is crazy," Taite said, but her heart was pounding, burning. She thought it might burst. "I-I can't be here right now. Knees shaking, she stood and glanced at Baylin, his face full of pity. She had to get out of there before he said another word. Throwing the door open, Taite rushed into the hall. She slammed into someone, mumbled an apology, and hurried away.

For the remainder of the day and the next, the long arms of Xander's jacket covered her hands as she hugged herself in the hammock. She hadn't worn it for weeks, but she needed it. True, it smelled a little off and places were stiff with dried blood. She didn't care and remained there in her cocoon.

Days crawled by as Taite hid in the dorm and sometimes lurked in the halls at night. Before, such small things had knocked her down. Tiny pebbles had sent her hurtling into confusion, lost in a mental fog. Since she had left the so-called care of Dr. Fermin, she had spiraled down and pulled herself back up so many times. It was exhausting, but the roller coaster seemed to be inescapable. She had been getting better at shaking off the small things. But once again, she wanted to jump off the ride. What was life anyway? What did it matter if she was here or not? No one else cared. That was for sure. Such thoughts cluttered her mind, fighting for life like a school of suffocating fish in a dried-up stream.

Whenever Cy sent people looking for her, Taite sent them away. He could handle things without her for a while. Meanwhile, the storm was dying above them, and the generators died below. Lately, the air seemed stale, suffocating. But there was no escape until the wind weakened. They had sealed the door tight, and only a few could open it. Since she came to this miserable planet, she had been locked up in one place or another. A prisoner. She wanted to scream until her lungs burst.

One day, Cy came looking for her — chasing her down as she sulked through the first meal she had eaten in over twenty-four hours. He had heard about what happened and was concerned. With a roll of her eyes, she told him to leave her alone.

"Taite," he asked, "do you want to talk?" He was trying to help, but dang, he was annoying.

"I don't want to talk about anything. Thanks, but please go away." He left, looking like a confused, lost puppy. Within a minute, the twinge of remorse faded.

Later, she stomped along the corridor toward the steps that led to the outer door. It was more of a hatch, a massive rectangle, steel probably. At least six inches thick. Placed at an odd angle, the door leaned inward so the blowing sand wouldn't bury them alive. At the thought of being buried forever, her heartbeat quickened.

She stared longingly at the door. A few inches of metal kept her from freedom and fresh air. The wind roared beyond, a starving animal that seemed to call her name, drawing her outside to consume her alive. To have the sand scour the flesh from her bones would be better than being entombed in this place.

Hours had passed as she sat on the frigid floor. Still, Taite stared at the hatch, remembering everything Baylin had told her, when his voice suddenly came from behind.

"Just a bit longer, Taite."

It was the first time in a week they had crossed paths. Perhaps he would just go away.

Instead, he asked, "What's with the jacket, Taite?" It was irritating that he kept repeating that name.

"Do you have to keep calling me that?"

"Do you prefer Aisea these days?"

"Forget it." How could she explain that even her name felt wrong? "The jacket is none of your business."

"Damn. Cy said you were acting weird."

Taite's eyes spun up in their sockets. "So, that's why you're here," Taite said without looking up again. "Another one of Cy's messengers."

"No, I was wondering how you were doing. Just thought you needed some time. Cy is concerned though."

"What did Cy say exactly? Taite's wearing the crazy coat again?"

A subtle smile played at the corner of his mouth as he said, "He wasn't quite so eloquent. But, well, last week you were stitching people up like a machine, and now... not so much."

Taite scowled. "Things have changed. Besides, there's no one to stitch up at the moment. Unless you're volunteering."

Baylin stayed silent.

"I want out of here. I feel like a prisoner."

"Breathe. Try to focus on something else. You'll get though it."

"Why? What's waiting for me when I'm through it? Nothing."

"You can't be sure of that. Things changed once. They can change again. That's what makes life interesting."

"Is that what you'd call it?" she asked, picking at the hem of the coat.

"Among other things. But really, what's the deal with the coat? Cy told me about it, but I thought you were over that. I realize things must have been a shock, but you shouldn't be wearing that filthy coat."

"Yeah, I thought I was over it too, but I was wrong. I need it."

"You don't need it. It's a jacket. A dirty, smelly jacket that's too big."

"No, you don't understand. It isn't the coat. It's Xander. But you still think I'm crazy, and I'm not so sure I'm not," she said, her voice trailing off. She took a deep breath and let it escape. "Anyway, did you want something other than to annoy me?"

"You're not crazy. You've been through a lot. I didn't know beforehand."

"What didn't you know? The attempted suicide thing or the part about my father?"

"Any of it."

"Baylin, I appreciate that you're trying to be nice, but I'm not ready to talk about this."

"Yeah, fair enough. If you change your mind, you know where to find me."

As he stood up, he put a hand on her back for a moment.

Without looking at him, she nodded. "Thanks."

Filled with mixed emotions, Taite watched him walk away. While she shouldn't have been so sharp, he wasn't supposed to give up so fast.

TWENTY-FIVE

The world seemed turned wrong-side-out. No, really, they had yanked it from beneath her feet. She didn't even understand who she was. Taite. That didn't seem right anymore, the name of a substitute father. While she hoped it wasn't true, she'd never be able to ask. Aisea didn't feel right either because that was what he had called her.

Cold on the floor, her joints were stiff from disuse when she untangled herself. She had sat brooding by the entrance well after midnight, after they reduced the lights to a few scattered bulbs. Despite the late hour, she wasn't tired at all.

As she crept down the empty hall, chills climbed her calves with each step. Her boots were heavy in hand, and questions filled her mind. With sleep beyond reach, she went to find the only person she could talk to about her worries.

The door to the storage closet was shut and knocking gave no answer. By the time the hinge creaked open, she had walked five feet back down the hall.

Baylin stood in the doorway, shirtless and a little bleary-eyed. A tattoo spread over one side of his rib cage, a circular design wider than her whole hand. Noticing traces of sweat on his neck, Taite suddenly wished she hadn't come.

"Taite?"

"Sorry, I didn't mean to bother you."

"It's all right," he said, hanging on the door. "You need something?"

"Well, I... but if you're busy," she said, the words coming out wrong.

"Busy? It's the middle of the night." His expression changed as he spoke, and his face turned a blotchy red.

"No. No, I'm not busy. I was asleep, but I'm wide awake now."

"Sorry," Taite said again. "Maybe I shouldn't have come, but I couldn't sleep. I thought you might be awake."

"It's fine. Ya might as well sit."

Inside the room, a bare light bulb cast shadows as it hung over a small round table in the center. On one side was a worn brown couch, still crumpled where Baylin had slept. As Taite looked around, it occurred to her she had seen this room on a late night wandering.

"Did I wake you?"

Baylin gestured for her to sit on the couch and reached for a shirt draped over a chair. As he pulled it over his head, he said, "You did, but you kinda did me a favor. Trust me on that."

Everyone knew Baylin slept here, but only a few realized why. Cy said Baylin often still had nightmares and refused to sleep in the men's dorm to avoid disturbing everyone else.

"You were dreaming," she said, trying not to stare as he adjusted the wrinkled t-shirt over his abs.

"That's one word for it, but you saved me from finishing it."

"Oh, nightmares. I remember that."

Baylin sat on the other end of the couch, propping himself up by jamming his bare feet beneath the cushion.

"Anyway, you wanted to talk?"

After dropping her boots to the floor, Taite collected her thoughts and said, "There were questions I should have asked. Things maybe I didn't give you a chance to say."

He said nothing now, so she continued. "It's been one thing after another for such a long time. The hospital, the camp, and now this. I didn't want to listen, but I've thought about this a lot."

Baylin cut in. "You want to hear what else we found."

"Did you find anything else?"

"Maybe, and Anthony's always getting more intel."

"Anything about my real parents? I never met my mother."

"No, nothing like that."

She sighed. "I don't even know who I am. My name doesn't even sound right anymore."

"I get all that, and I wish I had more information. But the way I see it, a name isn't that important. Just a label."

"You couldn't possibly understand, Baylin."

"Oh?"

"I've lost everything, my family, my home, everything, and now even myself."

"At least you're starting to get answers. It's better to know the truth."

Taite scowled. "I'm not sure about that."

"Well, I can't say if my sister survived or not. At this point, I would rather be sure either way."

At his words, the memory of Fermin's photograph jumped forward. She should have mentioned it before now, but she avoided thinking of anything concerning Dr. Fermin.

After a moment of hesitation, she said, "In the hospital, Dr. Fermin showed me a bunch of photographs. I can't be certain they were real, but they looked real enough."

"And?" he asked, anxiety in his voice.

"You may have been in one. Fermin said you killed a guard somewhere, but the other..."

"The other was what, Taite?"

"The other was Lanie, and..." she paused, struggling for the right words.

"What?"

Taite inhaled and let the sentence fly out of her mouth. "She was—she wasn't alive."

"Are you sure?"

"If the picture was real, then yes."

"And you're just now getting around to telling me this?" he asked, his voice rising.

"It happened a long time ago, and I assumed you knew."

"Lanie is unquestionably dead, and you said nothing?"

"How was I supposed to bring that up?"

"Any way would have been better than not at all."

Her temper flared, and she shouted, "Baylin, I've had some other problems."

"Yeah, but this—"

"You must have assumed by now."

"What I assumed doesn't matter, Taite."

"So, you're mad? I told you now, didn't I?

"Just go, Taite. Please."

"Fine," she said, pulling at the edge of her jacket. "I shouldn't be here anyway." Slamming the door behind, she stormed from the room.

+++

For a few days, Taite didn't see Baylin. Most likely, he was still pissed off. She meant to tell him sooner, but so much had happened since then. So, Baylin avoided her, and she returned the favor.

While planning to keep on avoiding him, she came across Anthony in the hall late one evening. Thinking he might have more information, she called his name. Instead of giving an awkward smile like normal, he buried his face in the stack of papers he held and pretended not to hear. He wasn't very good at pretending. Then he whirled around like he remembered an imaginary errand and disappeared around the corner.

Tempted to follow him, Taite took a few steps before thinking better of it. All right, if Anthony didn't want to talk, she wouldn't force him. Baylin probably had something to do with it.

Instead, she made her way to the infirmary to see what Cy was doing. To her surprise, a petite brunette was there with him. Cy was taking her blood pressure and laughing. The brunette grinned and fluttered her eyelashes. Taite puffed out a breath and rolled her eyes, then she straightened her back before stomping down the hall.

TWENTY-SIX

The storage closet door stared Taite in the face. Baylin was probably somewhere examining a machine or pissing someone off, but it might be worth a try. She pounded a fist on the door, but no answer came. She knocked again, then trying the knob, found it turned freely. After a moment of indecision, Taite pushed the door open a crack.

"Baylin?"

Met with silence, she ventured into the dimly lit room. To her alarm, Baylin stretched out on the ratty couch with one arm draped over his eyes. Still wearing the clothes she had seen him in last, his chest rose and fell with breath.

Surprised he was asleep for once, Taite crept back toward the door but noticed on the table, a pile of papers with edges crumpled from handling. A few stray sheets were strewn about. These had to be the transmissions Baylin and Anthony had been working on.

With a glance at the still slumbering figure, she crossed over to the table. Thick black marker lines had been drawn across the pages. A few sentences here and there broke the lines, but as she shuffled through, whole pages had been blacked out. The remaining sentences repeated some of what Baylin had already shown her, but someone was hiding something.

Her heart pounded faster against her ribs and stopped cold when a permanent marker rolled from between the papers and tumbled to the floor. As she bent to retrieve it, she bumped into a chair that scraped against the floor.

"What are you doing in here?" Baylin asked from behind, causing Taite to jump out of her skin. How could someone be such a light sleeper and still have looked so passed out? She spun around, collecting her thoughts on the way.

"Well, I came to find you, and the door wasn't locked."

"You've come to apologize or something?" he asked through a yawn while scratching his rumpled hair.

"Apologize? The thought never crossed— I mean, I am sorry for not telling you. And about Lanie, but—"

"Listen, maybe I overreacted. It wasn't your fault. I assumed as much by now, but knowing feels different." As he stretched and cracked his neck, he said, "So, why are you here then? You have a habit of waking me up lately."

"Yeah, sorry. I wasn't sure what to do with myself. Cy is strangely flirting with a girl in the infirmary. Anthony is avoiding me, and of course, you're avoiding me."

"Taite, I'm not avoiding you, and nothing's strange about Cy flirting," he said and straightened his back against the couch. He didn't wait for a comment before asking, "What were you doing over there?"

Taite's mind rushed back to the black lines, knowing Baylin would answer his own question soon enough.

"Funny," she said, an accusation in the air. "That's what I planned on asking you." With a loud screech, she pulled the chair out and scooped up the stack of papers. "What is all this?"

"What do you mean?" he asked, dumbfounded. The surprise on his face was almost enjoyable. Ambushed.

"It's the papers I told you about. You can see right there."

"Don't play stupid. You've been marking things out. What's in here?"

His mouth twitched as he bit his lower lip. "Look, Taite, it's late. You barge into my room uninvited and start an interrogation. This is ridiculous. We'll talk tomorrow."

"No, I want to talk now."

"Give it a rest. Trust me."

"I can't trust anybody who's hiding something. Here you are covering things up after jumping on my case because I hadn't told you about Lanie. This paper was all about me. You said so. What are you hiding? I have a right to know."

Baylin sighed and rubbed the bridge of his nose. "You aren't going to back down, are you? Would it help if I said sometimes things are better off left alone?"

"No, it wouldn't. You're keeping something from me. Like you said before, it's always better to know."

Baylin shook his head and muttered, "You would use that. No, Taite, I can't tell you."

Blood warmed her cheeks and anger climbed her throat. "You can't?" she asked. "You can't tell me something that concerns me? Baylin, you will tell me, and you'll tell me right now."

"Taite, you don't realize what you're asking," Baylin said, his jaw set firm and his eyes open wide now.

"That's my point. I need to know." Her voice cracked, rising in the quiet night air.

"God, why did you have to come in here in the first place? Now you're demanding things? Unbelievable."

"I thought I could trust you with this. Sorry to uncover your little conspiracy."

"Conspiracy? There's no conspiracy. You don't need to hear this and you won't want to hear it. Why can't you stop and think for a minute instead of being so obstinate?"

Arms crossed over her chest, Taite glared. With as much calm as she could muster, she said "You're right. I am obstinate, so you might as well tell me. We can yell until everyone in this whole bloody place comes running, I will still not back down."

Baylin ran a long-fingered hand over his eyes. In a gesture she took as an admission of defeat, he sat back on the frumpy brown couch. He said nothing but held out an empty hand.

"That's sweet, Baylin, but I don't want to hold hands."

"The papers. Give me the papers. Please." Sounding tired again, he slumped against the back of the cushion.

With a flick of a wrist, she tossed the stack of crumpled striped secrets on the couch beside him.

His eyes darted up in irritation. The pulsing light cast strange creeping shadows and made him look as ominous as the mood in the room.

"OK, I blacked things out and for a good reason."

"Which is?"

"Your mental health has been a bit... delicate. I wasn't sure you could handle so much at once. I was trying to protect you."

"Oh, not again. Poor little Taite might have a nervous breakdown at any moment. Great."

"This is different, but you're right. And I'll tell you, but it'll cost you."

"Cost me what? That takes a lot of nerve."

"The crazy coat, as you call it. I will not have you drooping around here because of everything I've said. Give me the coat or you get nothing."

She stared open-mouthed. "My coat? But I've explained this. It isn't just the coat. I need it."

"No, you don't. Why hasn't someone washed that thing? It's repulsive."

Pulling the sleeves tight around her, she said with a smile, "When one of the girls offered to wash it, I threatened to scratch her eyes out. Sometimes being the crazy girl has its advantages.

"Anyway, just tell me. How bad can it be?"

"The coat or no deal."

"Fine, but only after you tell me everything." While she needed the coat, she needed answers even more.

Baylin made a little noise, halfway between a snort and a sigh. "That'll do, but no backing out."

"I promise."

Baylin inhaled and said, "We learned Dr. Taite isn't your father, and that he made an agreement."

"Yes, we learned that. Thanks for clarifying. Moving on."

"The parts I blacked out explain who you are and why you're here."

"That's what I've been trying to find out. Why hide that?"

"You'll understand later," he said, ruffling through the papers with trembling hands.

"You were meant to go to the colony, but someone intervened and took you off the base where you first arrived. It might have even been your father, well... Dr. Taite, or rather someone he hired."

"But why, if he—?"

He held up a hand and continued. "Maybe he had second thoughts. I can't say. Or it might not have been him, but that's not the point. Anyway, Aises is the so-called new and better Earth. The Governor's name is Faren. Like a lot of leaders, he seems to use his position to put himself first."

"What does this have to do with me?"

"Patience. I'm getting to it."

"Well, get to it already."

"The Governor and his wife both came from Earth. They were married long before he was in charge of Aises, his own private Utopia. But the Utopia started falling apart early on. The colony wasn't thriving as it should, and his wife was ill with a genetic disorder.

"The papers weren't clear what illness. Only that she's dying, and she needs more than one organ transplant — heart, lungs, liver. Others, too. From the time she was young, they knew that she would need transplants later to survive."

"That's sad Baylin, but I still don't get it."

"You will. Stop interrupting. The hospital saved the umbilical cord and cord blood, in case the stem cells were useful. I guess they were thinking ahead. At some point..."

Baylin paused to best arrange his next words.

With strained eyes, Taite focused on the space those words would fill.

After a minute, Baylin exhaled and continued, "In the long run, they decided the best way to handle it was to create a clone. All the organs she might need, right there, healthy and alive when needed. Well, they're needed now. Anise, that's her name, is waiting to receive transplants from her clone."

As puzzle pieces whirled into place, Taite was lightheaded, breathless. What could this have to do with her? The answer was there, but she didn't want to see.

"I can't listen to anymore," she said as she looked toward the hall.

"No, you were right."

"Why? You weren't going to tell me. Just go back to that idea."

Baylin shook his head, scowling. "No, you should hear the rest." As he continued, he seemed more serious than ever. "During the time you were missing with Lanie and me, Anise was growing worse. She was running out of time. They put her in stasis until you were located."

"That can't be me, Baylin. They shot me!"

"In the shoulder. That was intentional. No real harm done."

"I don't want to hear more."

"When you were in the hospital, Anise was being thawed so to speak, recovering and all. She's very weak. Everything needs to be perfect before they can... So, they used the time to pick your brain about Duratio, find out what you knew.

"It seems there were a few mix-ups along the way. By the sound of it, that Dr. Fermin guy was a sadistic asshole who enjoyed messing with your head. Looks like he got himself into some trouble over it."

He cleared his throat and stifled a cough in his hand. "Fermin was drugging you against orders. Apparently, he wasn't fully briefed beforehand. When you tried to kill yourself, it was a pretty big deal. The Governor insisted you had to be moved.

"So, they sent you to the camp, less likely to hurt yourself. Plus, you'd be getting fresh air and exercise. They want you healthy. After a setback or two, Anise was improving. They had to make sure she was strong enough, to... to survive the transplants."

"I feel sick."

"You and your friends surprised them though," he said through a forced smile. "You got away and screwed them over."

"No, I'm serious," Taite said, ignoring his comment. With effort, she choked out her next words. "I'm gonna throw up."

"What?"

As she ran from the room, Baylin was left staring at the door.

When she returned moments later, Taite was pale, her forehead sticky with sweat. As she sank to the couch and put her head in her hands, she said, "Not to sound cruel, but I've been gone a while. Isn't she dead by now? Anyway, why bother with this? If I'm her clone, I'll have the same disease, right?"

"Are you all right?"

"I'm great. Are they still after me or not?"

"I doubt she's dead. They'll keep her alive. The last transmission was a month ago, and you're still a topic of conversation. The storm makes acting difficult. When it passes, it'll be easier.

"And I'm sure they corrected the genes during the cloning process. They wouldn't waste their time."

"I wanna go home. This isn't real," Taite groaned.

"It is, Taite. You see why I didn't want to tell you. But the storm is passing. You need to understand."

"I wanna go home," she repeated without thinking.

"That isn't possible."

"How can I be sure you aren't the sadistic ass messing with my head? Everyone is messing with me. I don't want any of this," Taite said. "I want my pathetic, boring life back where my biggest problem was picking a college major.

"First, you tell me my father isn't my father. Now, I'm not even me.

I'm a copy of somebody else. I don't even have real parents. What the hell am I supposed to do with that, Baylin?"

His silence was frustrating, so she stood and paced the floor. "Now, I have to accept that the same people who screwed up my life, who created me, are going to butcher me for spare parts? You say that as if it's the most normal thing in the world. And don't give me that look. Pity is not helping."

"It's a lot to take in, especially for someone who—"

"Go ahead and say it," she said, her voice climbing. "Someone who what? Is already crazy? Is teetering on the verge of another breakdown? What?"

"I was going to say, for someone who has been through a lot."

"That's one way of putting it."

As her mind failed to offer any more biting retorts, Taite took a deep a breath. The fire burned out, and she said, "I'm sorry. I want to go back home, where at least no one was trying to harvest my organs."

"It's OK. But you realize that won't happen, Taite."

With a sneer, she asked, "Which part, going back home or having my internal organs harvested?"

"Neither. We're not going to hand you over to them. You should know that by now. Your heart and lungs are safe here." He cracked a crooked smile before continuing in a more serious tone. "And there is no way back."

As he looked over at her, he said, "Don't take this wrong, but if there was a way to go back, I wouldn't help you find it."

"Oh, thanks for clarifying," she said, smirking. "I'm sure you have far more important things to do than help me. It's enough that you guard my guts. Don't worry, I wouldn't ask for more."

He stared at her for a moment and said, "That isn't at all what I meant, Taite."

"Then what did you mean?"

He brushed a hand through his hair and looked behind her at the wall, "I'm just kinda used to having you here."

"It isn't like we're exactly friends."

"Aren't we?" he asked, shaking his head. "Anyway, you seem to be taking this well. Besides the vomiting."

"It hasn't hit me yet. That's why I can't give up my coat. I mean, you weren't serious, right?"

"Taite," Baylin said, his voice dropping in warning. "We had a deal. Stop being dramatic."

"That was before. This will come rushing at me later. I need it. I'm only half awake, and later..." She trailed off, seeing how Baylin stared in disapproval.

"This isn't fair. It's mine. You can't make me take it off." Taite was nearing panic, like a child giving up her security blanket.

"Can't I?" Baylin asked, looking confident. "I would hate to do it, considering your traumatized state of mind, but I can. And it would be easy." His eyes sparkled as a smile teased at the corner of his mouth. "Save us both the trouble and hand it over. I'm tired."

"No," Taite said, standing up and backing toward the door.

As if to accept the challenge, Baylin rose to his feet. He looked awfully wide awake for someone who claimed to be so exhausted. And contrary to his words, the look on his face said he enjoyed this.

As Taite shook her head and fumbled back another step, she said, "You're not getting it." The words sounded small in the room, but she stood firm.

For a moment, tension filled the air, then like a spring, Baylin shot away from the couch. Before she reacted, her face was pressed against the floor, and her arms were behind her back.

"Ow. Why d'you do that? This floor is filthy."

"Sorry, but a deal's a deal, and you are not backing out of it."

"Come on, Baylin. Don't I have enough problems without being sat on? You're heavy, and these coat buttons are painful."

"You promised."

"Fine. Fine. Get off. But I will point out I could have strangled you with my sleeves."

"Of course, Taite. Of course," he said, stumbling to his feet, one hand still tight around the loose sleeves of the jacket. Then he guided her to the table, righted the chair with a foot, and sat her down.

"Baylin, I am sick of being treated like a kid," Taite said. "Everybody is always ordering me around."

An idea bloomed, and she said. "Oh, wait, I'm the freak. Everybody knows. I was just crazy before, but now I'm Frankenstein's monster. That explains everything, I'm not a real person to anyone. I might as well be Pinocchio. What does that make you? The freaking cricket?"

"Taite, you aren't making much sense."

"And so what? Just let go, and you can have the coat."

"Why don't I believe you? Perhaps because you threatened to strangle me?"

"Then what are you going to do? I can't take it off unless you let go."

"I'll manage," he said. While keeping hold of both sleeves in one hand, he released her arms inside. Taite jerked one arm free to slap him, but she couldn't turn around. He reached over and unfastened the two secured buttons. With the other hand, he pulled the jacket away.

Air rushed at her back, and Taite shivered in her t-shirt. As she curled her knees in, she glared at Baylin. While digging around in a pocket of his cargo pants, he walked over, trailing the coat in one hand.

"Happy now?" she glowered.

"Not yet."

"Ah... here we are." he said, producing the small target of his search. With a quick motion of his fingers, a blade folded out, gleaming in the dim light.

"No. Absolutely not."

"Yeah, 'fraid so, Taite," he said, drawling out the words, as he sawed at the collar of the jacket. Knife between his teeth, he ripped the crazy coat in two.

Taite's jaw dropped, and her eyes burned. She turned and stared at the wall. As he mutilated her coat — Xander's coat, another rip broke the silence, and she winced. With her jaw clenched, Taite was vowing vengeance when a dangling piece of stained fabric appeared before her eyes.

"Here ya go. A little souvenir," he said. With her eyes, she followed the suspended fabric to Baylin's outstretched hand above, and she snatched the fabric away. The strip of the coat, the whole length of it, was about three inches wide, and she ran the rough material through her fingers, feeling the roughness of the dried blood stain. Despite her best efforts, she wasn't angry anymore.

Earlier, she had said it wasn't the coat itself. He had listened. She thought of Xander; smiling and then dying. A doleful sigh escaped before she could catch it. Taite turned to see Baylin sitting on the couch, his head propped up by an elbow.

He watched through heavy eyelids, each blink lasting longer.

"Thanks," she said. "I hadn't thought to do that."

"Clearly." He laid his head on his arm.

Glancing at the torn fabric in her hand, she twirled it around her fingers. The mangled mark on her wrist leered back, an ugly reminder of an ugly time. She wound the fabric around until the scar vanished.

"I should let you sleep."

Baylin replied with a long blink.

"Could you do something for me first?" she asked, standing over him and holding out a wrapped wrist.

"Sure." He yawned and reached out to tie up the loose ends. His hands were warm against her cold ones and even half-asleep his long fingers moved with precision.

"Thanks," she said, bumping his shoulder with her fist.

With closed eyes, he smiled. "Goodnight, Taite."

Taite walked back down the hall, a foreign mood creeping over her. While she should be horrified to learn so many distressful things, she wasn't. Maybe she was going numb or had become immune to bad news. To think she was born with the specific purpose to die was bewildering at best. In a way, that could be said of anyone.

But this was different. What was she expected to do with this? People were trying to kill her. Yet somehow, as she ran a palm over the looped fabric on her wrist, there relief more than anything — to learn the truth, to let go, at least a little, of Xander. With relief came hope she might overcome it all. And perhaps she wasn't as alone as she had felt.

TWENTY-SEVEN

As the storm moved out of the area, and the sun was finally visible, Taite didn't see much of Baylin. He and Dakota were busy getting a team together to scout the area, check for signs of activity, and restock supplies. As usual, that would mean ambushing a colony convoy. While Taite had tried to talk them into letting her go, they had all agreed it was too dangerous. Ridiculous. But as she sat outside in the fresh air, she felt the distinct vulnerability of a sitting duck.

Nothing over her head but a wide pale sky, she savored being outside at last. She could see for miles in all directions, but any day, danger might appear on that open horizon.

Nothing would surprise Taite anymore. Learning she was a clone seemed like icing on the cake. It was too weird to have any real meaning for her, and she still hadn't had another major breakdown like she expected. Taite hoped Governor Faren would give up, and the whole ordeal would drift away. They wouldn't put so much effort into finding a singular person. She wasn't so important.

But Baylin had assured her they wouldn't give up, perhaps not even if Anise died. Taite was her new, improved duplicate after all. Not to mention a scientific commodity.

As thoughts whirled in her head, a searing wind blew through her hair. It would have been too hot had she not spent the last few months locked away underground. Though the sunlight didn't cause burns and dark tans on Aises, after forty-eight hours of continual exposure, it really started to warm up. She struggled to her feet in the shifting sand and descended the stairs to the cool darkness below.

She had spent a lot of time contemplating why this happened to her and questioning if being a clone made her less of a person. To find out your parents weren't your real parents wasn't so unusual. To learn you didn't have parents in the usual biological sense was something else. Staring at faces in the crowd, wondering if one of them could be her mother seemed so far away now. She should have just looked in a mirror.

But Taite hadn't crumbled into pieces at this latest development, and that was progress. Whenever panic took hold, she would run a finger along the fabric on her wrist. She often thought of Xander then, and the choices he would never get to make. No matter how bizarre his life had become, he would want to be alive. He would have kept fighting.

Once, he had asked her about the scar. She hadn't been brave enough to own up to the truth and had changed the subject instead. It was the only secret she had kept from him.

Taite snapped back to the present to see Dakota approaching from the opposite direction. She was tempted to turn around and avoid him. Lately, he had become a real smart ass. She was not in the mood to deal with him, but Cy was expecting her.

"Isn't it a little late to put a bandage on that?" Dakota asked, sneering as he gestured to Taite's wrist.

"Go away, asshole," she said, wondering why Baylin was even friends with the guy.

"Crazy bitch," he said through a cough as he walked past.

"Clever."

"Oh, Baylin was looking for you. Can't imagine why," he said over his shoulder as he disappeared around a corner.

"Where is he?"

She didn't get an answer, so she continued toward the infirmary where Cy was waiting. She would worry about Baylin later. If she showed up any later than she already was, Cy would be ticked.

In one continuous gesture, she threw the door open and stepped inside. "Sorry I'm late Cy, I lost track of time and— oh." Stopping herself, she realized Cy wasn't listening. He was collecting supplies and packing them into the pack Baylin held.

They both looked up, and Cy said, "You're late."

"Yeah, I was explaining. Oh, never mind. Sorry."

"If you were anywhere to be found I would have told you not to come in today. Change of plans."

"Oh?"

"The patrol is leaving today as soon as everyone is ready. As you can tell, I'm busy packing supplies," he said as he rose from a crouch and disappeared into the infirmary storage closet.

As she knitted her eyebrows together, Taite turned to Baylin. "Why so soon? I thought you were leaving next week?"

"With the recent developments, I thought it best to move it up. Didn't Dakota tell you? I asked him to tell you."

"That's what you told him to say? He said you were looking for me."

"Typical."

"And speaking of Dakota, when you get a chance, could you tell your best bud to leave me alone?" she asked with a scowl.

He looked up from the carton he was packing and asked, "What do ya mean?"

"To be clear, Dakota is an ass, and I want him to stop bothering me," she said before relating the story. "I don't understand why you had to tell him."

"Taite, I didn't tell him anything about it. Don't think too much of him. He's like that sometimes. Anyway, he won't be here to mess with you after today. Not for a while."

"Guess not."

"Dakota and I just decided yesterday morning. I wanted to tell you, but nobody had seen you today." As he spoke, he continued packing, his hands in constant motion.

"I went for a walk. I was out most of the morning."

His head snapped up and his hands went still. "What? You don't mean outside?"

"Yeah, so? I've been dying to get out of here. Now I can."

"Where did you go?" A note of irritation laced his voice. "What if something had happened?"

"Baylin, I'm not a child. I walked over to the rock ledge. I needed to think."

"It isn't safe, especially not for you." Back to packing now, his face was angled toward the floor. "That's almost a mile away. Anything could have happened. What would you have done then? Did you even bother to tell anyone where you were going?"

"No, I guess I didn't. But nothing happened." She held out her arms in a wide gesture. "I came back before anyone knew I left. It's all good."

"No, it isn't," he said, rising to face her. "You can't go out on your own while we're gone. It's too dangerous for you to be out alone."

"Oh, come on."

"Taite, the last thing we need is to worry that you're back here wandering around and putting yourself in danger."

"Fine. If that's what you need to hear, I won't go by myself. I promise to stay here like a prison inmate. Better?" she asked with pursed lips and an eye roll.

"No. I don't believe you."

"Why not? I said I promised."

Baylin's gaze shifted to the wristband.

"Oh, that," Taite said, tucking her hand in her back pocket.

"This has to be different. It isn't about what I want to hear. It's about you staying safe."

Dark eyes disclosed that he hadn't slept again, and a pang of guilt jabbed at her chest. She had caused them all so much trouble, especially Baylin.

With a groan, she nodded. "All right. I promise."

"Taite, it's important. Besides, if I find out you break your word," he said with a grin. "There's gonna be hell to pay."

"I won't. OK?" she said again, looking up as Cy came into the room with an assortment of boxes and bags in his arms. "How long do you expect to be away?" she asked, keeping her voice light.

"A week or so. It's hard to be sure."

"If we keep up all the yapping, it'll be a week before you get packed," Cy said, interrupting.

Taite said, "I can take a hint. I'll get out of the way."

Baylin looked up at her through his eyelashes. "See ya later and stay out of trouble."

"Always," she said, as she stepped backwards out the door.

The rest of the afternoon, Taite wondered when they would leave without knowing why it mattered. While spinning the fabric around her wrist, she roamed the halls until she found herself headed to the mechanical guts of the little fortress in the desert. She saw no one around and soaked up the solitude. That was the worst part of being here, the constant presence of... someone.

As she strolled further, her footsteps made quiet clangs against the metal grate walkway. The monotonous moan of a generator was almost soothing, and the heat of machinery warmed the air. Though not everything had been fixed, she observed no signs of the earlier explosion.

Out of curiosity, Taite climbed up a short ladder of cold steel. It led to a small landing that overlooked the main floor and equipment. Far at the other end, someone was checking gauges. She flopped down on the grating and stretched her legs over the edge of the ladder. The narrow landing allowed her to still lean against the rails behind her. Taite closed her eyes and focused on the breath coming and going from her lungs. The same lungs they would rip from her if they found her.

She was tired of worrying. It was exhausting on multiple levels. Only when she heard her name called and struggled to open her eyes, did Taite realize she had drifted off.

"Taite, are you in here?" the familiar voice asked.

As she sat up, she replied, "I'm here."

"We're heading out soon. Thought I'd tell you," he called up. Seconds later, boots clambered up the ladder, while Taite struggled to release one of hers from the railing where it had become trapped. Baylin's hands appeared first, grabbing her boot. With a slight twist, he dislodged it from the bars.

"Have you been up here the whole time with your boot stuck in the rail?" he asked with a crooked grin.

"I came in here to get away from everybody and must have dozed off. How did you find me?" she asked, attempting to right herself and shake off the remaining sleep.

"Someone saw you come this way over an hour ago. Besides, I know how you like to find strange places to wedge yourself into. Glad I came though, otherwise, who knows? You could have starved to death up here."

"Funny. Thank you for freeing my foot though. So, you're leaving?" she asked, as she grabbed the railing to pull herself up. Baylin nodded, but folded his long legs under him and sat, pulling her back down with him.

"Aren't you in a hurry?"

"I have a minute. Dakota was finishing a few things."

"Oh, all right," she said and watched him as he sat staring toward the door in a daze.

"You will keep that promise, right?"

"Yes, Baylin."

"How are you handling everything? You know... up here?" he asked, lightly grasping the top of her head, like he might squeeze out the answer.

With a shrug, she said. "OK, I guess. It's weird, but I'm getting better at dealing with weird."

After reaching for her wrist, he turned it over in his hand and asked, "No more of this stuff?"

"Too many people already want me dead. I at least need me on my side."

"I'm on your side."

"Yeah, thanks," Taite said. "It still bothers me about my father or whoever he is. I can't understand how someone could do that. Raise a child and then turn her over, knowing what waited. That's the hard part. It was all a lie, and I'm a lie too."

"About your father — I told you, he might have reconsidered. Maybe that wasn't all fake. Taite, you aren't a lie. They may have caused you to live, but no one can give life. That comes from somewhere else."

As he talked, his hand still encircled her wrist. Did he feel her pulse quickening? He said something else about her father. She didn't understand a word but wondered if her face looked as flushed as it felt. Baylin was staring at her, saying he needed to get going. His fingers had slid down to Taite's, and he did not seem to be going.

"Baylin."

"Yeah?"

"Can you tell me something?"

"Possibly."

"You know almost everything about me, including things I wish you didn't. I know next to nothing about you. Why do you do all this? Why you were at that camp with Xander?"

Before he could answer, someone yelled his name from the hall. With a sigh, he said, "Yeah, sure. Looks like it will have to wait though." With a squeeze of her fingers, he released her hand and rose from the floor. Offering Taite the opposite hand, he pulled her to her feet.

Dakota stood in the doorway, and called up, "Everything's ready. Move your ass, Maras." Taite glanced at Baylin from the corner of her eye. Maras?

"I'll be right there."

"You're the one who wanted to get moving early, so don't slow us down now 'cause of little Miss Misery."

226

"I said I'm coming."

Dakota snorted and stomped out.

"So I'll see you in about a week?" Taite asked, forcing a smile as she started down the short ladder.

"Something like that," Baylin said, following close behind. He stepped off the ladder and nodded, meeting her eyes as she turned.

Taking a few strides toward the door, Baylin paused a moment before turning back and retracing his steps. Frozen in place, Taite watched as he returned to stand in front of her. He shifted his weight from one foot to the other and looped a thumb in a pocket.

"Look," he said, running a hand through his hair and rolling his boot to his heel. "Take care of yourself, OK?" Then he gave Taite a solid pat on the back and walked away.

"Um... is that it?" she asked, but by the time she spoke, Baylin had already rushed from the room.

TWENTY-EIGHT

After Baylin left, Taite was a little off balance, foggy. So many thoughts spinning they became too much to process. Hopes and worries fighting for space, and too many neurons were firing at once.

On the third night, she woke in the dark for no obvious reason. Thoughts darted in and out, keeping her awake like a noisy neighbor. Anxious to escape herself, she walked the halls in bare feet and found herself hovering in front of Baylin's empty room. She hadn't intended to go there, but there she stood. Taite stared at the door and yawned. She wished he was there, willing to talk at any hour.

Baylin wouldn't care if she sat a minute, so she opened the door. Last time, she hadn't taken time to notice much, but now she looked around and noticed everything. The room was small with shelves on the far wall and a deep utility sink in the corner by the couch. Of course, he had cleared the papers from the table.

Other than a couple shirts folded on the couch, there didn't seem to be much of him around. The shelves were full of random supplies: bottled water, towels, even boxes of ammunition. Taite didn't touch anything, but flopped down on the worn old couch and kicked her legs out in front. A faint smell of soap and sand lingered in the air. Nothing else remained but the memory of Baylin's presence. She wondered where he was now and if he had found dreams or nightmares that night.

Taite was surprised to find herself coiled up on the couch when she woke the next morning, her head resting on the stack of folded shirts. After uncurling and stretching, she rushed to her feet in embarrassment, though she didn't know why. Everyone realized Baylin was away. Still, she crept out of the room like a thief.

No one seemed to notice her absence from her hammock the first night. Or the next. The room sat empty. And who wouldn't want a private room? When Baylin returned, she would retreat to the bunk room. No harm done. It was hardly even his room. It was a closet. Besides, she often woke at odd hours and worried about disturbing everyone else. She had been sleeping much better away from the others.

+++

A week and a half had flown by since Baylin left. Taite occupied her time helping Cy take an inventory of the dwindling medical supplies. While Cy usually avoided personal conversations, today was different.

"Taite," he said. "You doing okay?"

"Sure. Why do you ask?"

"You seem distracted. You look a little down."

"Well, it's everything going on. There's a lot on my mind, as I'm told you've heard."

"Is that why you've been missing from the girls' dorm these days?"

Taite lifted her eyes to meet his. "What would you know about that?"

"People talk. Someone mentioned it."

"Well, it's no one's business," she said as she huffed. Nosy gossips. Was she not allowed one minute of privacy?

"Are you... seeing someone?" he asked.

"What?" she said. "No, I'm not seeing anyone. I swear, if a man needs some solitude, it's no questions asked. If I want the same, everyone assumes I'm messing around. Such a double standard."

"You mean Baylin?" he asked. "Most people understand why he— "

"Of course. Well, why the heck wouldn't the crazy girl want some privacy?"

"Relax, Taite. See? You're on edge lately."

"No, I'm not. I don't like accusations."

"It wasn't an accusation. No one would care. It's allowed."

"Why would I be concerned about that?"

"I'm saying it would be OK."

She rolled her eyes and tried to tone down the sarcasm as she replied. "Thanks for your permission, but it isn't necessary. Besides, you forget I'm the resident psycho. Guys aren't scrambling for my affections. Can we get back to work now?"

"Yes, but I just want to say I consider you a friend and if you need to talk..."

She sighed. "Look, it's a nice of you, but there's nothing to talk about."

"OK. Forget I said anything. Can you hand me that box of bandages there?"

Taite exhaled. "Sure."

That was the last anyone mentioned of her not sleeping in her hammock. Cy didn't seem to be aware she slept in Baylin's closet, or he didn't want to delve into the subject.

Another week passed, and the tension built. Throughout, there was a new strained atmosphere as everyone grew uneasy, and an unspoken fear loomed. What if Baylin and Dakota had been captured or wounded? What if they didn't return at all? It wouldn't be the first time someone left on a simple task and didn't come back.

Sometimes, Taite would worry about what would happen to her if he didn't return. Then she would scold herself for being selfish and pathetic. But it wasn't the real reason she worried, so the guilt never lasted.

Though longing to walk off the stress outside, she kept her word and only ventured out in bursts for occasional sunshine. Even Cy said she looked pale and unhealthy.

Above, white clouds quilted the sky in an endless pattern. She sat with Anthony on a rare day when he tore himself away from his monitors and papers. Since he had deciphered it, he remained one of the few people who knew her whole story. He had never dared mention it. Taite wondered if he had been so engrossed in his work that he didn't concern himself with the results.

As always, he stayed quiet, seldom meeting her eye. If he was like this with everyone or just clones, Taite couldn't say. The silence was awkward though, and Taite broke it. "So, working on anything new, Anthony? Last time, your work proved... interesting."

"What's that?" he asked as he woke from a trance. "Oh, yes, I have a lot of work to do — a few encrypted transmissions we got a hold of, but that's what I do."

"That's why I brought it up," Taite said. Anthony was like most super smart guys — literal, always serious. The only lines he read between were lines of code.

"Have you heard anything about Dakota and Baylin?" she asked, showing her indifference by saying Dakota's name first.

He shook his head.

"Is that normal? Or would you expect to hear from them somehow?"

"They don't have a reliable way to communicate with us from out there. Anything we intercept is random. It's much more difficult to get a signal here on purpose."

Then Anthony launched into a long explanation of the complicated reasons communications could be difficult. Taite regretted starting the conversation, since she didn't understand a word of it.

Her mind had run off on a detour by the time Anthony drew his lecture to a close and said, "We should go inside, but would you mind if I ask you something?"

"No, go ahead."

"Just curiosity. I've never met a clone before."

"Oh, let's stop right there. I've never met a clone before either. And just because I apparently am one, doesn't mean I understand the first thing about it. A few weeks ago, I was a normal person." She paused and laughed. "OK, so that's debatable, but you know what I mean."

"You had no indication there was anything unusual about you?"

"None whatsoever, until I found myself in this mess. And so we're clear, I still feel physically normal as far as I can tell."

"Hmm, sorry for the intrusion. Like I said, it was curiosity."

"It's fine. I'm still trying to sort all this out myself." They dropped into a brief silence and her mind immediately jumped back to Baylin. "Are they usually gone this long?"

"Sorry, who?"

"Baylin and Dakota. The teams that go out."

"Oh, no, not with things like this."

"Taite, I need another bandage. He's bled through already," Cy said as he continued to apply pressure on a gushing wound.

"Here, and the needle is there on the tray," she said, tossing the bloody gauze in the trash can behind her. Blood had seeped through the new bandage already and smeared all the way to the elbow. Taite hadn't met the man, although he looked familiar. He had ripped his arm open on a sliver of twisted metal in the generator room. They were working on repairs again. Now that the solar panels were functional, it would be easier. While Cy adjusted the lamp and found the antiseptic, Taite applied pressure.

"OK, Taite. You're the master seamstress," Cy said with a smile. "Start stitching, while I find a blanket. He's starting to look like he's going into shock. I wish we had some anesthetic. That's not gonna help matters."

"Yeah, I'll try to be quick," she said, the needle already in hand. She was sorry to think it, but this was the kind of distraction she needed. Something she had to turn all her attention to. By now, Baylin and Dakota had been gone almost a month, and everyone was beyond concerned. Besides, like Cy said, she was good at this. She guessed the wound would need at least a dozen stitches.

Taite had finished number four, when the door flew open, making her flinch and almost drop the needle. In the doorway, stood a guy who didn't appear over fifteen, and that was a stretch. His face was flushed, and the doorknob still in his hand. Taite thought his name might be Aiden, and he didn't seem injured. Actually, he looked rather pleased.

Before she could wonder why, he said, "Cy, they're back. Finally.

Dakota told me to come get you. Baylin called a meeting in the mess hall. Something's going on. He seemed kinda pissed."

At his first sentence, Taite's hands were shaking, and it took all she had not to run from the room. Instead, she caught Cy's eye, raised an eyebrow and breathed slowly to steady her hand.

"Well, that's a relief," Cy said. "I was starting to worry."

Forcing herself to concentrate, she pressed the needle through the skin again. "Baylin being pissed is a relief?" she asked, recovering from the shock enough to find her sense of humor. Her patient gave a weak smile with one side of his thick mouth.

"Clever, Taite," Cy said. "You finish up. I'll go see what's going on." Watching over her shoulder, he added, "Watch those stitches. They're getting a little crooked there."

"Thanks for noticing. That's when Junior burst through the door and made me jump out of my skin."

Cy grinned his open toothy grin, one Taite hadn't seen for a while, and said, "I'm off to see what's got the peacock's feathers ruffled."

"Hey, tell me what's going on if I'm not finished in here," Taite said after him. As she listened to his footsteps fade in the hallway, she wiped the blood off the wound and dove in to her work, metaphorically. It might be the worst wound she had ever stitched, both in the experience and in the performance. Cy would have done a better job.

She tried to make light conversation with her patient to distract herself as much as him. But he was still rather woozy with shock, so he offered little help. His name was Jeremy, she got that much from him. As Taite tied off the last stitch and bandaged him up, she tried not to hurry, but her hands wanted to fly. Taite whirled around, knocking the tray to the floor with a clatter. Though she had finished with it, she scrambled to clean up the mess.

She apologized to Jeremy for the crooked scar he would have, but he said he didn't mind. It would only add to his image, especially once he enhanced the story. Finally, he was bandaged and resting. And Taite rushed out the door as fast as she could walk.

When she approached the cafeteria, or mess hall, as the others called it, the door stood open a crack. It wasn't long before the sounds of the commotion reached her ears. Taite picked out Baylin's voice among the others. She had to agree — he did sound pissed.

Standing outside the door, she still couldn't make out what they were saying. The tone of the meeting seemed worrisome, and Taite widened the door opening a little to catch the conversation without interrupting.

"Shouldn't she be here then?"

"No," Cy said. "That isn't necessary. In fact, this has worked out for the best. I'm not sure how she would take it."

Then Baylin said, "She'll have to know. You realize that."

"I spend more time with her than anyone, and I don't think it's a good idea yet," Cy said.

"That may all be true, but we have to decide what's best for everyone. Taite's been a liability since you found her," Dakota said, as someone shuffled papers on a table.

"Lanie found her if you remember," Baylin said.

In the hall, Taite gripped the door for a better position. She didn't like to be the center of the discussion, but what ticked her off was they all seemed determined to exclude her. With a scowl, she leaned closer.

Through the gap in the door, she could see Dakota, covered in grime, sitting at a table at the far end. He hadn't taken time to clean up, and she feared what the rush could be.

She had two real options: to walk away or go in. Each of these led to more choices. If she went, what would she say? If she left, would she pretend she had never been there? Somewhere, her mind was answering the questions, and she smiled as she inhaled and pulled the door open.

TWENTY-NINE

The room fell silent the moment the door flew open, but Taite played her part. Marching straight back to the kitchen, Taite didn't look at anyone, as if she was unaware of their presence at all. She fumbled in the kitchen, slamming a cabinet shut after pulling out a chipped mug. Her back had been to the room, but as she turned to fill her cup, seventy pairs of eyes stared at her. All turned in their chairs.

Just as she expected they would be.

Taite raised her eyebrows as she looked around. "Oh, the meeting! Glad I didn't miss it. Don't let me interrupt," she said with a flick of her fingers. "I'm just desperate for some coffee."

Taite scanned the room to judge how her act was going over, as she slid into a chair and propped her feet up on another. Cy was staring with a suspicious expression. Most of the others looked embarrassed for her, and it gave Taite secret satisfaction.

Baylin's expression was difficult to interpret. If he was amused at her performance or ticked that his important meeting had hit a snag, she couldn't tell and didn't care. It was a relief to see him in one piece though. Despite the sand and filth, he was a pleasant sight. Her mind began to wander down roads best avoided for the moment, and she tried to focus on more smart ass remarks. He looked irritated. So what? Let him be irritated. It served him right for making her worry and for holding a meeting so they could talk about her behind her back in unison. Let him be mad, she mentally repeated, shutting down the urge to smile when he met her gaze.

Taite found the awkward silence entertaining, but Dakota broke it. "Taite, you could have your coffee in the infirmary."

"She doesn't even drink coffee," Baylin said to Dakota.

"Good. Stuff's hard to come by."

"Oh, sorry. Am I interrupting something? Is this a private meeting with..." she paused and looked around. "Pretty much everyone except me and Jeremy. He's still recovering from the seventeen stitches I just sewed in his skin.

"And what the hell do you know about what I drink? Good to see you though," she said with a smirk, ignoring the serious mood of the gathering.

Dakota curled his lip. "It isn't a good time for your antics. We have serious matters to discuss."

As Dakota spoke, Baylin said over him, "Cy, come here."

Cy went to the front of the room, where Baylin was pacing the floor. While leaning in, Baylin whispered something to him. Taite tore away from her sarcasm and found the courage to be serious as she watched. She didn't care how many people were here. Most had never cared to understand her — just always assumed she was crazy.

Without thinking, she threw her feet to the floor and stood up as she said, "Why was I the only able-bodied person not included in this?"

"Isn't that obvious, you little— you just said that you were stitching up Jeremy," Dakota said.

Taite could always count on him to lose his temper.

"How convenient," she said, realizing this was a logical explanation. Then again, they didn't realize how long she had been listening at the door. "Here, I thought it was a members-only thing. I've never been part of the club." She planted a hand on one hip. Then she noticed Cy walking toward her.

Baylin interrupted. "Taite, we need to make some decisions. Cy will explain things to you, but there isn't time to go over everything you've missed. I'm sorry, but you need to go."

Taite didn't know what she had expected from him, but that was not it. With a blank stare, she weighed the options.

"You're serious. Fine. Just freaking fine. You all just go ahead and decide my future. I don't give a shit anyway." She squared her jaw to match her shoulders, stood up to her full height, and turned without another word or glance.

Taite almost slammed the door in Cy's face as she left the room. She had forgotten all about him, but he caught it and walked in silence until they were well away. Then she turned back, stopping him mid-step. She said nothing, but he knew what she expected.

"Sorry about that. I'm not sure what else to say."

"You can start by filling me in, like the Big Chief in Charge said."

"I only know so much. Let's go to the infirmary. Baylin asked me to do something."

"Fine. You can talk as you walk, right?"

"Somehow, he knows you're alive and that you're here. He's preparing to move."

"Who are you talking about?"

"You can guess."

She slowed her pace. This wasn't something she anticipated. The one person behind all her misery, past present, and possibly future, knew where to find her.

Fury reared up, leaving no room for fear, and she said, "The meeting was about me, and I am not allowed in. I have no say. Is this how it works around here? Everyone else gets together to decide the clone's fate?"

"Taite, there are very few people who have any details. All they've been told is Faren's searching for you, and it jeopardizes everyone. That's all we have time to worry about now."

Cy tugged at her arm, and they started walking toward the infirmary again.

"So, why am I not in the meeting?"

"Two reasons, Taite. First, you don't have enough information to make a decision about any of it. It would only slow things down like Baylin explained." Cy took a deep breath as he continued. "Second, Baylin's asked me to do something that involves you."

"What?" she asked as they reached their destination. They walked in where Jeremy sat with his feet propped up, still covered in a blanket.

"Think, Taite." Cy shut the door and folded his arms across his chest. "If they know where you are, don't you suppose we should find out how?"

"Why do we need to be in the infirmary? They just figured it out. Aren't too many places out here."

"Baylin, doesn't think so."

"What does the great and powerful Baylin think?" she asked with an eye roll.

"Taite, they had you for quite some time. If you wanted to keep track of something or someone. What would you do?" He didn't wait for an answer from her. "You'd find a way to track it... or her."

"I hadn't thought of that," Taite said, feeling deflated and somewhat guilty. Her presence had put them all in jeopardy.

"None of us did, but they did."

"So what do we do? Where's the tracker?"

"That's what we have to find out. Sit over there while I find what I'm looking for."

"Which is?"

"Metal detector. We keep it around for removing bullets, shrapnel — that kind of thing. It should come in handy." He opened cabinet after cabinet until he said, "Got it. Been a while since I've needed it."

In his hand was a flat black wand, much like security would have waved over passengers in an airport. With a high-pitched beep, he switched it on.

He muttered to himself, "Probably in a place you wouldn't notice."

"Stand over here. We'll see what we come up with. Behind her, Cy waved the magic wand, but it remained mute from head to toe.

"Are you sure that thing works?"

As he ran it over his knee, it emitted a sharp tone. "Yep. Metal pin from when I was a kid."

"Well, let's go," Taite said, as Cy came around to face her. He scanned her sides, under her arms. Nothing. Nothing until the wand beeped over her right collarbone.

"Success, it would seem. You mind?" he asked, with a gesture to the wide strap of her tank top.

"What choice do I have?" she asked, pushing the strap down.

As he moved the wand over the bone again, it screamed over the center of her clavicle. She sighed as she strained to see if there was anything visible; but it was a useless endeavor.

Cy prodded around the edge of the bone for anything that shouldn't be there, but there was nothing. He stood back to think, and Taite sat swinging her legs in worry.

"Guess we should scan it, 'cause I can't tell where it is. It will have to come out."

"Great."

Not much bigger than Taite's tablet back home, the Portable Internal Scanning System, or as she liked to call it, the PISS, fit in the palm of Cy's hand. After a few minutes to warm up, he floated the back side containing the sensor over her shoulder, while he examined the display on the front.

A warm sensation spread along her collarbone, and Cy said to the screen. "There you are, you little rascal."

"Can you get it out?"

"Oh sure, but they were clever," he said, touching the screen to freeze the image. "See, they've inserted it deep behind your clavicle." He pointed to a thin straight line on the picture of her bones.

"Behind?"

"Yep, like I said, clever. I'm guessing they injected it back there when you were unconscious."

"But how do we get it out?"

"Ah, good question. They definitely like to make things difficult." He slid a finger on the screen to zoom in as he spoke. "I would like to use at least a local anesthetic, but as you're aware, we don't have any right now. I'm not sure what Baylin brought back yet, but we'll do the best we can."

"That doesn't sound good, Cy."

"Nope. It won't be too much fun. Hey, look on the bright side, we've got bandages and potent oral pain killer."

Taite grumbled, "Let's get it over with."

Guided by the scanner, Cy marked her collarbone. Then he readied a tray with a scalpel, bandages, tweezers, and an assortment of other supplies.

While he gathered materials before him, Cy continued chatting. Taite knew this routine, and she had forgotten about being angry by now. With her stomach full of butterflies, she wanted it over with as soon as possible. It had been a while since she had been the patient, and she didn't like it.

As he wiped the incision area with alcohol, Taite shivered at the cold sensation. Cy remarked that she shouldn't do that. While guiding her to a chair, he repeated, "Seriously, don't do that again."

Backwards in the chair, Taite was in an uncomfortable position. Her shoulders pressed forward to increase the space between the clavicle and the ribs beneath. As Cy approached with the scalpel in hand, Taite tried to not focus on it, but she couldn't help but shrink.

"Keep your chin up, Taite."

At first, she took his words as encouragement. But then he lifted her jaw, and said, "You're blocking my light."

As the sharp blade pressed into her skin, Taite suppressed a tiny squeak and bit her lip. It couldn't be much worse than removing a big splinter, right? Afterward, she would disagree.

A trickle of blood was already running down her shirt, tickling through the spreading burn. When Cy turned to the tray for his tweezers, she wanted to cry. Pain began radiating out and down, dispersing through her shoulder and chest. And he hadn't even found the thing yet. Taite gritted her teeth and winced with every move.

Jeremy, who was feeling better by now, rolled up a towel to rest between her head and shoulder. There was a lot of digging and sponging of her leaking blood. As Cy explored behind the bone, Taite was getting dizzy. The pain was continuous and unrelenting. Her whole body wanted to send Cy flying backwards into the cabinet. To allow someone to do this went against every instinct.

Sweat dripped down her forehead, the chilly room now sweltering. She wished he would find the damn thing already. She focused on breathing. If it was supposed to work for childbirth, she reasoned it would work for this. It was helping, when a new, needle-sharp pain ripped through her chest.

"Found it," Cy said, a little too cheerfully.

She wanted to swear and to tell him to speed it along, but she couldn't get the words out. Not without worrying they might turn to sobs in her mouth.

"Ah, it's got tiny barbs, Taite. You wouldn't believe this little thing. Regrettably, I'll have to cut around it."

Minutes later, Cy was still fumbling to get a grip on the implant, and breathing wasn't helping anymore. She squeezed her eyes shut, and she didn't care to open them. Not even when the door opened.

But she recognized Baylin's voice when he said, "What the hell, Cy?"

Cy must not have looked up because the stabbing pain continued as he said, "You were right, Baylin. It's in here, but the bastards put it behind the bone. It's proving quite stubborn. You need something?"

There was a pause, then Baylin said, "No, I was checking in. I thought you'd be done by no—" He broke off when Cy said, "I got it! I got it. Taite, when I pull this, it's gonna hurt like hell. Tell me when you're ready, and we'll get it over with."

A warm hand was in hers, and she squeezed until her own fingers burned as she said, "OK."

She dug into the hand she held as the implant ripped free with a distinct tearing pain and a shriek. Then there was relief. She released her grip. The fingers held on, but Taite was too distracted to notice. She breathed a sigh that came out much louder than she expected.

After cleaning the wound, Cy started to stitch it up, as Taite had done for Jeremy moments before.

"I'm sorry, Taite. I didn't realize this would be so complicated when I asked Cy to do it."

She opened her eyes to see Baylin looking down. Taite couldn't devise anything witty to say. Angry and exhausted as she was, part of her was still glad to see him alive. She said nothing and squeezed his hand instead.

Cy was asking about smashing the device as he bandaged her up.

Baylin said, "Hang on to it for now. It might come in handy."

Taite unfolded herself from the chair. She was rather sore as she leaned back, feeling like she'd taken a beating. Her fingers moved to explore the bandage on her chest and replace her shirt and bra strap.

"Not how I planned to spend the day," she said, her voice dry and artificial in her throat. "But not as bad as having my organs removed I suppose." No one laughed at the halfhearted attempt at humor.

Cy said, "I think it's fair to say you get the rest of the day off."

"Otherwise I'll kill you. Where's that pain killer you promised?"

"I'm one step ahead." He smiled and handed Taite two glossy capsules and a small bottle of water.

"What now?" she asked after downing the pills.

"Go rest. Those pills will make you drowsy."

Taite glanced at Baylin, who was leaning against a cabinet. "That isn't what I meant," she said.

"One thing at a time," Baylin said. "Cy's right. Go rest."

It was then she remembered she was angry with him, so she said, "I've had enough of being told what to do for one day. Thank you."

"What do you want to do? Go for a hike?"

"Actually, I would like another drink and to go lie down for a bit."

Baylin smirked. "All right then. Come on, I'll pour you that coffee."

"You were right about that. I don't drink it," she said as she got to her feet.

"I know."

As she stood, she caught her reflection in the cabinet's glass doors, and stared. Her gray shirt was streaked with blood, stripes and splatters, smears and blobs.

"You're a mess. You should stop and change first," he said with a raised eyebrow and an attempt to hide a smile.

"Yeah, I should have a clean shirt." As the words left her mouth, she realized that her clean shirt was still in Baylin's room. Crap. How was she going to explain that? She had meant to move her stuff before crashing the meeting but had completely forgotten.

"I wanted to apologize for the way the meeting went. No one intended to exclude you, but you weren't there at the beginning. Things got complicated," Baylin said, interrupting her thoughts as they continued down the hall.

"It was kind of crappy."

He stopped walking, turned to her, and said "I'm trying to save your life, and everyone else too. It isn't always easy."

"When you put it like that I don't have a choice except to forgive you and get over it, huh?"

"Exactly. I assume you value your life and actually do give a shit." By the tone of his voice, she thought he meant to be lighthearted, but for Taite the words fell heavy. Her face must have shown it.

"What?" he asked, sounding surprised.

"Made me think of something." Taite started walking again.

"Yes?"

"What does all this make me? A person or something else? Maybe that's the pain killer talking," she said, noticing that they neared the women's dorm where she would not find her shirt.

But then the door of the dormitory swung open.

For a split second, Taite stared in disbelief at the familiar face on the other side of the door. Her auburn hair was a little longer, rougher now, but she was still August. Taite would have recognized her anywhere.

"What?" Baylin asked again. "You want me to introduce you?"

Taite glanced around. A few people were making their way down the hall as she said, "No need."

August wasn't looking at Taite, she was talking to someone inside the room. Taite stomped toward her, digging her heels in against the floor and pulling herself up as much the ache allowed. Her jaw was so tight she thought her teeth might crack.

"August," she said in a pleasant tone as she drew closer.

August whirled around. Her expression was confused. Then the confusion turned to amazement, and she smiled a fake, friendly smile.

Taite smiled back. "You seem surprised to see me, August. I can understand that considering you left Xander and I behind. Did you assume we were both dead by now?"

August scowled. "What do you want? You and Xander want an apology?"

The question sent Taite seething, and she said, "Xander is dead because of you, and you aren't even sorry."

"Taite, you're crazy. You were always crazy. Leave me alone."

"You're absolutely right." Drawing back, Taite landed a solid left hook across August's freckled face. August stumbled back into the door which gave way, since she'd been holding it open.

Her expression was priceless and worth the shooting pain ripping through Taite's chest. August's lip was bleeding, and her eyes were huge on her thin face.

"That was for Xander, you heartless bitch," Taite said as August stared up from the floor. Then Taite sighed and grinned. "So glad you're here, August. We should squeeze in some girl talk sometime."

August only gawked and touched her lip.

Taite spun around, Baylin's face a short distance a way. He didn't look happy. Oh well. With an inhale and forced cheerfulness, she said, "All right then, let's go."

"Taite! What was that about? You can't go around punching people!"

"I usually don't, and I prefer to use my other hand," she said, hearing the door slam behind her. August had slunk back under her rock. "Why is she here?" Taite asked.

"Dakota and I ran into her and a couple guys. They came back with us. How do you know her?"

As she talked, Taite started to walk back in the other direction. "She was at the camp. We were planning to escape. When it came down to it, she and a few others left as soon as they could. She drove off in the watcher's truck. The guards were all dead. Xander had been shot. It wouldn't have cost her anything to help, but she left. You couldn't have known about it."

"You're right. I had no idea. I doubt she would have come if she

248

realized you were here, not with the welcome you just gave her." He smiled and said, "I should consider myself lucky, huh?"

A guilty grin spread across her face. "Probably."

"Hey, don't you still need a clean shirt?"

Taite stopped dead in the hall and said, "I have a confession."

"Another one?" Baylin asked. "You're full of surprises today. I hope it's something equally shocking as the last show."

Taite blew a strand of hair from her eyes and felt the warmth of blood in her cheeks. She was still a little dizzy. From the pain killer, exertion or embarrassment, she wasn't sure. She looked up at him and said, "My clean shirt isn't back there."

"Oh?" A flicker of a smile flashed across his eyes.

"I've never liked sleeping in the dorm. Maybe it's the hammock," she said, wanting to get this over with quickly, much like removing a band aid or an implanted GPS device. "Your storage closet was empty. So, you see where I'm going with this?"

"Not really. You should explain it."

Taite huffed and asked, "You're enjoying this, aren't you? Fine. So I stayed in the storage closet. Your storage closet. Big freaking deal. My shirt's back there."

"Huh." He smiled. "You're the one making a big deal of it, Taite. So you slept in my room. Nothing to get worked up about."

"The storage closet. It isn't your room."

"If you say so, Taite, but I already knew that anyway," he said with a sidelong glace and mischief in his eyes.

"Who told you? I swear no one can keep their mouths shut around here."

"No one told me. The meeting wrapped up, and I went to clean up. You didn't notice I'm no longer covered in dirt?"

Oh. Why hadn't she noticed that? Well, she had other things going on at the time.

"Your things were in there," he said, still grinning like a Cheshire cat. He must have thought he was so clever.

"Odd that you have time to play tricks with everything going on."

"Relax, Taite," he said as he walked. "Anyway, I should lecture you about punching people, but yes, there's a lot happening. I'll tell you after you rest. Go on in and get cleaned up," he said as he reached for the door.

"Can't you tell me now. I'm not going to able to relax. How could I relax? Obviously, Cy told me why he had to do this." She gestured to her collar. "I won't be able to sleep." She covered up a yawn.

Baylin smiled. "Not that I believe that for one minute, but I'll summarize."

He pushed through the door, holding it for her to duck under his arm. He flipped on the light and slowly lowered himself to the couch with a grunt.

Taite sighed. "What did you do to your knee?"

"Hm?" he asked, looking up at her. "What do you mean?"

"I didn't notice before, but it looks like you've hurt your knee. You sat down like someone in their nineties."

"See? I told you back in the cave, I was too old for you."

At the reference, she smiled and thought a moment. "No, Baylin. When you figure in space travel, I am older than you by a lot."

"Oh, you're right. An older woman. Hmm..." Baylin said with a slow smile.

"Anyway, the knee?"

"It's nothing. Slammed it into a rock a few days ago. It's fine."

"Sure it is," she said. "Let me see it. I am a somewhat official medic."

"Taite, I'll have Cy take a look later. OK?"

"Oh, Cy can look at it? Stop being a baby and let me see your knee."

"You trying to get my pants off?" he asked with a lazy laugh.

"You can roll up your pant leg, idiot."

"Fine, but you need to work on your bedside manner."

"I'll keep that in mind. Now, do what you're told."

"Yes, ma'am," he said, rolling up the leg of his khaki cargo pants. Baylin's tall black boots were worn and dusty, though it looked like he had attempted to clean them off. His knee, he had completely neglected. A black bruise covered the side, along with a caked bloody smear where he had scraped it open again.

"Did you even bother to clean this out, Baylin?" Taite asked, as she shook her head and yawned.

"I forgot. You're tired. I'll deal with it later."

"How could you forget? You can barely bend your leg to sit. I swear." She rolled her eyes and pushed her hair from her forehead. "We'll deal with it now. At least wash it off. You'll get an infection. In the meantime, tell me what's going on."

"You win again," he said, watching her head over to the sink in the corner. She lathered the soap and grabbed a towel from the shelf.

"Sit still and start talking," she said, crouching by his extended leg.

"Look at yourself, Taite," he said. "Blood caked on your shirt and you're scrubbing off my banged knee. Give it here and go change."

"Not with you in here, so I might as well clean your knee while you talk. Stop changing the subject and get to it. This won't take long."

"All right. Cy told you about the tracking implant. Did he tell you that removing it now was a little too late?"

Nodding, she picked a bit of rock out of his knee.

"So, yeah, they know you're here, and they know exactly where here

251

is. The R.A. built the place. They seem to be waiting for something. I'm not sure what, but it's only a matter of time before we have visitors."

As she scrubbed his knee and his leg muscles tightened, and he winced. Taite frowned. "So what do we do now?" she asked, looking up to meet his eyes.

"We leave, but at least they won't be able to track us now."

"Everyone? They only want me right?"

"Yes and no. They want you, but they wouldn't mind having any of us. We aren't exactly on good terms."

"I guess not," Taite said as she gave his knee one last wipe with a damp edge of the towel. "You should put some antiseptic on that."

"Yeah, I will," he said, rolling down the leg of his pants.

"A cold pack might not be a bad idea either." She sat on the couch next to him, knowing he wouldn't give his knee another thought.

"Where do we go now?"

"That's what we were trying to decided earlier. Of course, Dakota always makes things more difficult with that mouth." He rested his head against the wall behind and closed his eyes.

"Did you decide anything for sure?" she asked through another yawn. The pain killer was taking hold. She could no longer feel most of her shoulder at all, and her eyelids were growing heavy.

"I think so." The corner of his mouth turned up. He had to realize how frustrating his cryptic answers were. He peeked out and shut his eyes again.

"Looks like I'm not the only one who needs a nap," Taite said, willing herself to her feet. The drowsy haze was threatening to overtake her. "I'll go. I'm sure you need your rest as much as I do."

Baylin's eyes fluttered open. "Don't be stupid, Taite. It's a big couch, and you're too exhausted to take advantage of me. You can stay."

Too tired to appreciate his sense of humor, Taite stood trying to make a decision as Baylin continued. "Please go put on a clean shirt though. I don't want to see any more blood today. I won't look. My eyes are closed as it is."

"Oh, fine," she mumbled, as she made her way to the table where her shirt and pack sat. With her back turned, she struggled to swoop one shirt off and the other on with as little pain as possible. If he peeked at her bra, she was too tired to notice or care. She tossed the wadded, bloody shirt to the floor and stumbled back to collapse on the couch.

Baylin hadn't moved. He was still leaning back in the cushions, legs stretched out on the floor. "Don't bump my knee please."

"If you watch out for my shoulder."

He laughed. "We're both in our nineties."

Pulling off her boots, Taite lowered down and curled up on her left side, careful to avoid hitting Baylin's knee. Taite slept a sweet, black sleep, and if she dreamed, she didn't remember.

As she came around later, she was first aware of something rather heavy lying across her waist. Her eyes flew open to see it was Baylin's arm. At some point, he had stretched out behind her. His warm breath stirred the hair on the back of her neck. By his breathing, he was still asleep, though she couldn't see him. His arm pinned her down and her collarbone was far too sore to do anything about it.

By the stiffness in her joints, it seemed she had slept for hours. She lay awake, wishing to change positions, when she remembered what Baylin had said. They were still looking for her. They had found her. Jolting upright in a moment of panic, her pulse raced. Shouldn't they be doing something? Shouldn't they be getting out of here? They couldn't sit around and wait.

"What is it?" Baylin said as he rubbed a hand over his eyes.

"How long have we been here? You said we had to leave."

He fumbled around in a pocket, pulling out an old brass pocket watch before he said, "It's late. Relax. Nothing happens until morning. Dakota won't leave without us. Not without me at least." A slight smile played across his lips. "Anyway, everybody's asleep by now. Speaking of which..."

"Sorry, I woke up and freaked out."

"You can stop freaking out and go back to sleep. Come tomorrow you'll wish you'd had more rest. Gonna be a busy day." He tugged her back down to the couch.

"Yeah," Taite said, as she lay on her back to relieve the pulling pain in her collar. Taite settled and tried to slow her pounding heart.

Moments later, Baylin cleared his throat. In the dim light, she forced her heavy eyelids open. She assumed he was back to sleep already but found him staring instead. His face above her head, Taite raised an eyebrow in a silent question.

Baylin said nothing but brought his hand around to trace the line of her exposed, tattooed collarbone. Her skin prickled, and a warm flush washed over her face. She reached for his hand, planning to push it away. But his fingers curled around hers.

She craned her head to see his face. Something about the way he was looking at her, through half-dazed eyes, gray with exhaustion, was a little alarming. As he leaned closer, the invulnerable mask he wore seemed to drop from his eyes.

But in an instant, her collarbone seemed to burst into flames and she let out a squeak.

"Are you ok?" Baylin asked as he pulled away into the back of the cushions.

With a groan, she said, "I think I popped a stitch."

"Sorry. You can kick me in the knee if it helps," he said, pink blotches splattered across his cheekbones.

"I'll pass."

She peered under the bandage to see a slow trickle of red. "It'll be all right until morning. I don't want to wake up Cy." As she settled back, Baylin wrapped an arm around her, careful to avoid her bandaged shoulder.

"Well, goodnight again." His voice hoarse with weariness. Closing her eyes, she leaned into his chest, and the hours slipped away.

THIRTY

When Taite woke, Baylin had already gone. As much as she had expected it, she was still disappointed. No doubt he had risen hours before with some internal alarm clock and was already knee deep in his day. She stretched away the sleep hanging on her bones and rose to her feet. The dull ache in her chest reminded her of the first stop she needed to make. A small spot of blood had soaked through the bandage. As she pulled on her boots, she considered if Cy would be in the infirmary already.

Although occasional footsteps sounded through the hall, things felt too quiet. It was the calm before the storm, and Taite was afraid. With a shake of her head, she pushed the fear away as she waited for the footfalls to pass and slipped out the door.

Further toward the infirmary, the mood had shifted. A hurried, expeditious speed had replaced the casual pace which they had kept recently, as if everyone was jolted alert in unison. Everyone but her.

On the way to see Cy, she stopped by the dining hall. She was hoping Baylin might still be there. He wasn't. August was sitting at a table though, holding ice to her lip. Taite gave her a enthusiastic wave as she stepped through the door. After snagging a granola bar and a water bottle from the boxes of half-packed supplies, she hurried on her way.

In the infirmary, Cy was stuffing medicine into plastic totes and crates. Without so much as a glance and without bothering to disguise his irritation, he said "It's about time you got here. I've been expecting you all morning."

"What time is it?" Taite asked, tearing into her breakfast.

"It's 10:30 already. Time's wasting away, Taite. We have a lot to do."

"Sorry. I was knocked out."

"Well, you need to wake up and help me. I realize you can't lift." He looked over at her for the first time since she had walked in. "You've bled through a bit there."

"I have?" she asked.

"Let me have a quick look," he said, walking over and pulling at the bandage. "It's fine. You just aggravated it. Try to be more careful. I shouldn't have to tell you."

"I told you, I was sleeping like the dead."

"OK, let's just get to work."

For the remaining hours of the morning, Taite arranged supplies so they would fit in the boxes and be easy to access, but her mind was elsewhere. She worked fast though, eager to leave the base as much as the next person. More even, considering it was her life most at risk.

Weaving between various people rushing here and there, Cy and Taite made their way to the mess hall hours later. Boxes and carts were carried, pushed and pulled through the building.

Just ahead, as he walked backwards down the hall, Dakota was shouting directions. As he turned around, he slammed into Taite.

"Hey, watch it!" she said, holding her arm up protectively.

"Stay out of my way." He stormed down the hall without another word.

Cy ignored the incident, and Taite squelched the urge to knee Dakota in the groin.

She turned to Cy and asked, "How are we going to take all this stuff? We can't carry everything."

"Trucks, Taite."

"Well, yeah, but where are they? We're underground in case you didn't know."

They sat together at a table near the wall, and he said, "We've got trucks."

"That was helpful. Thanks."

"We need to take supplies over anyway. You'll see after lunch."

"Fair enough," Taite said and let the subject drop. She scanned the room full of people in silence, recognizing some by name, but she could remember each one of their wounds she had treated. Others she didn't know at all. They must have been more cautious when they worked.

After returning from lunch, Cy led the way down the hall and reached for a door Taite had never been through. She remembered she had tried it once. Since she found it locked, she hadn't given it a second thought. Cy swung the door open and marched off down another long hall, pushing a cart full of medical supplies.

Taite hadn't been aware this section existed. Two doors stood on each side of the hall and seemed to lead to the main storage areas. Crates spilled out now, and Taite was curious how they had accumulated so much stuff. She asked out loud.

Cy smiled and answered, "Various ways. Some bought, traded, some gained by more forceful means."

"Yeah, the stolen goods again."

"Appropriated," he said. "Besides, we can help our cause while hurting theirs. It's a win-win. You should be glad, otherwise, you wouldn't have those bandages."

"I guess," Taite said, as she stumbled into a cart someone steered from the next room. "Sorry," she said to the small brunette as she continued after Cy.

At the end of the hall, a set of double doors stood waiting — thick steel with heavy locking bolts. The bolts were open, and Cy pushed the massive doors with one hand. With a loud squeal, they opened to release a flood of sunshine that filled the dim hallway. A wave of warm air hit Taite in the face. Everything inside the room was black shadows and silhouettes against the bright backdrop.

As she squinted, she tried to make sense of what she saw. The room opened up to both sides, full of rows of silhouetted forms that she took to be the trucks. Several sat on rolling tracks like the trucks she remembered from the camp. There were two rows of about ten each. Some were covered with canvas, others were taller, box-shaped with hard sides. At the far end, sunlight was pouring in through a huge door at the bottom of a long ramp. Rolled to the side on giant casters, it must have been thirty feet wide.

Shadowed figures moved here and there; lifting boxes, shoving crates, shouting to each other. The ceiling soared above her head, and Taite was astonished she hadn't known about it before. How could this all be underground? Where did this place come from?

Cy started an explanation before she even asked. "The doors open out onto a hillside. It isn't all sand out there, but there's a layer that conceals everything pretty well. The storm always comes from the opposite direction — blows the sand out of the way, instead of completely burying the gate. Until now, you've only used the hatch on the opposite side. The R.A. built the whole thing, and abandoned it before it was complete. Wasteful spending as usual. Until now, either they hadn't figured out we were here, or they hadn't cared."

Cy had enough talk and said, "Let's get going. There's more work waiting in the infirmary."

"Where do we take this stuff?" she asked, though Cy was already guiding the cart over to a boxy truck near the door.

"Baylin said he wants it here at number five. See the truck is marked there. They'll load it. We bring everything up."

"OK, so, truck five," she said.

"Well, trucks five and six beside it there. We always split up the essential supplies when we can."

Simple enough. She followed Cy back out the door, missing the slim figure stepping down from the back of a truck as they passed.

"How's it going?" Cy asked as they walked. Taite looked around and saw Baylin fall in step beside Cy for a moment.

"Not bad, but I'd like to speed things up a little." Without another word, he turned and headed down the row of trucks to the right. Taite followed him with her eyes, making a mental note of the way he favored his leg.

They spent the rest of the day making trips back and forth. Sometimes, Taite walked with Cy to help steer the end of a heavy cart. Other times, she pushed her own. She couldn't do much without her stitches threatening to open and her chest burning. Through the day, she saw Baylin only one other time, almost running into him as he hurried from a storage room.

"Sorry," she said before asking about his knee.

His mind seemed to be in a thousand other places, as he asked, "My knee? It's fine. Just a little sore."

She stared after him as he looked back over his shoulder, hesitated, then rushed toward the gate.

Taite refocused on the empty cart she pushed. They had cleared the medical supplies out and now were moving the remains of the food supply. The speed at which everything was cleared out was impressive. When they needed to be, they could be really efficient.

By evening, the constant hustle had worn Taite thin. As she walked back to Baylin's room, it seemed a little presumptive to make herself comfortable there when he was still working on the trucks. But it didn't feel right to grab her stuff and disappear either. She sat at the small table tapping her foot.

On the floor by the shelf, a box sat partially packed with supplies. It was the perfect excuse. She jumped up to finish packing it and then folded the top closed. Leaving it behind, she went back down to find Baylin.

She found him sitting on the gate of a truck, chugging down a bottle of water. Red in the face and sweat plastering his hair to his temples, he wiped his mouth with the back of his hand.

"Hey," she said, trying to sound normal. "I'm sure you're busy, but I had a quick question."

"Fire away," he said, dangling one leg off the back of the truck.

"I went to get my stuff and noticed a box there. I finished packing it. Should I bring it down now or wait?"

"Just leave that for now. Did you say you were getting your stuff?" He looked a little confused. "You aren't putting that on the truck yet, are you?"

She shifted her weight and looked at the floor of the truck. "No, but I didn't really know where to go."

"Just sleep on the couch, Taite. You leave in the morning anyway. I imagine I'll be here a while yet."

Taite exhaled with a small smile. Then she scowled. "What do you mean, I leave? Isn't everyone leaving in the morning?"

As he raked a hand through his hair, he asked, "Didn't Cy tell you?"

"Cy told me to be ready by morning. I assumed everyone was leaving."

"That was the plan at first, but we aren't going to be finished. Still have the electronics to load and a lot to sort through. Besides, it's safer if we travel in two groups, ya know?"

"So, who leaves in the morning then?" Taite was growing agitated.

"You. Cy will stay, since we don't want all the medics in one place. Dakota will be in charge of the first group, so he's going. Sorry about that. We've divided in half."

"Why can't we all wait and leave together?"

"It's safer this way and easier for smaller groups to travel."

Taite moaned. "Does it have to be Dakota? He can't stand me, and the feeling is mutual."

"Sorry, but I have to stay here. Too much to do."

"I'll stay and help then."

Baylin gave her an exasperated look. "You know why you're going. Don't make me explain it to you."

She sighed. "Yeah, I guess."

Taite was about to hop up beside him when Jeremy walked over, asking Baylin to have a look at one of the trucks.

Baylin said, "See ya, Taite," and followed Jeremy down the aisle.

Taite stalked off to the main building.

After flipping the light on, she yanked off her boots and sweaty socks. The concrete floor was refreshing on her tired feet as she cleaned up and collapsed onto the couch. She tried to empty her mind and relax, but she kept thinking she didn't want to go without

Baylin. It wouldn't be good if he didn't leave in time.

As she positioned herself as to not be a complete couch hog, the night before came to mind. Was it her imagination or had Baylin been about to kiss her? She wasn't sure, but she smiled to herself as she drifted off.

Hours later, Taite jumped awake. The couch was empty beside her, and she sat up in the dark before it occurred to her that the bulb had burned out. She needed some air, and she couldn't quite get her bearings.

Taite stumbled toward the door, but after a few wobbly steps her foot caught against something, she plummeted to the floor, only just getting her hands up in time. Her collarbone was on fire, and she was dizzy. With a groan, she rolled off her face and away from her stitches.

"Taite," a voice said in the blackness. "What are you doing? Are you OK?"

"Baylin?" she asked. "What am I doing? I thought I would do some sit-ups. What do you think I'm doing? I tripped on you. Why are you on the floor? Why is the light out?"

"I was sleeping. When I got here, you were pretty well stretched out on the couch. And I rarely keep the lights on. Sorry."

"Right," she said, sitting up and rubbing her sore wrist.

"Were you going somewhere?"

"I'm not sure. I woke up confused, I guess."

"Still confused?"

"No."

"Sit down and stay a while," he said, his voice hoarse from shouting over the noise in the truck garage. "But no funny business, Taite. I'm dead tired." Even in the dark room his voice held a hint of a smile, but she could tell he didn't have the energy for a real one.

"I'm already sitting," she said, ignoring the other comment. "We should all leave together. I don't like this."

He sighed. "We aren't going through this again, Taite."

"Well, I don't like it, but I'll go if that's what you want."

"This isn't about what I want. It's the way it needs to be."

"Well, it sucks. You haven't even kept your promise. I kept my promise, you know."

"I'll tell you whatever you want when we get there. Now please let me sleep."

Taite inhaled. She wanted to ask what would happen if he didn't leave soon enough, but she bit her lip and instead asked, "On the floor?"

"What?"

"You're gonna sleep on the floor?"

"To be honest, it's killing my back, so if you don't mind, I vote we share the couch."

"Then get up and try not to step on me," Taite said, pushing her worries back. She would deal with them one at a time.

Baylin's head was resting on Taite's shoulder as she listened to his breath slip into the steady pattern of sleep. She was jealous, sleep escaped her. In the quiet, the anxiety of the next day crept up from all corners of her mind.

+++

"Taite," Baylin said from across the room where he sat tightening the laces of his boots.

She peeked out and closed her eyelids again. "A few more minutes," she mumbled, throwing an arm over her face.

"Afraid not."

She cracked her eyes open again, watching him stuff something in his backpack. She moaned in defiance.

"Come on. Get moving," he said in his all-business voice.

"I don't wanna go," she said as she scowled and willed herself upright, hair falling in her eyes.

"Not my first choice either, but it's the way it has to be."

She threw her bare feet to the floor but sank back into the cushion. Baylin walked over, looking way more rested than he should in her opinion. As he took her hand, he pulled her to her feet, drawing her towards him.

"Taite, everything will be fine," he said as he looked down at her with eyes that seemed to read her mind.

If he was trying to wake her up, it was working. With an exhale, and another, she lifted her head. "Fine. I'm awake, but I'm not happy about it."

Baylin took a step back, his hands on her shoulders. He curved his mouth into a reassuring smile, but clouds of doubt shadowed his gray-green eyes. "You've only got a few minutes to get ready. I'll wait in the hall."

Baylin was leaning against the wall when she stepped out, feeling fresher but not happier. She glowered, but then Baylin flashed a mischievous smile. "Thought I might have to come in after you."

Though she didn't intend to at all, she grinned back. Her traitorous mouth had a mind of its own. After following the halls together, they came to the garage where several people loitered around. Others already sat in the backs of a few trucks.

Baylin walked over to talk to a driver for a few minutes. Marching back, he said, "About five more minutes till they're ready to go... if everyone's on time."

"Great," Taite said, as she adjusted the bag on her good shoulder.

Baylin squeezed her arm and led her over to a truck.

"You will be careful, right?" Taite asked him, as he held out a hand to help boost her up.

"I'm always careful."

Taite sat on the edge of the seat and shoved her pack underneath. As she glanced up, something caught her attention on the seat in front of her. The paint was etched with a familiar drawing of a bullet. Up close it looked like a distorted letter 'D' with smoke trailing behind. While running a finger over it, a sad smile pulled at the corners of her lips.

"That's so weird," she said, turning to Baylin as he watched. "This is the same truck from the camp. Xander drew this. That's crazy."

"Not so much," he said. "I told you we stopped at the camp. We took the truck. That's Duratio's... signature."

Taite laughed. "Figures he would draw that of all things. He was obsessed. So you were really there? I guess I hadn't believed you."

With a raised eyebrow, he said, "I'm offended. Feel better now that you're on familiar territory?"

"A little," she said, looking down at him, as the boy named Aiden jumped up. A line was forming, and Baylin stepped out of the way. He had plenty of work to do and should probably be off shouting orders at someone already.

The engine turned over with a growl, and her eyes darted to Baylin's. He looked grim. Taite wished he would smile again, but he didn't. She thought of the last time she saw her pseudo-father and bit her lip.

As it pulled out into the sand and sun, the convoy seemed like a funeral procession to Taite. The huge doors, the whole life she had known for the past months, and even Baylin grew smaller until they disappeared against the sand and glare.

Ten vehicles rumbled across the desert together. Heat rose off the sand, and a dry wind blew through the trucks. They traveled for hours; the sun creeping through the sky. About four hours in, the driver of the lead truck slowed to a stop, creating a domino effect as they all braked in a single file line. The driver stepped down, and to Taite's disappointment, it was Dakota. Was it necessary that he be on the same truck? Apparently so. He swaggered to the back, standing by the flapping canvas.

"Break time. If you want to stretch your legs, now's the time people." Taite swung her legs over the rear end of the truck and hopped down in the sand.

As soon her feet hit the ground, Dakota grabbed her arm, "Now, sweetheart," he said through a sneer. "You stay close."

"Where do you think I would I go?" she asked as she glared at him. Sometimes, Taite thought it was rather unlucky that looks couldn't kill.

He stepped back to let the others down, returning her icy stare. "Do what you're told."

With the base far behind, the wide openness of the desert was both exhilarating and terrifying. The last time she had been out in unsheltered sands, it had almost killed her. She was in no hurry to repeat the experience, so unfortunately, she agreed with Dakota and stayed close to the trucks.

Taite had met most of the people in the group, but she didn't know them well. Added to the mix was the fact everyone realized it was her fault they had to leave the comfortable conditions of the base. She was having a splendid time.

From what she understood, they would journey all day and then again the next day and the next. Possibly until sundown. And that assumed they didn't have problems. She wasn't even sure where they were going. Regardless, they were soon rolling again, and Taite's eyes drooped from the lack of sleep the night before. When the truck came to a sudden stop, she was fighting to stay awake.

Dakota jumped out and shouted to the driver of the truck behind. In an instant, Taite was alert and alarmed. The other driver ran over to Dakota, who she could see through the windshield up front. They looked straight ahead, Dakota pointing toward the horizon. Maybe they were lost. She strained to hear anything that might tell her what was happening.

"Shit," Dakota said. "Shit. Shit. Shit."

Classy. Taite rolled her eyes to the ceiling then leaned forward for a better look. On the horizon, blurry in the radiating heat of the sand, was a black speck. As her eyes adjusted, the speck became a small rectangle. A truck, and it was the wrong direction to be Baylin.

"Shit," she muttered under her breath, earning a glance from a girl sitting across from her. Taite's heart threatened to leap out of her chest, and her hands shook. She jiggled her legs, she couldn't just sit there. The next second her feet were slipping on the sand, running around the truck to Dakota and the other driver.

"Get back in the truck," Dakota said as soon as she came within five feet.

"Tell me what's going on. Who are they?" she asked.

"I don't have patience for this. Get in the damn truck!" he shouted.

"No. This concerns me more than you."

"Well, who do you think they are? You got a plan? Every second we waste, they get closer."

"No, I don't have a plan, but I know what will happen to me if they find me. You, they might put in prison or something."

"They throw you back into a camp. So what?"

"Baylin really didn't tell you?" she asked in disbelief. "They're gonna kill me."

"What do I care?" he said, staring her in the face, "They killed Lanie. Why would I care if they kill you?"

"What does Lanie have to do with this?"

"Baylin isn't too big on sharing information is he? The only reason I'm not turning you over to them is because of Baylin, period. I'm not risking anyone else to save your ass."

"Fine," she said. "I wouldn't expect you to, but they're coming. What do we do?"

"We can't go back. They'd follow us right back to the base and Baylin. They would be thrilled to wrap their hands around his throat."

"And we can't outrun them. Besides, we don't have enough fuel to waste running miles out of the way," the other driver said.

"There's only one thing to do, isn't there?"

THIRTY-ONE

In the last truck of their convoy, Taite sat wedged behind a crate as they rumbled along. With nothing more than a smile and a wave, they would attempt to pass by the other truck. Everyone realized that wouldn't be the case.

That's why Dakota had moved her to another truck and shoved a small pistol in her hand. He didn't bother asking if she knew how to use it. Everyone else was all geared up, ready to go charging out with guns waving if needed. Sit and be quiet, they had told Taite. Had they all traveled together like she wanted, this might not be such a problem. This whole evacuation had been a terrible idea. All of it.

She thought over the coincidence of Faren's men traipsing across the desert and stumbling into them. It seemed a little odd to her, and she wondered if they could still track her.

How the others felt, she didn't know, but Taite was shaking with anticipation and terror. She tried to visualize how it might play out, but all that would depend on how many trucks followed their first. And how many people sat in those trucks. The waiting was horrible. It reminded her of Cy digging for the implant. The stitches were still sore.

Over the roar of engines, she couldn't hear anything, and she couldn't see much either. All that remained was the growing anxiety within her chest. Time moved at a snail's pace. She hoped the oncoming truck would rattle past without incident, but that wouldn't happen.

When the shouting started, Taite wasn't surprised.

Then the truck rolled to a stop beneath her. The engines were all cut off, and she caught hints of muffled voices in the air. Voices full of questions: Who were they? Where were they going? Dakota answered in a low and restrained tone. Taite prayed it didn't end in shooting.

The conversation grew louder, and as she pieced the sentences together, it only confirmed her fears.

"We know the girl is here," a man said. "And we are willing to let you pass and turn a blind eye to your presence if you turn her over." The statement was a command and a threat all wrapped up into one little package.

"I'm charged with bringing her back alive at any cost to the rest of you," said the voice.

Taite strained to make out words, strained to breathe. She had no idea how many men they had, but even a few might do a lot of damage with the right weapons.

Dakota said to the man, "We got a few girls, but I don't know what you want with any of 'em."

"Don't play stupid," the man said. "The clone. We want the clone."

"Hey, I don't know anything about any clone."

"Then we'll have to search your trucks."

"Be my guest."

After a few minutes, more voices shouted, "She's not here."

"Yes, she is. Keep looking."

Taite held her breath. They were getting impatient.

She couldn't sit and wait to be discovered or worse.

"I can always start shooting your little troop one by one."

Dakota said, "If you kill us all, she still wouldn't be here, and then you have no one to question."

"I said shoot. I didn't say kill. You need to learn to pay attention, boy."

Dakota must be buying time, weighing the options, and wrestling with the decision. A decision that he and everyone else could live with. As much as she disliked him, perhaps he had his reasons for being a jerk. She couldn't put herself above at least thirty other people.

Before she talked herself out if it, she was walking alongside the trucks. The sand was gleaming in the sun, but Taite imagined snow. She remembered watching the snowflakes flutter down and settle on the bus window, lost among the miniature drifts. Maybe she wasn't one of a kind, but disappearing into the crowd would be a luxury for her now.

"There you are," the man said as she appeared, shaking, from the shadow of the truck. He was tall and abrasive, as intimidating as his voice. The brim of his blue cap sat low over his eyes, and his wide jaw was set firm.

Dakota's eyes widened, but for once he stayed quiet. Five other men pointed rifles in her direction, and she saw more men in their truck. Three more trucks idled behind that one.

"That is amazing," the man in charge said. "You are the spittin' image. Who would've thought it possible?"

Taite stayed silent, but inside she was reeling.

Dakota asked her on a hiss of air, "What are you doing?"

"I'm saving your stupid ass," she said under her breath before turning to face the man in the hat.

"You can let them go."

"Sure, sure," he said. "Eventually."

He nodded his head at the soldier to his right. A squeeze of a trigger, a single earsplitting shot. Dakota dropped to the ground, red pouring from his upper arm. A shriek escaped Taite's mouth.

"I won't tolerate a liar."

Taite grabbed the pistol from her belt behind her and shoved it against her temple.

"I'll shoot myself if you hurt anyone else."

"Let's not be dramatic, miss," he said. "You won't do that."

"Really?" she asked. "They'll kill me anyway. At least this way, I have a little control. This way she dies too."

At his blank stare, she said, "You know who I am. and if I die out here, it'll be your heart on a skewer instead of mine." The barrel of the gun pressed into her head, her hand shaking.

"You can't do it," he said, jeering from his position in the sand.

"Seems you haven't been doing your research lately," Taite said.

He hesitated a moment, then gestured to the shooter to lower his gun. "Fine, Aisea," he said. "We'll play it your way for now."

"Stop the bleeding," she said, not making a move.

"Don't you think you're pushing your luck, Aisea?"

"No, but you might be pushing yours."

"Oh, hell," he said with a sigh. "Anderson, see what you can do. Clean up your mess." He gestured to the man who had fired.

Taite stepped over, standing several feet behind Dakota's head to supervise. As Anderson applied pressure, she said, "Put him in a truck. After they leave, when they're out of sight, I'll put the gun down and go with you."

"Do you understand how long it'll take before they're out of sight?"

"Do you need to be somewhere?"

273

He shook his head. "If you were anyone else, you'd be dead where you stand."

Taite stood firm, a sudden rush of adrenaline in her veins. Except for the inevitable conclusion awaiting her, she kinda liked it. She stayed well away from Anderson, or anyone else, aware that if they got a hold of her gun, she had nothing. It surprised her they went along with it at all. In moments, they hoisted Dakota into a truck, where August took over with his bullet wound. That was a little ironic.

As Duratio's trucks pulled away to retrace their path, Taite exhaled. Nothing prevented someone from following, but at least they had some time.

Her arm ached from holding the gun, and her mind turned to a new terror, but she was alive for now. That was something. The future wasn't written. Long moments later, the quiet was disrupted, pulling her from her thoughts.

"OK, cupcake," the man said. "They're out a sight. Time to hand over your weapon and take a seat."

It was true. The trucks had vanished in the distance. As she dropped the gun in the sand, almost immediately something crashed into her skull with a thud. In a fog, she stumbled to the ground, watching as a fine spattering of bright scarlet appeared on the pale sand. A pair of rough hands pulled her up and toward the truck. As she swayed on her feet, someone handcuffed her and pushed her into the back.

"Mission accomplished," an arrogant voice said from somewhere to her right.

"The mission will be compete when she's out of our custody. Not before."

While she started to fade out of consciousness, she caught bits of conversation. A lot of swearing, and some derogatory comments about herself, but she blacked out somewhere along the way.

+++

"When will you be ready?" a woman asked as Taite struggled to open her eyes.

A deep baritone answered, "In a few days most likely. I need to run some tests first. Anise should have regained some strength by then."

Taite's head throbbed as footsteps echoed from the room. Her eyelids fluttered open. Straps coiled around her ankles and wrists, tying her down to a hospital bed. But it was not a hospital room.

Heavy brocade drapes were pulled shut at the windows. Beneath the center window, sat a wooden bench, complete with striped cushions and a pillow. Covering the walls was shimmery, cream-colored paper. Over a stone fireplace, hung a large painting of a garden. The only thing that seemed like a hospital was the bed where she was tied. Strange. She tugged hard at her strapped arms just the same.

Much to her embarrassment, she now wore a hospital gown, and someone had bathed her. Her arms lacked the dust from the trip, and her hair fell in shiny waves over her shoulders. Xander's tags were gone, as was her wristband. They had taken everything.

For hours, she saw and heard no one. The little light that the wine-colored drapes allowed through had changed, but nothing else had. As she sat twisting her arm to loosen the strap, the wooden door opened, and a large-framed woman walked in carrying a tray. Her thick-soled shoes squeaked on the waxed wood floor.

"What is that?" Taite asked, as the nurse punctured the top of a vial with a syringe.

She ignored Taite, not even offering a glance. It brought back too many memories. Within seconds, whatever the syringe contained was flowing through her veins.

Taite didn't remember much after that, not until she was confronted with a tall man in an expensive suit. It hung in graceful folds and had a slight shimmer to it when he moved. He was nearing sixty. Standing at the foot of her bed, he looked at her, she would have said fondly, but she remembered why she was there.

An older man in a white coat crossed over from somewhere outside Taite's vision. As he placed a hand on the sleeve of the gray suit, he said, "It's best if you don't talk to her."

Taite blinked her eyes hard to clear her blurry vision. "Why the hell not?"

The man in the suit looked taken aback, as if the animals at the circus had started speaking.

Drugged and angry, she couldn't make herself shut up. "Why shouldn't he talk to me? He's here staring at me. He must want something."

While shaking his head, the suit retreated a step. "No, Dr. Linton, I don't think I should speak with her." His voice was smooth and controlled like someone who had had a lot of practice. Then he turned and hurried from the room.

The physician walked to the bedside. "You should remain quiet from now on. We may need you alive, but it doesn't need to be pleasant."

"It doesn't need to pleasant for you either."

He closed his pale eyes for a moment before leaving the room.

It wasn't clear how long she'd been here, but she had to get away. Time must be running out. She tried scraping the straps against the metal bed frame, but it didn't work. By folding her thumb, she attempted to force her hand through. Taite even tried spitting on her

276

skin. All that accomplished was making her thirsty and disgusting. With a frustrated yell, she pulled at the straps one last time.

Later in the day, the door opened, and an older woman stepped in, pushing a small cart and smiled. This small gesture piqued Taite's interest. No one smiled at her here. Close to Taite's height, the woman held herself as straight as an arrow. Pure white streaked her light hair, but there was still something youthful about her face despite the smile lines and crow's feet.

On top of the cart sat a tray with food. Real food, hot and steaming, and Taite's stomach rolled in response. Being spoon fed diminished the experience, but she was not in a position to complain. It was still better than anything they had at the base. The woman even seemed well-practiced at tipping a drinking a glass for someone else.

"Your meals will come through a tube later, so enjoy," she said with a trace of sympathy in her voice. "If you're allowed anything at all. I'm not sure about that." She spoke again in a whisper. "I want you to understand that I don't like any of this business." Her voice was calm and friendly, and Taite decided to be nice to her.

"Who are you?" Taite asked.

"My name is Josie. You might say I've been a nurse to Mrs. Faren, Anise, for years. I've also been more of a companion. She and I have always been good friends. We talk about everything."

"That's nice, I guess," Taite said, a little confused.

Josie looked over her shoulder to the door and continued. "Anise never approved of this. She didn't realize for years what he was up to."

"Why are you telling me this?" Taite asked.

"I wanted you to understand. I care about her, and I don't want you to think ill of her." With a soft pat on Taite's arm, she replaced the tray on her little cart. As she stood up, she said, "I'll try to pay you another visit if I can before... You look just like Anise when she was your age."

"I am basically Anise when she was my age. On a biological level anyway," Taite said in astonishment.

Josie smiled again, shook her head and left the room. What a disappointment that turned out to be. Taite had hoped she would help her somehow, but she only wanted to preserve the image of her friend. Why did they care what she thought? She would be dead soon anyway.

All was quiet in the night. All except Taite. She tugged. She pulled. She scraped, and she tugged some more until her wrists were burning and raw. It was all pointless and exhausting. Her mind still worked at it too, but she was thinking herself in circles.

If she had still been struggling, she wouldn't have noticed it. But she wasn't, and she did. Footsteps rushing down the hall not too far from Taite's room, and a sob of a woman's voice. Was it Mrs. Faren? The original to her copy. Somewhere down the hall, dying of whatever disease she had. Taite felt a pang of pity.

The tormented moan that met her ears was heart-wrenching. While she sat in the dark, Taite wanted to cry, for herself or for Anise, she didn't know anymore. But she decided to stop fighting. It wasn't so much despair, but a simple, peaceful acceptance.

Taite never had any definite plans like some people do. Life seems unpredictable no matter what plans a person makes, with nothing certain except change and the inevitability of death. Taite only existed because of Anise. In a way, she was her. Maybe she had never had the right to the life coursing through her veins. It had always been Anise's to claim. Her head sinking into the pillow, she closed her eyes and slept.

A creak, and a stripe of light crept into the room, curving and bending as it slid over the bed before her.

Suddenly, Josie popped her head through the door and whispered, "Miss, are you awake?"

"I am now."

"If you don't mind, Anise has asked a favor. She would like to come speak with you."

"Can she do that?" Taite asked, not hiding the surprise in her voice.

"I won't tell anyone about it."

"I mean... isn't she, well, dying?"

"Oh, that," she said. "I've given her some medication, and she's feeling a bit better at the moment. I'll wheel her in."

"OK," Taite said with hesitation, realizing this would be one of the most surreal moments of her life. Josie had already opened the door wide, light pouring into the room.

Although she hadn't looked into a decent mirror for a while, Taite had a pretty good idea what to expect from Anise. When the wheelchair entered the room, it still came as a shock. It was like looking into her own possible future... not that she would have one.

Somewhere in her late forties, Anise was very sick. She was too thin, propped up by pillows and covered in a blanket. Her feet, dangling limp before her, were lost in fluffy pink slippers. Even in the pale light of the room her face was a spectral gray, a deathly mask. But her features were Taite's own, just older with lines furrowed across her brow, from pain or worry. Her hair, the same light brown as Taite's, was streaked with gray. As she regarded Taite with tired eyes, dark circles on her undernourished face, she said nothing for a moment. And Taite's mind was a blank page.

"So," Anise said in a weak voice. "This is awkward, isn't it?"

"Yes. Yes, it is," Taite said as she found her voice, surprised that they thought alike too.

"Josie tells me she had a talk with you. I won't bother repeating it, but I will tell you it's true. This wasn't want I wanted."

"Guess that makes two of us," Taite said. Quick to add, "Not that I don't want you to get better, but I..."

"Want to live. Most people do," Anise said, her voice like a pale echo of Taite's. It was a touch creepy she had finished her sentence.

"I do. There was a time when I didn't care, but I want to live," Taite said, recognizing that no matter how much she tried to accept this fate, she never could.

"What changed?" Anise asked with a slight tilt of her head.

Taite paused a moment. This woman didn't care, but she had nothing to lose. "When I found out about everything I had lost, I didn't think I could live with all that. I didn't even know what was real. Now that I've learned the truth, I guess I've adapted. I had started to think I could still have a life here."

"I've learned to adapt over the years too. It was devastating to learn about my disease as I grew old enough to understand it. I wanted to live. I tried everything. Every treatment and every experimental procedure. My whole life became about trying not to die.

"I look back, and I think of what a waste it was. I might have had children early on, before it took over. Then I lost that too." She trailed off, looking sad for a moment before righting herself and managing through her weakness to look dignified.

"I was never meant to live this long. I decided years ago that I would face this as it came. True, it came slowly at first, but it comes. I want to live, don't get me wrong, but all our days are numbered." She paused for breath before continuing moments later.

"I'll continue. Don't feel bad. I believe in God. My husband, he's a different story. His faith is in science, only science. Bless him, he thinks he's doing right by me, but this isn't what I want. It was never what I wanted. And I won't tolerate it."

"What are you saying?" Taite asked, not daring to even hope.

"I will live on here through you. The daughter I never had. I couldn't cause you to be destroyed any more than if you were my own. It pains me that my husband can't see that.

"The acts of a desperate man. Mr. Faren keeps trying to prolong my life. He has, but what life is this? Sometimes, it is difficult to accept that part of love is letting go."

"He won't listen to you. He'll do what he wants. Can't you see that?" Taite asked.

"Of course, I can. That's why I'm taking matters into my own hands. Frail as they may be," Anise said. "Aisea, I first heard about you a little over three years ago. Before that, your existence was unknown to me.

"With Josie's help, I have interfered when possible. Josie and I even disrupted your transport after your arrival, but that didn't go as planned."

"That was you?"

"Yes, but that was before they put me back in stasis. The deep sleep I call it. You've been mistreated on my account. I've heard things. I want to help you before it's too late."

"How?" Taite asked in a suspicious whisper. "I would never get out of here."

"Josie will help you with that."

Josie had returned to the room. Anise gestured to her with a graceful hand as she said, "There's an event here tomorrow for the scientific community. My husband and his pet medical team arranged a display of their... accomplishments. I'm surprised someone hasn't told you about it yet. You'll be the main attraction."

"No one has mentioned it," Taite said, realizing the man in the suit must have been the Governor. "What are they going to do to me?"

"Not to worry. They won't be doing anything. Only talking and explaining what they've already done, what they plan on doing, and the future ramifications of the research. We won't let them go through with the procedure later. It's a bad idea. I can just imagine the further perversions of this twisted science. That's why you'll be leaving before it takes place."

"And then what?" Taite asked. "I don't know where I am or where to go. He'll hunt me down."

"I've considered that," Anise said, sounding as if she grew more tired by the minute. With a self-assured expression, she looked up at Taite. "And well, you see, I've taken some liberties. I have more information about you than you might think. I have arranged for some help at the symposium. You shouldn't run into too many difficulties. Josie will explain the details."

She exhaled before continuing, "I only ask one thing in exchange."

Taite sat in silent curiosity as Anise went on.

"Do you see all these wires and tubes?" she asked, raising her hand an inch off the chair to show all the plastic running from her body.

"Yes."

"I can't live without them. Sometimes, I've considered pulling them out myself. I get so tired." Taite watched her, as Anise said, "You're right. He will keep coming after you. He'll put me in his chamber to keep me alive, like a lab specimen. Unless you stop it."

"How?" Taite asked, confused.

"You know the only way," she said, her voice drifting off to nothing. "It's the only way we can be sure, but I can't do it myself. I can't meet my creator that way, but you do it. Tomorrow. Promise me you will."

Taite shook her head, horrified and speechless.

"We're all aware I should have died long ago. This is stolen time I'm living on. Time stolen from you. Tomorrow, take it back, Aisea."

"I can't do that," she said, still shaking her head. What kind of choice was this?

"You can. I want you to," she said, forcing a faint smile. Anise may be the closet thing Taite had to a biological mother, and now she was asking Taite to end her life.

"No. No," Taite said. Taite was desperate to get out of this place, but there had to be another way.

As if reading her mind, Anise said "It's the only way. It might not seem right to you. You're a good girl, but none of this has been right. Help make it right. Otherwise, he will kill you. He can't let go."

"Why not Josie? Why doesn't she do it?" Taite asked, her voice rising an octave.

"Josie has been with me for years. She can't bring herself to do it. It's all I ask of you," Anise said with tears in her eyes. As she shook her head, Taite's vision blurred, and her eyes overflowed. How could she ask her to do this?

"Promise me. I'm giving you your freedom. Promise me you'll give me mine."

"OK," Taite whispered, teardrops streaming down her face by now. "I promise."

"Good," Anise said with a sad smile. "I'll make it easy on you. I'll be sleeping by that time of evening. Josie will explain. I'll leave you now. I'm so tired."

Again, she smiled, and then she and Josie made their exit. Taite was alone in the quiet of the room, dread and hope rising in her at once.

THIRTY-TWO

As Baylin watched the trucks pull away, the sun poured in, nearly blinding against the interior. Though he and Dakota agreed to splitting in two teams, and his experience said it was for the best, he was already regretting the decision. Perhaps it was the fact that Taite hadn't wanted to go, but then he hadn't really wanted her to go either. But he pushed her into it anyway.

Someone called his name from across the room, breaking his stream of thought and forcing him to turn his attention back to the matters at hand. Dakota, Taite and the others were on their way. There was no changing that now.

Striding through the rows of remaining trucks, he found Anthony. He'd been trying to track him down all morning.

"I've got the majority of it packed," Anthony said as he approached. "Where do I load everything? I want to make sure nothing gets damaged."

"Sure, Anthony. I'll help you bring everything down here. We'll put it in the second truck there." Baylin pointed down the line as the two of them started back through the doors.

As they marched through the hall, Baylin asked, "You got that re-calibration taken care of beforehand, right?"

"Should be ready to go. I tested it first thing this morning. Nice strong signal."

"Good," Baylin said. "Thanks. I'm sure you have a million other things to do."

"No problem," Anthony said with a dismissive gesture of his hand.

While walking through the bunker as part of the final check, he knew they couldn't take everything, and it was frustrating. As claustrophobic as this place could be, he would miss it. The base had been like home for them, and they had everything they needed. It could be some time before they came across another place like that.

The abandoned half-built bunker had been Duratio's base since before he had heard of Duratio. When he had first joined, Samuel had told him all about it. Built by the R.A., they planned a much larger structure. They had only completed the underground section before the storm hit, more damaging than expected. In the strength of the wall cloud, they abandoned it for a safer site. It was a nice bit of luck until now.

A sudden thought springing up, Baylin trotted back to his storage closet and pulled up the threadbare couch cushion. As he ran a hand over the familiar worn leather book he had almost forgotten, he sat down and thumbed through by habit. In the last few weeks, he thought about the book often. Once, he almost returned it, stopping himself short. It might only bring up unhelpful memories and trigger more problems than she already had.

All morning, the idea he had made a terrible mistake hounded him. They'd be leaving within minutes, but he questioned if it would be soon enough. He removed a pen from a pocket of his jacket and opened the book to a blank page toward the back. He inhaled, and the pen scratched across the page. Without a plan, he wrote, and minutes later, snapped the book closed. As he slipped the photographs into a pocket, he decided to return it at the first opportunity.

When he returned to the garage, Cy was in the middle of a head-count as those that remained boarded the trucks. Everyone was accounted for and the vehicles were at maximum capacity. Cy looked toward Baylin for the final go-ahead. With one last look around, Baylin called, "Move out."

+++

Over the last few days, Baylin slept little. After driving for over two hours, it wore at him until he finally relinquished the wheel. After exchanging places with Jeremy in the back, Baylin's eyes grew heavy as he rested his head against the side of the truck. Tired and sore as he was, he couldn't give in to sleep.

He should finally be able to relax, but there was still something nagging at him instead. He chalked it up to general anxiety of leaving the bunker and forced it from his mind.

The noise of the engine was giving him a headache, and he rubbed his temples and tried to decompress. Another half hour had passed when he realized Jeremy was shouting something through the open cab.

Through the noise, he strained to listen as Jeremy repeated, "We're coming up on Dakota's team."

"What?" Baylin asked. "They should be miles ahead."

"Well, they're up there. Engine trouble?" Jeremy asked.

"Guess we'll find out."

Within ten minutes they saw that Dakota's team was driving toward them. Baylin grew uneasy.

"So much for engine trouble. Be cautious. I've got a bad feeling about this."

"You and me both," said Jeremy.

Both teams of trucks came to a slow stop, thirty yards apart. As he took a swig from his canteen, Baylin jumped down, instructing everyone else to wait for orders. As he walked forward, Baylin saw Dakota's sleeve was ripped off, his arm wrapped.

Baylin slowed his pace in the sliding sand and asked, "What's going on, Dakota?"

Dakota said nothing, but stopped and waited for Baylin to reach him. Finally as Baylin neared, Dakota said, "Bastard shot me. Taite's gone. They took her."

Baylin stood silent for a second, closing his eyes to gather his thoughts before he said, "Say that again."

"Yeah, I'm gonna be fine. Thanks for asking." Dakota adjusted the bandage on his arm and frowned.

"Just tell me what happened."

"I had everything under control," Dakota said after summarizing the events. "And then she went and screwed it up."

"Dammit," Baylin said as he threw his canteen in the sand. "I'm sure she was trying to help."

"Oh, she did. She helped me get shot."

"You would have preferred she stayed in the truck and let them shoot you all one by one?" Baylin asked, rubbing a hand over his eyes.

"Well, they have her now," Dakota said, though it didn't make much difference to him. "I guess I don't get what the big deal is anyway. Were you aware she's a clone? That's what they said."

Baylin sighed. "Yeah, I knew."

"Why the hell didn't you tell me? We're supposed to be a team. You

287

can't keep something like that from me."

"Usually, I would agree, but you've made it clear that a different set of rules applies to Taite. It's no secret you two don't get along."

Dakota led the way towards one of Baylin's truck as he said, "She doesn't get along with anyone except Cy and you. You hear she punched August in the face?"

"I was there," Baylin said. "In her place, you would have done the same thing."

"I don't punch women."

"You get what I mean."

"I need to know what you know. Things might have been different if I'd known."

"Maybe," Baylin said, before relating to Dakota some of what he knew, but not everything.

"Well, I guess that explains some of her crazy behavior."

"Yeah, I still don't understand yours all that well though," Baylin said, sitting on the back of a supply truck and looking off into the distance. His mind only half-involved in the conversation. "What's your problem with her?"

"Do I need a reason? You're telling me she isn't even a person. Not a real one anyway."

"She's a real person, Dakota. Don't be a jackass."

"Whatever," he said on an exhale. "If Lanie hadn't picked up that little freak along the road, she might still be here."

"You shouldn't say that. It isn't true."

"No? Well, you spent hours obsessing over a lab rat and no time at all trying to find your own sister."

Baylin stood up and squared his shoulders, as he looked down at Dakota. "You know nothing about it, Dakota, so drop it."

"Drop it?" he asked in exasperation. "Lanie could be alive somewhere, and you want me to drop it?"

"Lanie's my sister. Don't act like you're the only one who cared about her. I wish she was alive too, but she isn't."

"You don't know that." Dakota was close to shouting.

"Yes. Yes, I do," Baylin said, jumping to the sand and forcing a change of subject. They didn't have time for this conversation now. "Did they get the bullet out of your arm?"

Dakota glared but relaxed and nodded. "It isn't too bad now. The bleeding stopped. What do we do now? We'll have to change plans a bit. Head in the other direction," Dakota said.

"We'll be changing plans all right, but I'm not going in the other direction."

"What are you talking about, Maras?" Dakota asked, suspicion seeping through his voice.

"This has all seemed off to me. Anthony reconfigured the tracking device they found on Taite. I attached it to one of her boots last night, and we had a signal this morning." He continued with a sigh. "I'm gonna go get her."

"You're joking."

"No, I won't leave her to be dissected. You can come or you can stay. It's up to you."

THIRTY-THREE

By lunch the next day, there had been no mention of the evening event. Taite was beginning to think Anise was wrong. Perhaps in her illness, she was confused. Or it could all be a trap to get her to attempt an escape. But she didn't see any motive for that.

Taite grew restless. The day wore on, and she stared at the recessed ceiling and prayed in desperation

It must have been late afternoon when the door burst open, waking her from the slumber she had fallen into. A frumpy nurse waltzed in, carrying shimmering silver fabric over one arm and a metal tray perched between her hands. Taite frowned at the sight of the needle on the tray.

"What's all that for?" she asked. The woman smiled as if she were presenting Taite with a gift. "The doctor's instructed me to make you look your best for this evening's little get together."

"Get together?"

"Yes, a little meeting that Doctor Linton has arranged. I suppose he wants to show you off."

"Why the needle?"

"That's something to calm you. I've heard you can be feisty now and then. We don't want any of that."

"Of course not," Taite said as the prick of the needle pinched her shoulder.

The woman rattled on as the well-known warmth spread over Taite. Watching her numb arms being moved around and pulled from sleeves was like watching someone else. She was sitting in a chair now, struggling to stay upright, hands gripping the arms of the chair beneath her. Taite's hair was brushed and pinned back, trailing over her bare shoulders. The room seemed to pitch beneath her.

The nurse bustled out, leaving Taite sitting in the hard-backed wooden chair. Close to an hour must have passed before Dr. Linton and a guard entered the room. The doctor wore a crisp black suit, and even the guard wore a formal dress uniform with the high collar buttoned tight. With a threatening pressure, the guard grabbed her arm, forced her to her feet, and led her away.

"You will be on your best behavior this evening," the doctor said as they exited the room. "You are to remain silent unless you are asked a direct question."

Taite nodded, noting the building layout and turns as she was pulled along the corridor.

"If you misbehave, I will simply render you unconscious. Is that clear?"

"Yes."

"Good," he said as they descended a staircase of richly stained wood. The end post was thicker than her thigh, carved as if twisted by a Titan's hand.

Her feet were still bare as she walked down the soft, carpeted steps. Twice the guard's black boots landed on her toes. Another staircase lay ahead, but they turned off the landing and marched down a long candlelit corridor. The stark contrast with the base was astounding.

Up ahead, a giant chandelier dangled from a vaulted ceiling as the hall opened up into a circular foyer. Beneath her feet, the burgundy carpet was patterned with Celtic knots embossed into the thick pile.

The men pulled her toward large double doors at the opposite end, thick and heavy with carvings.

As they approached, she recognized a man as her well-dressed visitor, Governor Faren. He wore a black tuxedo with no lapels. It made him appear a bit too much like a priest, and she found herself anticipating her last rites.

Moments later, Taite stood between Dr. Linton and Governor Faren, each having one of her arms in a firm grip beneath his own. For all appearances, she supposed she looked like a willing participant. As they stood waiting to be announced, a clatter of party noises seeped from behind the ornate doors. Silverware against china, and soft voices chattered away.

As the doors opened, Taite saw over one hundred people sitting in the candlelight of the ballroom. As she trembled, she contemplated how she would ever sneak out unnoticed.

The pair guided Taite to a row of empty chairs at the front of the crowd. From the ceiling fluttered a banner printed with the words 'Symposium of Genetic Replication'. At the left side of the room, in the center of a low, illuminated stage, stood a transparent acrylic podium. The man behind it was short with gray hair and had just announced their entrance.

As a hand pushed her into the chair, all the staring eyes felt like they would bore into her. And she couldn't ignore the uniformed guard sitting behind her. The doctor went to the podium, leaving

Taite with Governor Faren, who glanced over at her every few seconds.

The doctor spoke for quite some time, using many medical terms she didn't fully understand. He talked about her creation and her purpose though. He droned on about mitochondrial DNA, enucleation, and things Taite didn't want to know. As he spoke, projected images scrolled behind him.

When she dared to glance, there were images of twisting DNA and chromosomes. Then a photograph of Anise and one of herself, looking rather like the same picture. He spoke about Anise's medical condition, and Taite tried to think of other things. She didn't need to hear this.

Anise was on her side, she reminded herself as she glanced at the crowd. So many gathered to celebrate her impending death. Across the room, a figure sat still in a chair, and she couldn't help but think he resembled Cy. But Cy didn't know where she was and couldn't have made it here if he did. Wishful thinking. Or the medication.

They concluded the formal speeches with talk about saving lives and preventing the death of the colony and humanity. Taite's pulse quickened. As she squirmed with impatience, she watched the skin at her scarred wrist throb with rushing blood.

The Governor rose to his feet, taking her arm. Taite's breath was tight in her chest as he led her away and across the room. Taite had expected to be taken straight out. Instead, they stopped to talk to a group of men, all intellectual scientists of one kind or another.

The oldest one of the group said, "Governor Faren, this is fascinating, but I am not sure I understand the transplant process as the doctor described. Will the team remove all the organs at once then?"

"Ah, yes. Dr. Van Denend is confident it will be easier on Mrs. Faren if we accomplish everything in one surgery. There's no possibility of rejection, so I tend to agree. She'll only need to recover once. The procedure will involve several doctors working in shifts, of course."

"I see. Dr. Van Denend, is it?" the man asked as he gazed over at Taite like she was a painting on a wall.

"Yes. He's the supervising surgeon. I'm afraid he didn't make it this evening, but he will head to this location first thing tomorrow."

Blood drained from Taite's face, and the floor seemed to shift beneath her feet. With the continued buzz of ambient noise, the evening took on a surreal quality as if Taite was watching it all from far away.

"Governor, your subject seems uncomfortable with our discussion," a younger man added with an awkward chuckle.

"Don't be ridiculous. This is merely a replacement clone."

Taite groaned. This man was so blind. In her head, she screamed that his wife thought differently. But she didn't say a word out loud. Still, the Governor shot a stern glance at her that stopped even her thoughts cold. She couldn't afford to be sedated.

When her presence was otherwise ignored by the group, Taite forced herself to relax. They continued talking about her as if she wasn't there, and she turned her thoughts away. Minutes later, the Governor steered her toward the double doors, holding her arm tight.

While replaying Josie's instructions in her head, Taite kept her eyes on the doors. As the Governor pulled her briskly along, she wove herself through the encroaching crowd. Her shoulder grazed the sleeve of a nearby guard before the Governor stopped short of the door and turned back.

As the Governor muttered something to the officer, Taite was pushed aside into his custody. Wrapping a hand around her forearm, the man squeezed. Taite snapped her head around to glower at him. He was tall, his jaw squared and his hat low over his eyes. His gaze seemed fixed straight at her, and for a moment she thought she was hallucinating again. It was impossible.

She stared at the low hat, trying to see past the uniform and shadows. He looked like Baylin. The brief second stretched out and as the guard returned her stare, she was certain it was him. She didn't know how, but it was Baylin.

Time regained its hold as a hand snatched her other arm and tugged her away without a word. A raft pulled out to a sea of faces. The mirage vanished, and the Governor guided her roughly through the threshold. With a few quiet words, he passed her abruptly to a shorter guard with a small pistol tucked under his coat. Then Governor Faren disappeared back into the expansive room, and the doors shut with a resounding boom.

The guard pulled her through the circular room. As they neared the main staircase, she started to panic. This wasn't supposed to happen.

Then the man spoke. "Mrs. Faren wishes to see you."

"What?" Taite asked in surprise..

"She instructed me to bring you to her."

A warm glow filled the room as Taite stepped inside and reached to close the door. The guard was already walking back down the hall. Turning back with a sigh, before her opened an ample room dominated by a huge wooden bed with a carving of a swan, its wings outstretched across the headboard. The small figure of Anise seemed swallowed up by a mass of white blankets on the bed.

As Anise promised she would be, she was asleep. Her brown and gray hair loose against the pillow, her face serene in sleep. Plastic tubes ran from her thin hand to a liquid-filled bag hanging from a metal stand. Snaking out from beneath her blanket, wires tracked the rhythm of her beating heart on a monitor that sat on the bedside table.

She couldn't do this. Even if it meant they would kill her. Taite bent down close to Anise. With a shake of her head, she stood up again.

Then Josie appeared behind her, and Taite jumped in surprise. Dabbing her red eyes with a handkerchief, Josie only sniffled.

"I can't do this."

"You promised. You must keep your promise. It's want she wants," Josie said.

"It's horrible. I'm not a murderer."

"It isn't murder, miss. On her own, she would have died long ago," she said. "Her body is a prison. He keeps her like a possession. If he cared about her, he would have let her go. He only cares about himself. You promised her. It was her last wish. And if you don't keep your promise, I'll call the guard. It's your only chance."

Taite had promised, but as she turned back to look at Anise, she said to Josie, "If you loved her, you would have done it by now."

"No, I can't. The Governor would have me tortured. You don't understand. She doesn't even know how terrible he is."

"Then you shouldn't let anyone see you here."

Josie nodded and said, "I suppose you're right. I'll be down the hall." She squeezed Taite's hand and scurried from the room.

Seconds passed as Taite steeled herself.

Don't think, just do.

Taite reached her hand out to Anise, a vision of her future self, but her illness was a fate Taite wouldn't share. Momentum carried her forward and fingers gripped plastic. Taite's eyes were a blur of tears as her hand shook.

She squeezed her eyes shut and took a deep breath. It's what she wants. It's the only way. Then her fingers seemed to yank the tubes free on their own accord.

Her eyes flew open. Tubes and wires hung limp in her hand as Taite stared at them in horror. She couldn't make herself glance at Anise. Tears rolling, she bolted from the room with her heart racing in her chest.

Taite ran until someone grabbed her hand, pulling her from the hall into a small room. Josie. In a hushed voice, she said Anise would slip away before anyone intervened. Taite needed to be out of the house as soon as possible.

Josie rambled off the instructions to get off the floor, "Down the back staircase is the only way. Take a left down the hall to the side entrance. He'll meet you there." Then she twisted Taite's hair up into a loose bun and wrapped a soft blue robe around her shoulders as she spoke.

"Who?"

"Go. Quickly."

Taite turned and ran. From one side, twinkling stars peeked in the windows as Taite tried to remember the way out of the building. Heavy wooden doors lined the hall as she hurried forward. The clawing fingers of anxiety crept up her arms, into her chest and her pounding heart. Every second that passed, she expected someone to come rushing at her from the shadowed recesses.

She turned the corner where Josie had instructed. A faint glow spread from underneath a door ahead. She sucked in her breath, hesitating as she questioned moving forward or turning back. But it was the only way to get out unseen, so she clung to the wall and crept forward as fast as she dared.

The door was only a few feet ahead. Taite held her breath and tiptoed forward, the folds of the soft robe brushing against her bare legs. And then she stopped in her tracks.

"I was on my way to see you. What are you doing out here?" a slightly slurred voice said from down the hall. It was the Governor, his voice full of concern. "You aren't strong enough to be walking. Not yet, dear."

He thought she was Anise. It was dark in the corridor after all, and he seemed to have had one too many. As she glanced down at the pale blue robe, she realized it must belong to her. Taite stood frozen. She leaned against the wall, knowing at any moment, he would realize how wrong he was. Her entire body quivered as she held onto the wall.

His footsteps stopped, and he asked, "Anise?"

In an instant, survival instincts took over, and her feet darted into a sprint toward the next corner. From behind came the shatter of a dropped champagne flute, and the Governor yelled for her to stop.

A door opened. Another shout.

Taite rushed around the corner and scanned for the staircase leading down, finally catching the glimmer of the polished post at the far end of the long corridor. She dashed ahead, breath pulling hard at her chest. The sound of voices and running feet urged her on.

From nowhere, a hand wrenched her arm back, pain running through her stitched collarbone. She shrieked, spinning around and pounding her fist into her attacker.

"Got her," the man said.

Taite flailed and twisted, but he twisted her arm behind her back. His second vise-like limb crushed her against a broad chest. She could barely squirm, but she was liquid adrenaline. She aimed a backward kick into the man's knee. When his grip went slack, she threw an elbow to his face, wiggling away as he staggered. With the stairs in sight, she ran.

The folds of her dress gathered in one hand, she surged down two steps at a time. She plummeted down the remaining four steps to the landing where she came to a sudden halt as a voice said, "Fun's over."

When Taite turned to look behind, a pinch and pressure hit her hip. At the top of the stairs, the man was a dark blur, holding something small and black. While pulling a dart from her flesh, she turned and ran down the next flight. But her feet were already growing heavy. The room began to sway in the dark like treetops in a breeze.

THIRTY-FOUR

"Are you really going through with this?" Dakota asked as he leaned against the brick wall surrounding the Governor's expansive estate. They were a few hundred yards from the massive house, lurking in a remote and shadowed corner.

"Not up to it?" Baylin said, as he pulled a black nylon bag from beneath the wall, exactly where the message said it would be.

"I'm not sure it's worth the trouble," Dakota said. "This isn't some outpost. If this is a setup or if it doesn't work, we're dead."

"It'll work."

"Baylin, it's the Governor's estate. This is big. I don't know why I let you talk me into this."

"Neither do I. You surprised me there," Baylin said with a smirk. He took a quick look at the distant house through the scope before handing it to Dakota.

"We could have done this on our own. You had the GPS signal. I'm not comfortable relying on other people."

"You know we lost the signal miles back. You could have stayed if you're so worried about it," Baylin said, rifling through the bag.

"Somebody's gotta watch your back." He did his best to sound annoyed.

"You'll have to watch it from here. I go in with Cy. You stay here unless there's trouble."

"I know the plan, and I still don't agree with it," Dakota said. "I'm against the whole idea, but I should at least be going in."

"You aren't. I need Cy inside. Besides, the tux won't fit you," Baylin said, as he shook out a suit jacket and tossed it to Cy. Baylin slid into the pants of the military uniform, surprised to find they actually fit.

After buttoning the jacket which fit a little snug across his shoulders, he asked "What do ya think? Can I pass for one of those assholes?"

Cy chuckled as Dakota said, "You don't need a uniform to pass for an asshole."

"Ah, you're just pissy 'cause you don't get to come to the party," Baylin said.

Dakota flipped his gloved middle finger up as he glanced around. The lights from the house were glowing and flickering. "Whatdaya think they got to drink in there?" he asked under his breath.

"Be good, and I'll snag a bottle," Baylin said before turning to Cy.

"Got the invitation?" he asked the medic as he holstered his pistol.

Cy reached for his pocket and presented the crisp white card that had been left there.

When the transmission had come through to the only portable device they possessed, Baylin had thought it was a mistake. The message was simple with brief instructions 'to prevent the death of Miss Aisea Taite'. It was signed Anise Faren. Baylin couldn't imagine why Mrs. Faren was helping them or how she managed to reach them. While it was likely a trap, he was prepared for that possibility. He would make it work. The hardest part was getting in the estate, and that problem had been solved, regardless of the motive.

Cy checked the time, clapped Baylin on the back, and said, "Time to go, Mr. Maras."

Baylin nodded. "Be casual, but don't get into conversation if you can help it. If you can't avoid it, just throw some medical jargon at them. Taite's expected to be part of the presentation, so try to keep track of her. You don't have to do anything else until I get there."

"Got it," Cy said as he adjusted his suit for the fifth time. With a slow exhale, he pulled his shoulders back and started toward the main gate. Baylin watched as Cy approached the house and shifted to a casual stroll up the walkway.

"I'll be back in a few," Baylin told Dakota as he jogged off in the opposite direction. Dakota replied with a bored scowl from his crouched position.

+++

Baylin hurried through the front gardens, tripping twice on the irrigation system that kept it lush and green when the sun beat down for days. The side door was up ahead, right past a stone statue of a woman that looked a little like Taite. Perhaps it was Anise or else he was seeing that face everywhere.

As promised, the door was unlocked, and he slipped inside. He slowed his pace to the purposeful but unhurried gait of a soldier of the Order. He remembered how to play the role. After making his way through back corridors, he finally emerged into the main house.

The glossy floors of the foyer gleamed in the light of four chandeliers overhead, and he was immediately angry. The Governor shouldn't be living like this. He didn't even want to think about how much electricity they generated to power the place. He clenched his teeth, forcing himself to focus.

Cy would be inside and seated by now, Baylin thought as he looked up at the wide, wooden staircase. He ignored a middle-aged woman that was making eyes at him from a bench nearby. He made his way up to the second floor where the symposium was taking place.

Since he wasn't sure how to get in the room without drawing attention, he was relying on a little luck. As usual. Providence, as some would call it. In other words, he would wing it and hope an opportunity presented itself.

Ahead of him, a few people were making their way through the corridor. Waiters carried trays of glasses, and a wealthy socialite laughed on the arm of an older man, a physician or genetic engineer.

Another huge chandelier dangled menacingly overhead as he walked across the wide circular space before him. As he approached a pair of mahogany doors, there was a small sign for the event, and he heard the muffled droning of the speaker. He glanced behind him, considering if Taite was already inside.

With luck, the door swung open in the next moment. A tall man dressed all in white hurried through carrying a stack of papers. Before it shut, Baylin caught the door and stepped inside in one smooth motion.

At the opposite side of the door, a guard in the same style uniform he wore stood staring straight ahead. As he took a similar stance, Baylin surveyed the scene. The room was scattered with round tables. White tablecloths fluttered as servers buzzed by to fill empty wine glasses and clear abandoned plates.

In seconds, he spotted Cy at a table near the back of the room. He was sitting next to a skinny man wearing glasses and a heavy-set woman showing too much cleavage. Cy looked uncomfortable, sitting as far away from the pair as possible. Baylin might have laughed under different circumstances.

Next, he turned his attention to the other side of the room where an unfamiliar voice lectured about somewhat familiar things. There was a lot of terminology he didn't comprehend, but he caught enough to understand they were talking about Taite. Talking about her as if she was a lab experiment.

The speaker made a sweeping gesture to his side, and Baylin followed with his eyes to see Taite's small figure sitting beside a man he recognized as Governor Faren. The color had drained from Taite's face, her lips pale and tight as she stared at the floor. She wore a silver dress with a sheen to it like liquid metal as it gathered at a hip and rolled off her knees. As he recalled the frothing red water of his dream, he scowled and bit his cheek.

Taite seemed like a ghost of silver and gray, all but her hair and the lashes of her lowered eyes. Even from a distance, Baylin could see the quivering of her white-knuckled fists in her lap. He saw himself striding across the room, but he hadn't moved. And he couldn't move. He had to wait. So he inhaled, forcing himself to remain stoic in his soldier guise. A guard shouldn't pay attention to the content of a meeting like this, wasn't supposed to care.

Baylin shifted his eyes to see a projection of images playing behind the man — images of cells, DNA. The man continued speaking about the success of the project. Baylin focused on the wall in front of him for the remainder of the speech.

With a face made of stone, he stood through the talk of the surgical removal of Taite's heart. And in his head, he cursed them as they referred to her as a replacement source. He hadn't thought of how difficult it would be to listen without reaction. By the time Taite was pulled across his field of vision, his face was warm with a wave of fury.

As he pulled his brim low, he watched the Governor seize Taite's arm. She looked like she might pass out. He wanted to punch him in his face. No, he wanted his gun in his hand. Instead, he stood statue-still and gritted his teeth as the man pulled Taite toward the door.

She brushed by him, and he was close enough to catch the floral scent of soap on her skin. He could have reached right out to her, but he couldn't even allow himself a glance.

Then without warning, Faren thrust Taite toward him and said, "Hold this a moment. I've forgotten something."

The Governor hurried away, but Baylin didn't see where he went. He only saw Taite staring up at him, her blanched face angry and confused. The moment passed.

Before he could utter a word, the Governor stormed by, yanking her away as he might have grabbed his coat from a chair. The door closed behind them, and Baylin counted off a minute in his head before reaching for the handle of the broad wooden door. But it was pushed open from the other side, and for a brief second, Baylin was face to face with the Governor.

"Excuse me, sir," he said, mustering all the civility he could manage as he stepped out of the way to let the Governor pass.

The Governor said nothing, only threw a cool stare with piercing, unwavering eyes. Then he snapped his attention away and charged into the room with a smile.

Baylin stepped out in time to see Taite being led up another set of heavy stairs, her feet and legs bare to her calves. He and Cy were supposed to meet Taite outside. Watching her climb the stairs in the rough grip of an armed guard, he had doubts whether she could handle it on her own. While she was tougher than she looked, she looked as brittle as porcelain. Probably just the dress, so unlike the Taite he knew in cargo pants and heavy boots. He was still staring as she disappeared up the stairs.

On the third step, a firm hand on his shoulder stopped Baylin in his tracks. "Where do you think you're going?"

Baylin spun around to a taller man in uniform, several years older than himself. His furrowed brow a deep ridge through his bronze complexion. He didn't wait for an answer before yanking Baylin backward by his shoulder, almost sending him off balance.

"The third floor is off limits. You know that."

The grip tightened on Baylin's shoulder. As he stepped off the stairs, his mind and heart were racing. He said the first thing that came to him. "I... wasn't thinking, sir."

"Right," said the guard, looking unconvinced. "Come with me."

"I need to get back to my post, sir," Baylin said, backing away.

"Odd. I don't recall assigning you to a post. I don't seem to recall your face at all."

The burly officer pulled Baylin by his collar, leading him through a doorway and down a gloomy hall. As he stopped in front of a door, turning to look behind, Baylin reacted in an instant. Like a coiled snake, he lashed out with a fist aimed at the man's face.

Taken by surprise, the officer took a step backward as Baylin's knuckles made contact with his temple. His head jerked backward, and he staggered on his feet. He lunged at Baylin, his heavy hand crashing into the side of Baylin's face.

Despite the ringing in his ears, Baylin jumped back and ducked another punch. He shook his head, and the officer grabbed his gun and cracked it into Baylin's cheekbone. Another blow to his ribs, and he dropped to the floor — the metallic taste of blood on his tongue and pain screeching through his head.

The guard was a looming blur above him, and Baylin was running out of time. Not pausing to catch his breath, Baylin threw a hard, sweeping kick to the man's knee that sent him down.

Baylin rolled, grabbing the gun from the floor where it fell. And in the next second, the officer's weapon was aimed at his own skull.

"The rest of your weapons," Baylin said.

The guard cursed as he pulled another gun from his leg holster and slid it across the floor to Baylin.

"Keep going," Baylin said, kicking the pistol behind him. Even here, the man would have another holstered to his back and a knife strapped to his calf.

"Now get up," Baylin said, his whole body tense on a biochemical high. This was not part of the plan, and he swore under his breath. He shouldn't have lingered at the stairs, and now he had to waste time cleaning up his mess.

His head burning, he was unsteady on his feet. A warm trickle ran down his chin, and his lip was already swollen. For the moment, Baylin ignored it, and ordered the man through a small doorway to the side.

Behind the door, the passage opened up to an ornate library with shelves to the ceiling. Thick volumes lined every wall except the exterior which was a full row of windows covered with heavy blue drapes. The room smelled of dust, as if they rarely used it.

Baylin pushed the officer to the floor, aware he was waiting for the ideal moment to make a move. He wouldn't give him one. Before he took time to think, he was binding the man's hands and feet with the drapery cords. After using the guard's own dress tie to gag him, Baylin gave him a final boot to the kidney that doubled him over. He rushed from the room. There wasn't much time before the whole place was in an uproar.

He jogged along the corridor, pressing a hand to his bleeding cheekbone. Most of the attendees were still behind closed doors, but he slowed to a walk as he caught sight of Cy loitering near the staircase. Cy met his eye, shaking his head in answer to the unasked question: No, he hadn't seen Taite.

Baylin gave a brief nod and ran upstairs, not bothering to worry about appearances this time. The mansion had three floors, but it seemed to sprawl out in every direction. Reasoning Taite would be held in some obscure room away from the crowd, Baylin ran forward.

Then voices down a corridor caught his ear, frantic and loud. He stopped to listen.

"Gone?"

"How can this be? Who's done this?" The voice grew louder. "I will not allow it. Do something! Get the doctor up here immediately! Where's the guard?"

"Went after the girl, sir."

Baylin's pulse pounded in his temple. Someone was dead, and Taite had ran. He rushed in the opposite direction, ignoring the throbbing in his skull. As he turned the corner, he saw a security officer crouched at the top of another flight of stairs. Baylin stopped and watched as the man stood up, holstered a weapon, and trotted nonchalantly down the stairs as if his shot had hit its mark.

As he grabbed the gun from his belt, Baylin rushed forward to the stairwell. He jumped down three stairs, using gravity to slam the butt of the pistol into the guard's unaware skull.

The guard lurched headlong, grabbing for the railing as he tried to spin around. But Baylin had the advantage. Again, pistol met bone. While he could have shot him, it would have drawn too much attention, so he clocked him a third time.

The guard slumped to the stairs, sliding down a couple steps before his folded leg brought him to a rest. Catching sight of the guard's target, Baylin hurtled the slumped man and knelt down.

As Taite lay limp across the stair landing, her blue dressing gown puddled around her. A small red stain seeped through the fabric at her hip.

"Taite, wake up."

With a stirring of dread, he hesitated a moment before spotting a small dart on the floor nearby. It seemed they had only sedated her. He sat back on his knees, watching the shallow breath expand her rib cage. Then rolling her to her back and sweeping the hair from her face, Baylin scooped her up and over his shoulder.

Baylin had lost his sense of direction within the house, but the hall at the base of the stairs was empty. He crept down it. Up ahead, a clatter gave him fair warning that he was nearing the kitchen. The room was a clamor of activity as the staff scrubbed dishes, and waiters milled about complaining of tired feet. Then the door to the kitchen opened, and a short man hurried down the shadowy corridor.

After lowering Taite to his bent knees, Baylin crouched within a recessed doorway, watching the man scurry away. A faint moan escaped Taite's throat, and she shifted her head. Her eyes were open, but glazed over.

"Taite. Can you hear me?"

For a second, her pupils seemed to come into focus. She mumbled something unintelligible, as Baylin pulled her to her feet. Head rolled to the side, and she slumped into his shoulder, her knees too weak to support her weight.

Hazy himself, Baylin lifted her again and carried her along the zigzagging corridor. Until at last he registered where he was. The windows staring from across the hall told him he had to be on the far side of the house. The side door he had come through must be ahead, and he surged forward with renewed energy. He would have to come back for Cy. Pushing the door open with his shoulder, a welcome gust of wind greeted him.

+++

Dakota was pacing where Baylin had left him, and as Baylin approached, he stopped and raised his gun.

Unconcerned, Baylin only asked, "Have you seen Cy?"

Dakota relaxed but said, "No. He's still inside. What happened to your face?"

"Ran into some trouble," he said, pushing Taite's limp form into Dakota's chest. "Take her to the truck. I'll get Cy and catch up with you."

"You're a mess. I'd better go." Dakota refused to extend his arms to catch Taite.

"He was right inside. I'll get him," Baylin said, his biceps starting to burn. "Take her to the truck."

"Fine," Dakota said as he slid his arms behind Taite's back and knees. "Hurry up."

Baylin returned to the house and paused before the main door for a moment, hoping Cy hadn't wandered off. But as his hand reached for the handle, a sinking feeling hit the pit of his stomach. His luck had

310

turned. Things were going all wrong, and somehow he knew it would prove to be a mistake. He pushed the door open anyway.

From outward appearances, there was no sign they had disrupted the dwindling Symposium. Baylin knew different. As he stepped inside, the main foyer was deserted. Baylin ran straight for the wide staircase, almost tripping up the steps. He was only halfway up the flight when he saw Cy, still lingering near the top.

The streak of bad luck continued as Cy was facing away. No doubt expecting Baylin to signal from the back. Several other attendees milled about. Some laughed as they sipped from elegant glasses. Others whispered in small groups, aware that some unknown event had transpired.

As he slowed to a casual pace up the stairs. Baylin adjusted his cap lower, hoping to bring less attention to himself and his swelling face. There were three guards spread out among the thinning crowd. While Baylin hadn't noticed them before, as he approached Cy, it was clear they had already taken note of him. Expressions and postures shifted from dull to watchful. Baylin glanced at Cy. The medic usually stayed with his bandages and splints, and that work suited him best. He still had not turned.

His eyes on the floor as he strode past Cy, Baylin bumped his arm hard. He turned toward Cy in a false gesture of apology, and muttered, "Go. She's safe. Keep her that way."

The guards had already been watching, no doubt leery of Cy's awkwardness and failure to mingle. The whole exchange with Baylin only heightened their interest. Cy wasn't unaware of it, but he hadn't known what to do about it. As he made his way down the stairs, the two guards closest slid into step after him.

Cy heard the footsteps and quickened his pace as his pulse raced. In confirmation of his fears, they matched his new speed. Then one of them called out, "You! Stop!"

Only feet from the door, Cy risked a quick glance backward. Baylin was nowhere in sight, but the guards were closing in on him. Better for them to have two separate targets. That's probably what Baylin was thinking.

Cy broke into a run, slamming through the heavy doors and bolting across the lawn into the shadows. As he darted around trees and bypassed hazy patches of light, he ignored the commands to stop. And then he came to the wall.

The guards were still on his heels, threatening to shoot. In a quick leap that Cy surprised himself by making, he cleared the waist-high barrier. A second later, a bullet ricocheted off the brick with a puff of dust.

Cy kept running to the truck almost a quarter mile away. Though they had partially hidden the truck among vegetation, Cy could see Dakota behind the wheel where he was scanning the surroundings with his scope.

Cy yelled, "Start the truck! They're coming!"

Dakota tossed the scope next to him and asked, "Where's Maras?"

While throwing himself inside the cab, Cy gasped for air and said, "I don't know, but we can't stay here. He told me to get her out."

"Where is he?"

"I don't know!" Cy shouted. "There are at least two guards behind me, and you can count on more coming. Start the truck!"

Dakota growled but obeyed, and the engine roared to life.

THIRTY-FIVE

Through half-open eyes, Taite peered out as everything spun around in a groggy blur. Her head was heavy like iron and sounds amplified in her ears. Whispers were painful shouts. An ambient clamoring attempted to deafen her altogether. When the clamor faded away, only familiar voices and shuffling sounds remained. From the string of words, she caught a phrase about getting out of a truck.

As she tried to sit up, her limbs were as useless as a puppet's. Her mouth felt like dry paper, and she couldn't form the words she wanted to say. She surrendered back to the surface supporting her and closed her eyes. Within seconds, the blackness of a heavy sleep surrounded her like a comforting blanket.

Hours later when she pried her lids open again and sat up, she was grateful her arms didn't buckle and her vision didn't spin. If not for her recent memories, she would have felt refreshed. On a small cot, Taite glanced at her surroundings.

As the moonlight poured through, it revealed she was in a small tent. A chill hung in the air, her breath rising before her eyes. Little shared the space but a black bag and a small cardboard box.

Taite was alone, still wearing the thin gown and robe from the symposium. The memory seemed foggy and dreamlike.

Where she was or how she got here, she didn't know, and it didn't matter. Back at the estate, Taite had wanted to live so badly she ended a life, but now she didn't remember why. In her mind, her conversation with Anise played itself out again, light casting deep shadows along the edge of Anise's eye sockets. Her faint words echoed through Taite's memory.

Lost in thought, Taite barely noticed when the tent flap swept back, beams of light flooding in around two black shadows.

"Taite, glad to see you're finally awake," Cy said and stepped into the tent. "I was beginning to worry what they gave you."

"Cy," she said, as if to reassure herself. "Where are we? How did I get here?"

"There's time for all that later. First, I should take your pulse and blood pressure."

"Oh, OK," Taite said, as she held out an arm.

"Afterward, there will be time for explanations," Cy said again as he took her wrist and gestured with a nod to the second shadow, which she had forgotten.

Dakota stood near the flap of the tent, stooped under the peak. He said nothing while Cy attended to her.

Cy didn't mention Baylin. But she could guess why he hadn't visited He must have learned what she had done. He must be appalled. Dropping her eyes, she watched Cy clamp a monitor around her finger.

"Looks like you're getting back to normal. Your pulse was weak earlier. Now, it's actually a little quick," Cy said, standing up. "You get some rest. I'll see you later."

She nodded, as he stepped around Dakota and pushed his way out through the tent flap.

Dakota remained taciturn. Taite thought he might stand there forever as she fiddled with the hem of the robe. But then he broke the silence.

"How are you doing?"

In an instant, suspicion flowed in. Something was going on here. Dakota was never nice. While she felt rather ashamed, she refused to tell him that.

"All right," she said, glancing up with a shrug. He still made her uncomfortable, and her gaze did not linger long. "How's your arm?"

"It's fine. Kinda forgot about it with everything else happening," he said as he stepped in front of the cot and looked around the tent.

"What's happening? Where are we?" she asked, curious where all his venom had gone.

"We're days away from anywhere."

For a moment, Taite expected him to say something else, to explain things, but Dakota was still Dakota. Closed.

He finally said, "Thought I should check in with you and... I wanted to thank you for what you did. Turning yourself over to them. It was stupid, but thanks."

Taite snorted. "I'm not sure if it helped anything. They shot you, though I may have enjoyed that a little. I didn't enjoy the rest of it."

Dakota smirked, "Yeah, not the first time I've been shot, and it probably won't be the last. It'd better be the last time we need to track you down though."

With that, he stepped out into the night. Taite wanted to ask about Baylin, but he didn't give her the time. The stiffness of her joints starting to ebb, she pulled herself to her feet. When she noticed a jacket folded over the cardboard box in the corner, she walked over slowly. She recognized it as Baylin's, black stitches scarring the surface. Stitches she had sewn.

The jacket smelled of leather, the heat of the sand, and something else she couldn't name. But it too reminded her of Baylin. As Taite stooped to return it, something else caught her eye. Inside the box sat an assortment of everyday things: a bar of soap, a razor, a comb, but what held her attention was a small brown book. The image of the tree of life embossed in the worn cover.

Though it had been ages since she held it, Taite recognized it at a glance. She assumed it, along with everything in her pack, had long ago disappeared, but there it sat.

As she turned the first few pages, a painful lump formed in her throat. Memories of home flooded in — thoughts of her father, who wasn't even that. He hadn't had that change of heart either. It was Anise who saved her.

The leather of the cover displayed creases and wear. The pages more careworn than she remembered. A brief wave of agitation and discomfort washed over as she tried to remember all she had written within its pages. That led to anger. Baylin probably read it and never mentioned it. With a disgusted snort, she slammed the small book shut and threw it to the cot.

Only minutes later, Cy ducked inside. "Hello, again," he said. He looked glum and asked, "What did ya make of the news?"

"What news? Dakota didn't tell me anything," Taite answered with a scowl.

"Oh," Cy said as he fidgeted and finally sat down on the cot.

"Well, I guess we should talk then."

"All right."

"You remember being at the symposium?"

"Yes, but after a certain point it's all a blur."

"Someone hit you with a tranquilizer dart it seems."

"Figures," she said, wondering where all this was going.

"Did you see me there? Or Baylin?"

"Yes. At least I thought I did."

"You did. And, well, things went a little... wrong at the mansion. Baylin got you out to Dakota. You had been sedated by that point. I was still inside. He came back for me, but..."

"But what?" Taite asked. A knot of concern swelled in her stomach.

"We got separated, Bay and I," he said, agitated as he stood and walked the floor. "The guards were chasing us, chasing me, all the way out to the truck. We couldn't wait. He wanted us to get you out."

"What? What are you saying?"

"Baylin was left behind. We can only assume they detained him. That's what we hope. It's my fault, I'm afraid."

"You hope?" she asked in disbelief.

Cy shook his head. "If he got out, we would have heard something from him by now. When we were a safe distance away, we waited. But he never came."

+++

The next morning, bright sunlight streamed in the narrow opening at the front of the tent and forced itself through even the weave of the canvas. Inside, Taite was still drowning in a tidal wave of guilt. Baylin might be a prisoner. If he was lucky. A prisoner whom the Governor would most likely blame for his wife's death. Did Cy even know about that part?

This was all her fault. Cy tried to take the responsibility, saying he

317

should have waited for Baylin or should have left before Baylin came to retrieve him. But it came as little consolation for Taite. She was reliving all the moments of the last few days, her mind full of what-ifs. What if she hadn't turned herself over to them? What if she hadn't kept her promise to Anise? What if Baylin didn't come back?

Then interrupting Taite's thoughts, Kassidy popped her head into the tent, carrying a bundle of clothes. "Hey, kid!" she said with a grin. "Heard you've had yourself a bit a trouble."

Taite nodded. "You could say that."

"Brought you a new outfit. It's not as swanky as what you're wearing, but it's much more practical."

"Thanks, Kass. Anything is better than this."

"OK, then," Kassidy said as she tossed the clothes over with a broad hand. "Ain't got no boots, but I'm sure we can find some." Before she turned to go, she dropped into a playful curtsy and said, "You're always welcome in the ladies' quarters down at the far end."

Taite thanked her with a small, forced smile. Her head throbbed, but she ignored it as she slipped the light khaki pants on under the silvery gown.

Moments later, Taite began pacing the floor, grabbing for the ribbon on her wrist. It wasn't there. They had stolen that too. An exile without a refuge, smothered with worry, she finally grew too tired to pace and flopped down on the cot. Something poked her rib cage — her journal.

Again, she held the soft leather in her palms, running a finger along the cover. It seemed like an ancient relic from a forgotten life. As she read her own slanting writing, the words seemed to belong to someone else. She recalled sitting on her downy bed with pen in hand as she vented her frustrations. It was so far away from her now. Worlds away.

Earlier, Taite had hoped to see Baylin — to ask how they found her and yell at him for reading her journal. Now, she just hoped he was alive. While leafing through a few journal pages again, it amazed her how boring her problems had been. Back then, missing a party had been a disaster. Her trivial misfortunes must have seemed pathetic to him. They seemed pathetic to her.

Fearing what problems he might face because of her, she rolled onto her knotted stomach, book in hand. Falling open at random, the book stared back with writing that wasn't her own.

She flipped through three pages of the loose, hurried black letters and found where it began with her name.

Taite,

I wish I had said this in person, and now I'm not sure I'll get the opportunity. This morning you left with the others. At the time, I considered it the best option, but I regret it now. I hope it doesn't prove to be a disaster, but if something happens, there are things I want you to know. With any luck, this book will find its way back to you. By the way, I'm sorry about your journal. I was only trying to find some clue to help you before.

First, I promised to tell you a few things: My father and mother, always loyal to the R.A., insisted I train for the Order. Being young and ignorant, I agreed. When I learned the truth of the Order firsthand, I couldn't be part of it anymore. The Order was my father's dream for me. Mine was a world where people were free to live their lives. Where the people I cared about weren't subjected to the whims of others, tortured, mutilated, killed.

From there, it was Dakota who recruited me into Duratio. I had heard about it before — everyone in the Order had. But when said he was considering joining, it got my attention. You might wonder about Dakota. I've known him longer than anyone really. Trust me, he isn't as bad as he seems.

319

At nineteen, I packed a bag and became the enemy. When I deserted for Duratio, my parents legally disowned me. I've barely seen them since. And my family's name, Maras, is one that doesn't really fit anymore. You and I have that in common.

Samuel, the founder of Duratio became like a second father. He told me everything he remembered of Earth, and everything he knew of fighting. After he was killed, I guess it was natural for Dakota and I to take over. Samuel said standing up for what you believe often went hand in hand with being alone, with losing everyone. He was right. In one way or another, I tend to lose everyone too.

When Samuel died, things felt wrong and strange, and I questioned everything. Death becomes easier with practice they say. But not for me. It never gets easier. I never meant to drag Lanie into any of it. I told her to stay away, but she had suffered herself. In some ways more than I had. Anyway, I couldn't stop her.

I tried to find you both. That's why I was at the camp, but as usual I was too late. Too late for you. Too late for Lanie from the beginning. I blame myself for her death, but I guess at least she understood the risks. Every day, I live with the fact that she's gone forever.

Then there's you, unaware of any of it — a different set of rules in your head. At first, I didn't know what to think, but I do now. After everything that's happened, everything you've learned, you're still you in the ways that matter. When I first saw you again with Cy, I expected you to be broken. But you weren't. You're stronger than you believe.

At the same time, I see I have something in common with Gov. Faren. I have tried to protect you and Lanie, but I have failed miserably. Maybe that's all Faren wants to do, save someone he cares about. While I don't agree with his methods, I can't say I'm entirely against what he did. You wouldn't exist otherwise. I'm not sure what kind of person that makes me. A selfish one, I guess.

But it doesn't matter if you are a clone or crazy — you aren't — or sick or anything else, I'll be there. I can't say where all this will lead, but I hope you're safe. I should have listened, and I'm sorry if my decisions have put you or anyone in danger. If I get the chance, I won't let you down again.

– B

The first time she had read the letter, soggy circles had formed on the page. Now, emotion seemed beyond her. A horrible numbness had replaced everything else. Taite couldn't bring herself to think about what he had written.

Tents scattered behind her, foreign stars scattered above, and Earth, the home to where she could never return, winked somewhere across space. Taite no longer knew if it was a reassuring sight, reminding her of her humanity. Or an unsettling one, making her question it.

She knew nothing of the future. She understood little about her past. But like a sword tempered by fire, Taite sensed she was damaged, but somehow stronger for it. She was confused and scared, but deep within she found what Baylin wrote about her rang true. Despite all the chaos, or maybe because of it, she had somehow become more herself than she had ever been.

Acknowledgments & A Word From the Author

Many thanks to my family and friends for your emotional support, encouragement, and feedback while I struggled with all the unique aspects of writing my first novel. And then re-writing it. I'm sure there were times when I was quite obnoxious. Special thanks to Sidney, Taylor, Libby, and my mom, Suzanne.

Thank you for reading *Fearfully UnMade*. I had the initial idea for this book many years ago before I possessed the confidence to attempt to put it into words. When I finally did take that plunge and began tinkering with the story over time, it developed into something far different than I had planned. I found it wouldn't fit in one book, so my one novel became two.

I hope you enjoyed reading *Fearfully UnMade* and look for the sequel. Find a sneak peek on the following pages.

For updates, please follow or sign up at

www.jmrutherford.com

or

facebook.com/jmrutherfordwriting/

ONE

The table beneath her was frigid metal — a slab in a morgue. Straps held her ankles and wrists firm. The hard edge of the leather bit into her skin. Taite struggled and tugged with all her might, but she couldn't move. From beyond, a shadowed figure watched her efforts. As he stepped closer, Taite gasped. Dr. Fermin, the Vermin, as she thought of him.

He sneered as he twirled a bloody knife between his fingers like a member of a sadistic color guard. Her pulse quickened as sweat began to bead on her upper lip. Taite shook her head, but Fermin only smiled.

Behind him, a faint light glowed over another figure on a slab. Blood smeared the surface, dripping from fingers that dangled lifeless from the edge. Taite's breath rattled as her eyes followed the hand to the shoulder, the shoulder to the face — a tanned, blood-smudged face surrounded by messy, sand-colored hair.

"Baylin," Taite said, exhaling in a choked sputter.

The Vermin laughed as he said. "That was all you, sweetie. Don't blame me."

He slowly pressed the point of the knife into her abdomen. Taite screamed, a frantic, desperate sound of a dying animal. Then she bolted awake, throwing herself upright. Gasping for breath, shivering despite the early morning heat. Sweat ran from her hairline. Drops coursed along her cheekbones, but perhaps those were tears.

Tiptoeing through sleeping figures, corpse-like in their slumber, Taite made her way outside into the open air. As she threw back the tent flap, she inhaled the open space. She missed the tickle of grass between her toes, drops of rain sliding down her face. She missed many things about Earth, but most of all, Taite longed for the simplicity of life before now. The freedom of not worrying about survival every day, of not having the weight of guilt on her shoulders, the fear of what came next. She missed Baylin, the sense of someone watching out for her, a relative safety in a battlefield. And she worried.

There are mistakes in life that can be overcome and left behind, but then others are the haunting kind. Mistakes that can never be corrected. You cannot go back, but forward is a dark and lonely path. You cannot see the way, but still you go on because there is no other choice. The problem is that sometimes it's impossible to tell what you can overcome. You just get through it, or you don't. Still shaking from her nightmare, Taite wondered if her mistakes were the haunting kind.

A breeze rustled her shirt as she walked further away. It was a stifling breeze, but Taite was thankful for it all the same. She closed her eyes and tried to clear her mind, focusing on the sensation of the air tickling the fine hairs on her arms. Motionless except for the push and pull of air through her lungs, the rise and fall of her rib cage, she stayed this way.

A strand of hair blew across her forehead, and as she brushed it off, someone called her name. Her eyelids squeezed tighter, and she wished them away. She didn't know what they would say, but it would be a painful reminder of everything she struggled to escape at the moment. A cold, hard slap in the face. She sighed, her breath full of the scent of scorching sand. The voice called again. It was Dakota, and he was coming closer. Even better. Taite couldn't stand him, and he only talked to her when necessary. He never had good news. Never.

He came closer, silent in the sand, but she sensed him approaching with a chill up her spine. She searched for something likable about him, knowing that for some reason he and Baylin were friends. She didn't see why. He seemed arrogant and abrasive, an overall jackass. But still she tried, for Baylin's sake. He was a link, the only thing she had left.

Taite winced as he stood over her and said, "You need to come back to the tent for a while. We're having a meeting this morning, in case you've forgotten."

"I didn't forget," Taite said, aware of the defensiveness in her voice. She hated that he made her voice rise an octave. "I just needed a minute to collect myself, OK?"

"Yeah, well, your minute's over," he said as he turned to go.

"Always the gentleman," Taite muttered under her breath.

"What was that?"

"I said I'll be right there."

As he walked away, Dakota snorted and replied, "You will be if you give a shit."

Taite rolled her eyes, cursing him silently as she bit her lip. While she tolerated him, she really wanted to claw his eyes out. She unfolded her legs, thinner than they used to be, and pulled herself to her feet. Her body felt coated in lead, weighing her down with every step. Every day was the same, a crushing weight on her chest, like any minute she would suffocate. A knot in her stomach that refused to relax. She had been forcing herself to eat. Sometimes it stayed down, and sometimes it didn't.

Brushing sand from her pants, Taite half-walked, half-stumbled to the clustered tents. It was important. She had to hear what they said, but she dreaded it at the same time. If they had news, it wouldn't be good. Nothing good ever happened. There was no joy here. Nothing but sorrow and emptiness.

Baylin had been missing for over three days. Missing, captured, maybe dead. No one knew. Taite boiled with fury, depression, fear, so many things she couldn't separate the individual emotions from the tangled mess she'd become. She blamed herself for existing at all. She blamed Cy, who should have gotten out of the estate on his own, so Baylin didn't have to charge in after him. Of course, she blamed Dakota for no other reason than he was Dakota.

Standing before the tent flap, Taite may as well have perched before an eager maw waiting to devour her whole. The tightness in her chest squeezed until she thought her lungs might collapse, but her hand drew back the canvas, and her feet moved forward as she forced out a breath. The aroma of day old reheated coffee and sweat hit Taite in the face as she stepped inside. It was nauseating.

Taite paced through the tent— to the door, to the opposite side. Back again. Perspiration plastered hair to her forehead. The taste of salt seemed to linger in the suffocating air. Dakota spoke to the gathered group, but Taite found it difficult to concentrate on what he said. She should be listening. She wanted to know, but the mere mention of *his* name caused her heart to contract. She would explode.

How many times can a world shatter? How many times can a person tear apart? This was her fault. That singular thought ran laps through Taite's mind. If she hadn't given herself up, none of this would have happened. Then again, the R.A. might have killed them then and there. It was a pointless argument that she had with herself, but the thoughts kept circling, regardless. Footfalls in the soft, sinking sand of the tent floor, she paced as thoughts swarmed.

It wasn't only guilt moving her feet; it was apprehension too. But it was better to focus on guilt than on what they may do to Baylin, what they might have done. She turned to make another round, chewing her nail.

"Taite."

She kept pacing, but the voice repeated, "Taite, will you please sit?" Phrased as a question, he barked the words as a command. Dakota continued, "You're distracting everyone."

"Mmm... sorry," she said absently as she stopped in her tracks, folded her legs beneath her, and dropped to the ground like a stone.

"Does anyone have any better ideas?" Dakota asked the group as he looked around, exhaustion in his eyes.

No one spoke. Some shook their heads glumly.

This was bad. Taite had guessed most of it. They remained optimistic that Baylin was a captive. Held by the people who wanted him dead, who wanted her dead. People who held him responsible for her absence, for the death of the Governor's wife. The worst-case scenario was that he hadn't been captured at all. Taite's stomach turned. Lanie, Xander, Anise, Baylin — blood on her hands. It should have never happened.

Aiden broke her stream of thought. "We have to do something!" His words caught in his throat. At sixteen, he idolized Baylin like a big brother.

Dakota said, "We're doing everything we can, kid."

Not much. They had no indication where the Order would have taken Baylin. There were too many options. He might still be in the Governor's estate, but that was unlikely. It didn't matter, since the place was now the most well-guarded building on the hemisphere. He may have been taken to an R.A. base, but who knew which one? He could be in the colony. All options were far away, under heavy guard, and... impossible. They needed more information. Until they had it, their hands were tied.

If they had still been at the bunker, they might intercept a clue where Baylin had been moved, but as it stood, the portable equipment just wasn't strong enough this far out. They had been at the make-shift camp for three days now, waiting. For what, nobody knew, but they had to get moving soon. They had to set up a more permanent camp. That was the other topic of the meeting. Where to go now? From what Taite saw, there was a vast, empty land as far as the eye could see. There was nowhere.

About the Author

J.M. Rutherford creates things: Art, stories, messes, and whatever else she feels like. She has a Master's degree in painting, so she is currently attempting a double life as an artist and author. This is her first finished novel. Others float around half-completed or as vague impressions in her head.

She resides in Illinois where she can sometimes be found sipping tea with her daughter, attending art shows, working her day job, or complaining about taxes.

www.ingramcontent.com/pod-product-compliance
Lightning Source LLC
Chambersburg PA
CBHW051335250626
47155CB00007B/2602